EPISTOLARY

By

Lisa Lambros

TABLE of CONTENTS

"Si tu ne m'aime pas, je t'aime. Si je t'aime, prends garde à toi." - George Bizet, Carmen La Habanera

This book is dedicated to Mrs. Ida Thomas, who taught me how to read and write.

PART ONE: GRAND CANYON

Letter 1

Miss Amanda Hood to Mr. Adam Hood

(June 1996)

Dear Dad,

Greetings from the Grand Canyon!

It might seem a little weird to write letters to you since we normally speak on the phone, but my phone privilege is only on Sundays between six and six twenty in the evening, in the main office. Please don't forget that I will call you then. In writing, however, I can tell you as much as I like, but you can pick up and put down my letters at your leisure, as opposed to gluing your ear to the phone for twenty minutes straight. See how thoughtful I am?

I do hope your workload lightens up, Mr. Lift Equipment Manager (sorry, couldn't resist) so you can enjoy a little bit of this summer. Last month's graduation shifted me from full time student to an undetermined status, but this counselor gig changes me to full-fledged worker, which I am not used to. However, I hope I adjust well because the position will act as a nice steppingstone before I begin as a Junior National Park Ranger in the Fall. The practical experience with teenagers, as well as an arid setting in which I can become more familiar with desert forms of life won't hurt either. Of course, none of these jobs will provide an income that matches yours, but I think I will be equally fulfilled in my career. I don't think I had shared this many of my thoughts and feelings on this subject with you before, but letter-writing brings out my deeper side. Please tell me if it is too much.

Thanks again for wiring me the money. It arrived very quickly as I'm sure your bank account will prove. I'm sorry I didn't anticipate how much I would need for this trip. Mostly it's been miles of cornfields, but life's little emergencies tend to occur more frequently than I was prepared for. I'm relieved the car conked out in the good-sized town of Amarillo. Once the engine misfirings started and the loss of power began, it wasn't difficult to find and pull into a gas station. You were right - the distributor cap cracked. Not only that, but the spark plugs were also looking a bit overheated as if the air-cooling system wasn't working well. Frankly, I wouldn't be surprised if the summer heat in Texas is too much for this seventies Beetle. Yesterday, the temperature reached one hundred three degrees in the shade, per the local radio. Mercifully, I could focus on the tune-up. The attendant who let me place the call to you lent me a pan to drain the oil while I went to the bank and the auto parts store. There was a handy parts guide in the aisle, so I found the necessary supplies with ease.

I also rotated the tires for good measure since I've put so many miles on it. In full disclosure, the attendant had also offered to help me swap everything out, but I declined because I didn't want to spend the money, nor wait for him while he helped other customers. I thanked him for his help with a ten-dollar bill then skedaddled out of there so fast, I forgot to use hand cleaner.

Dad, the hotel room you booked for me that night was such a treat, thank you. I'm sure I looked ridiculous approaching the counter with my blackened hands, but the lady at the desk acted professionally, even offering a clean towel with which to wipe my hands. She gave me an old-fashioned skeleton key that weighed down my pocket, then led me through a complicated maze of hallways and short staircases, whose walls and ceilings were covered with the same green flocked wallpaper so if I hadn't followed her so closely, I might have gotten lost. Though this mid-nineteenth century hotel has been refurbished, the low wattage bulbs they use in the modern sconces only dimly light the passage because the ceilings are still twelve feet high. The wall-to-wall carpet must have been upgraded as our steps made no sound. Between the hush and the shadows, I felt like I was trailing a spirit through an ancient forest. Finally, she proceeded down a dead-end hallway and stopped in front of a large oaken door. Dead-end is quite the right word because it was so utterly silent from other rooms that lined the hallway - no blaring televisions, no light escaping under doorways, just the low lighting and the saturnity. We stood before the stately door whose white lace curtain covered the transom from inside the room. I placed my bag on the floor, pulled the key out of my pocket to turn in the lock. Satisfied that I could open the door, she disappeared so quickly that by the time I reached for the bag I had previously put down, she had evaporated, and I felt like the only soul around.

I walked through the door, switched on the light, and marveled at the sheer charm that greeted my eyes. The same green wallpaper wrapped the walls and surely the ceiling was just as high, but here it had purpose, for the focal point of the room was the enormous four poster bed in the middle. I'm sure you've seen poster beds, but Dad, I don't think you've ever seen one quite like this. Each post was shaped as a tree trunk and from the tops of each "trunk" carved leafy boughs reached toward the middle where they intertwined to form a delicate, but very elaborate canopy. I was so enthralled; I quickly hopped onto the white chenille bedspread and lay down so I could look up at it from underneath. It's possible I never even closed my mouth once; I was so agog.

Easily overwhelmed if I looked too quickly from one direction to another, I decided to be logical and turned my gaze to the post nearest to my right hand. A spray of climbing roses spiraled around an oak trunk and joined the leafy boughs above. Moving my eyes to the trunk closest to my right foot, I took in what looked like a hibiscus tree, its flowers and leaves reaching in equal measures to form the tall canopy overhead as the oak and roses had done. When I surveyed the canopy, I could see some birds and bird nests among the branches, but I couldn't identify any particular species. The trunk nearest my left foot was a weeping willow and while some of the boughs reached toward the center canopy above, a few draped around the post in a mournful stance. There were a few fallen flower petals scattered around its base, as if the wind had blown them from the other trees. Lastly, my eyes traveled to the tree by my left hand which by its leaf shape was a hickory, but there were no flowers on it. Instead, a little lower down the trunk a thick branch extended, from which hung a beehive whose belly had been carved away to give the viewer an intimate look inside. I sat up and peeked inside. And what I saw there was something I had only ever seen in a video in an advanced Botany class.

I don't know if you also learned this when you studied Biology, but in my course on pollinators, I learned about Asian hornets that prey on honeybees and devastate their colonies. The fascinating thing is, when the honeybees work together, they kill the few hornets that infiltrate the hive. By creating a "bee ball" around each gatecrasher and moving their muscles, they raise the temperature around the hornet to about one hundred seventeen degrees Fahrenheit, which cooks it to death. When people speak of a "hive mind" they may not have any idea how fatally effective it can be, but I've certainly witnessed its power in my studies. In the carving, the shape of the hornet surrounded by honeybees was discernible enough, but I started to feel drowsy and lay back down.

Still, the bed is gorgeous, and I reveled just lying in it. I fell asleep and dreamed of wandering through a labyrinth that somehow resembled a honeycomb until I happened upon a large room, in which stood a single table on whose surface sat a glass jar filled with a honey so precious that upon tasting it, I fainted. I'm not sure how possible it is to become even more unconscious while one is already asleep, but I woke up feeling very refreshed.

After I climbed down from the heavenly bed, I showered in the lovely, tiled bathroom that didn't have a tub, but more of a shower...nook? It was just tiled walls with the spigots and showerhead coming out of them, no tub, but a tiled floor, and big sliding glass doors to finish it. I've never seen such a thing before, but it made me feel regal to wash there. Breakfast was a granola bar and I dressed hurriedly to leave as soon as possible, so I didn't take the time to observe the beehive more closely. I hated leaving this sanctuary, but I really wanted to get to Arizona as soon as possible, so I checked out and hit the open road.

From the hotel in Amarillo, the sunny drive took only another eleven hours, twelve if you count all the pitstops. I arrived at Grand Canyon Youth Campground and checked in at eight o'clock last night. I am happy to report there was no further trouble with the car. The Assistant Director, Ms. Nyimsava who is kind of sharp, gave me my keys for the various buildings and told me my phone privilege assignment. She then dismissed me to my bunkhouse (Number Three) where I made up the only unmade twin bed with the sheets that had been stacked on top of it, lay down, and fell asleep without even changing my clothes. Imagine how startled I was to wake up in exactly the same position and in my same clothes when the revelry rang out at seven the next morning. After my heart calmed down a bit, I managed to open my eyes and look around. My bunkhouse is equipped with a full bathroom and sleeps four people - two in a bunk bed and two in twin beds. There are also four desks with corresponding chairs for when we would rather sit, I guess. I hope I don't have to do any paperwork, just supervise children, but I'll know more later in the week.

As I was looking around, I saw a young woman about my age already dressed and making up the other twin bed. She introduced herself to me as Beatrice, a counselor who has led camp groups here for a few years, so she knows the ropes. She wears so much makeup that she's kind of orange, but her hair is frosted lemon yellow, and I bet it is a rare day that she doesn't wear lime green accessory. With a watermelon smelly sticker on her name badge, I've decided not to tell her what a tacky fruit salad she is, but only because she is sweet. Okay, that pun wasn't actually intended. After I showered and changed, she traded home addresses with me so we can write to each other after the summer ends, then walked me to the mess tent, and pointed out the other counselors, one of whom I almost failed to recognize as Gilbert DeRoquedu. He has changed tremendously since we last saw him.

I think you might remember Gil as one of my teammates on the Quizzies trivia team in high school, yes? He was a conservative boy with horn-rimmed glasses, lovely wavy brown hair, and who always wore an Oxford shirt and tie. He looked at me from across the mess table with his ice blue eyes, but they were peering out from a pair of crooked granny glasses, and he has grown his hair awfully long into a rather tangled mess. I waved an awkward hello, which he returned with a bandaged hand. Some of the other counselors noticed and burst into an impromptu rendition of "Feelings," the Morris Albert hit, dissolving into snickers aimed at Gil after a few lyrics. Gil just looked down his glasses into his oatmeal and stirred it slowly with his other hand whose fingers were splinted.

After breakfast, most of the other counselors cleared the tables and began to rearrange the chairs for the general morning meeting, so I approached him.

"Hi, good to see you," I said.

"Hi," he returned, kind of quietly.

"How are you?" I asked.

"Fine," he said, but his tone was depressed, and he didn't even ask me how I was.

"What happened to your hands?" I asked, hoping it wasn't too painful a subject.

"I accidentally fell into the Grand Canyon."

"Ohmygosh, that's terrible! How did that happen?"

"Well," he started slowly at first, but then found his confidence to speak normally, "we were orienteering as a kind of bonding experience for the counselors, though the trail was mostly obvious. When I needed to take a leak, the only cover I could find was this scrubby tree high up the rocky hillside, away from the trail. They had advised us to hold it until we came across the porta potties, but I just didn't feel like it, plus porta potties are really gross, so I slowed down, pretending that I was adjusting my gear to let people pass. When the coast was clear, I left the trail and scrambled up the hillside. The dusty rocks were a little slippery, but I made it and answered Nature's call. Then, on the way down, my feet shot out from under me, and I slid down the steep hillside very fast, crashing onto the trail below but not veering into the ravine on the other side. Ultimately, the ground caught my fall, but in my panic, I had put my hands out and they smashed against some rocks. Mostly, the abrasions are superficial, but I broke my pinky finger and cracked my ring finger on the same hand. Other counselors heard my fall and hiked back to help me. Since I was in pain, someone walked with me back to the campground, then Ms. Nyimsava drove me to a hospital in Flagstaff where they patched me up pretty well. They said I might have arthritis when I'm older, but I'm not worried."

"Wow. I'm glad you weren't hurt more than that. And Ms. Nyimsava? What did she say to you?" I pressed.

"She was pissed that I broke a rule, but she understood on some level and warned me never to do it again. Then she put out an announcement that counselors really need to use the bathroom before hiking the trails, so this kind of thing doesn't happen again. She said I could still work as a counselor, but she recommended that I guide the kids in arts and crafts instead of riding or hiking for a while. That seemed like a good deal to me since I wanted to stay and I'm not as inclined to lead the physical activities."

"Well, I'm glad you didn't fall deeper into the canyon. You could have suffered many more injuries or even died. I would like to hear more, but it looks like meetings are about to start. Maybe we can catch up sometime later?" I asked.

"Yeah, we can meet after dinner. The counselors have some free time then."

"Okay, sounds great!" I replied with some fake cheer because I didn't know what else to do to lift this conversation to a better place. We agreed to meet in front of the mess hall after dinner, then parted to attend the meeting which was very dull.

"So, how do you know Gil?" Beatrice asked afterwards. We were on our way to a different meeting specific to preparing us for the campers who arrive tomorrow. Our first activity with them will be a hike through the Canyon. Eventually, the teens will hold a campout along one of the trails, but we must familiarize them with the territory first. We walked past a Sonoran lyre slithering across a rock and I froze.

"Don't worry, Mandy," Beatrice said, because I had stopped in my tracks and my eyeballs nearly popped out of my head, "those kinds of snakes aren't that venomous. It's the rattlesnakes that you need to really watch out for, but they usually rattle before they bite."

"Oh, okay," I said, thawing, then resuming my walk. Now that I could breathe again, I told her how Gil and I were trivia teammates in high school.

"Oh, that's interesting," she exclaimed. "Trivia is what Gil is known for here. He placed second all by himself in one of the tournaments last week and some of those opposing teams had four people. I don't do it myself, but sometimes I watch from the sidelines. Would you like to play? It's on Tuesday and Thursday evenings. There's even a championship game against the park rangers at the end of the summer."

"Absolutely!" I gushed; perfectly sure I would team up with Gil. We dominated as state champions in the past and this way, he'd have an ally instead of being a solitary outsider. I'd rather reconnect with someone familiar than just make more acquaintances which is what most of the other counselors are since we come from all across the country. I'm just not worried about the social capital I'm forfeiting, but I'm used to making these kinds of sacrifices as a nerd. Gil was the same, but here he seemed extra ostracized and downright miserable. I asked Beatrice if he has been down like this the whole time he's been here or if something had happened.

"Yeah, he used to be a lot friendlier, but last week, something happened, and he's been quiet ever since," she replied.

"You mean his hand injury?" I asked.

"No, something else entirely," she said.

"Please tell me. I won't repeat it," I promised her.

"I sense you wouldn't, it's just kind of sad," she confided, "You see, he asked out a girl named Serena and while everyone else seemed to know that she was necking with some beefcake named Tyler behind Bunkhouse Ten, Gil had no knowledge of this. So, when a bunch of us saw him start to give her attention for every little thing she said and did for two days straight, it wasn't long before we figured he'd make a move."

She continued, "On the night of the Counselor Cookout Gil attempted to pass Serena a note while we stood around the fire roasting hot dogs. He was asking her out, but he wrote a sonnet too, which I memorized because I really like it. Do you want to hear it?" she asked.

"Yes," I told her. I didn't know Gil ever wrote poems; this was new.

She began.

'In Spring, the Prickly Pear Cactus blooms red,

And the Columbian Monkshood yields blue,

Blackbrush turns yellow where raindrops tread,

And   Grassleaf   Peas   affect   a   purple   hue.

Paintbrush Flowers burst crimson in July,

Apache Plumes burn white through Summer's day,

And Trailing Four O'Clock reflect the sky,

To complete this patriotic display.

The Grand Canyon tickles the poet's heart,

And the buzzing attests to its nectar,

Rendered sagebrush or agave to start,

Our national park induces wonder.

This floral calepine offered to view,

Is because I bear strong feelings for you."

"Wow," I said, completely awed. "He wrote that?"

"Yes," Bea answered. "I don't know any guys our age who write like that."

"I don't know if he wrote such things in high school, but if so, he never shared it. Still, he didn't quite get to the point, did he?"

"Actually, he did. He followed the poem with the following lines:

"Serena, would you like to go out with me? We can meet to make plans behind Bunkhouse Eight, tomorrow night at nine, if you like. Gil."

"I guess I memorized those too," Bea blushed. She went on to describe what happened though.

"He tucked the folded piece of paper in a pocket of a sweatshirt that she had laid on the ground and walked away to resume his place nonchalantly on the other side of the fire, though we all noticed. What he didn't see through the smoky haze and flickering firelight was that one of the other counselors fished it out of the sweatshirt. That guy shared it with me and some other counselors, so one of the girls wrote a fake response that she "Serena" couldn't meet him behind Bunkhouse Eight, but Bunkhouse Ten instead, where we know Serena can usually be found with her tongue halfway down Tyler's throat. That response was then passed to Gil.

The next night, at the pre-arranged time, Gil left his bunkhouse, carrying a small bouquet of wildflowers, and headed to Bunkhouse Ten. We followed at a safe distance until we could skirt around the bunkhouse from the other side, then waited in the shadows, and it paid off spectacularly. Not only was Serena there with Tyler, but she was kneeling in front of him and moving her head very, very vigorously." (Dad, I hope this doesn't shock you, but that's what Bea told me.)

"Ohmygod," I said to her, remembering what a sensitive person Gil was in the past.

Beatrice resumed, "When Gil came around the corner, he saw them, stopped, spilled his sad little rainbow of weeds onto the ground, and just stood there, trying to process it all. Then the others burst out laughing, giving our position away. I didn't laugh, but he saw us and fled with embarrassment. Oh, and Serena and Tyler had no shame, she, having pulled off, and Tyler just told us to leave, which we totally did."

"Ohmygod," I repeated. Poor, dear, innocent Gil. That must have been an awful moment for him. Not only was his affection thwarted, but his complete humiliation was public. Additionally, I was a little concerned about the pit of vipers I seemed to have fallen into having come to this camp. I mean, how could they pull that kind of stunt? It was just so heinous. No wonder Gil wasn't his normal self. I thanked Beatrice for the info, careful not to relay my judgment of their behavior because while I considered her a friend, I wasn't entirely sure which part she really played in this heartbreak. I just mildly summed it up with "Well, I guess he learned his lesson," but inside, I vowed to be choosy with whom I shared any confidence. More importantly, I pledged to work to raise Gil's spirits so he could be returned to some happiness. He really has so much to offer, and he deserves to shine.

Dad, this letter is already long enough so I'll wrap it up. Please give my love to Mom and I'll write more when I can.

Love,

Mandy

Letter 2

Mr. Adam Hood to Miss Amanda Hood

(June 1996)

My Dear Mandy,

Your letters will never be "too much" for me because I am honored to be your father. Sometimes I cannot quite believe how I managed to raise a daughter so beautiful, educated, resourceful, accomplished, and kind as you are. When the doctors placed you in my arms for the first time, my heart melted, and you have left it in that warm, syrupy state ever since.

It comes as no surprise to me how much you are interested in writing because girls are better in the Soft Sciences like languages, while boys tend to excel in the Hard Sciences like math and science. Of course, I am no stranger to writing letters which I mostly sent to your mom when we dated, and I turned in a couple of research papers in college. Had I not dropped out of my Entomology major, I might have taken a class titled, "Advanced Pollinators" in which I would have learned about that interesting honeybee counterattack. Since both honeybees and hornets belong to the Order of Hymenopterans, I don't know why hornets are so susceptible to the temperature change when the honeybees aren't, but that's probably just a difference between the species.

The hotel sounds almost gothic in nature. I might have to check it out if I attend the American Equipment Convention in Oklahoma City next Spring since it's roughly a four-hour drive away. I only found it because my coworker Bob happened to mention a few weeks ago that he is from Amarillo. I called him at home, and he gave me the name which Directory Assistance used to connect me with them. They seemed to understand that you would pay cash instead of reserve by credit card. Incidentally, I am glad to help you when I can, but I cannot always. You might consider carrying more cash next time, though I know things are a bit tight for you before you receive your first paycheck. At least your dear old Dad taught you how to maintain your car, right?

I vaguely remember the young man you mentioned in your letter, but then, I barely noticed other kids beyond you on those trivia teams. When you weren't answering the questions, I was reading my paperback mysteries. Mandy, most young men are over exuberant in their attempts to woo a young woman, so they're also remarkably familiar with rejection. While it may have been meaningful in the moment, I highly doubt he will remember it in five years, much less ten. And no, I'm not shocked by what you described. In fact, if I recall, I lent my copy of The Happy Hooker by Xaviera Hollander to you so you would understand more of the types of ways men and women can relate to one another. I would be surprised if you haven't engaged in some of those behaviors already since you are an independent young woman. And I certainly won't judge you if you have.

In other news, your mother referred to my mother's silver soup terrine as a "soup latrine" at a family dinner so my mother smiled one of her rare smiles and gently explained the malapropism while the rest of us were trying to hold our laughter in. Sometimes, the difference in our backgrounds is startling, but I try to remember that she did birth you, so that's something, and as far as I know, I'm the only person she's ever been intimate with, so there's that too.

Your mother is calling me to take out the trash, so I'll end this here. Write back when you can.

Love,

Dad

Letter 3

Miss Amanda Hood to Mr. Adam Hood

(June 1996)

Dear Dad,

Thank you so much for your last letter. You had never written one to me before, so I will cherish it always. I've never received a letter from Mom either, but she and I had a lively conversation on the phone this morning while you were away at work. As I continue to grow into a woman, I do appreciate more about her that I hadn't thought of before. For example, she laughs at her own mistakes, like what she called the soup terrine when she told me her version of events. She also laughed at the fact that she had broken another coffee carafe - the sixth in as many months. And I treasure her laugh which tinkles. I hope you find this a valuable trait in her as well. Come to think of it, Mom has a few other traits - persistence, diligence, forgiveness. I mean, not every person put herself through college while working at a grocery store and earning a 4.0, no? And I can't count how many times I let her down by not helping her with the housework, but she always makes sure I have clean clothes and healthy food. She's pretty special and I don't ever want to take her for granted, even if she did snoop through my diary when I was thirteen.

Lately, I've begun to ask myself - who on either side of our family has openly expressed admiration for the serious accomplishments of any grown woman? I've been struggling to come up with one. I know you're proud of me for my academics, you always have been, but I haven't really accomplished anything in the real world yet, so I'm not ready to count myself as an example. If you think of someone, please write about her for me. I think I would really enjoy reading your words.

As you know from our phone conversation, Gil and I partnered for trivia nights and yes, we are wiping the floor with the other teams. It doesn't bode well for making many friends, but I don't know that we'll ever see these people again anyway. It also feels good to win at something after long days of teenagers complaining about what they did, what they're doing, and what they're going to have to do. Very little that I do with them seems to make these young people happy. Honestly, when I see groups of kids rafting on the Colorado River, setting out on the mule trips to the bottom of the Canyon, or engaged in arts and crafts, they seem excited, and I feel a twinge of jealousy.

When they're with me on the trail hikes, the Yavapai Museum of Geology, the Grand Canyon Museum Collection, the Visitor Center, or other points of interest, they roll their eyes, spit on the ground, talk to each other over me, throw wads of paper around, and are just rude in general. It takes all of my energy to address their behaviors and keep them focused on the task at hand, though I know not to lose my temper. Sometimes they even wander away. For that they receive a penalty of loss of television privileges, but I'm handing these out more often than I think is normal. I don't know why they drift off when I'm telling them so many interesting facts about the flora and fauna of the Canyon, as well as the fossils that they're supposed to sketch, though the beautiful vistas always draw the eyes and hearts. But what I'm explaining can enrich their explorations, help them make connections, and divert them from dangers otherwise hidden. Their obtuseness about the education or its value drives me up a wall some days. When I can work with small groups or one-on-one, it goes great with the particular teen(s) I'm attending to, but then, the others fare worse.

Just the other day, I had taken my morning group to Waldron Basin. After we disembarked from the bus at the Hermit Rest, we proceeded along the Hermit Trail at a good pace that would return us to Hermit Road in four hours at the most. In fact, the descent from the Hermit Trailhead into Waldron Basin went very smoothly. After an hour and half of hiking and pausing to talk about the different forms of life we saw, we reached our stopping point where we hydrated and ate a midmorning snack. For those who needed it, the porta potty was available. Having checked that everyone packed up their trash and was still in attendance, I started them on the hike back to Hermit Road. By an hour into the ascent, our pace had slowed, and we walked more in a straight line of pairs rather than one large group, but I was at the rear, ready to help anyone who faltered. In fact, I had to spend a considerable amount of time helping a teen patch a hole that had opened on the sole of his shoe. (I found a ponderosa pine dripping sap, so I gathered some into a wad, let it fill the hole so it would stick inside under the liner, then dusted it with dirt, which lasted.) Since we didn't pause as much as before, I didn't take attendance as often, and so, by the second hour, I discovered that two teens had snuck off to be private. Everyone who hikes together has walkie talkies, which is something the camp provides so we can stay in touch with each other, but the ranges are only about a mile, so they only help if other parties are within that range. For the next forty-five minutes, my calls to the teens went unanswered. It was tremendously frustrating not only for me, but for the kids with me as well. I tried to close my mind off to the things the missing kids could be up to. The rest of the kids had turned off their walkie talkies as instructed, but they were bored. I couldn't abandon them to look for the teens, nor could I dispatch any minors to look for the others. Retracing our steps was a risk of losing more people along the way. I didn't know what else to do, but call and call, hoping the missing teens would eventually turn their walkie talkies back on. And then, who should appear around a corner, but Beatrice! She had had some free time this morning and had also decided to hike the Hermit trail. Having heard my latest calls, she hastened to our group, guided by the strength of the signal. I explained the situation to her, and she offered to look for them in a mile radius. Then, we had to wait for her too.

I tried to engage the teens in some games, but after a couple rounds of the Havasupai Stick Dice and Vaputta, they just petered out and talked with each other instead. Finally, after another hour, Beatrice crackled through the walkie talkie that she was with them. Those two delinquents had indeed turned off their walkie talkies, then had lost the trail so that by the time they turned the mikes back on, we had already walked far enough ahead to be out of their range. However, Beatrice had spotted them with her binoculars near the Santa Maria Spring Trail at just the right moment and called their names. They ran the half-mile straight to her and drank the water she offered to them though they were not dehydrated, nor in any need of medical attention. After having been lost, they had become scared, then relieved at the sound of her voice. After that, all three hiked back to us. I also felt relief to see them, but admonished them for sneaking off, as well as wasting all our time returning to the campground. When we were less than a mile from Hermit Rest Area, I radioed the bus driver of our return. He had been worried when we hadn't communicated within the flexible hour of our scheduled return and, following procedure, had radioed Ms. Nyimsava of our absence. She in turn had sent other counselors to search for us once she found cover for their activities. Not only had these teens caused our lateness, but they had also created a disruption for the entire campground as kids were shuffled from one building or area to the next and schedules were compromised to send the adult search party. However, as soon as their bus arrived, we appeared on the scene, so they returned to the campground, never having left their bus. The kids received detention for a couple of days, but were back in my group afterwards, though those particular kids didn't wander away again.

After that, I was called into the office to explain what happened. I noted that I followed procedure with regards to taking attendance, but I was reminded that too frequently, students wandered away, as evidenced by the mountain of television privilege loss slip copies in my file. I tried to explain that I was doing all I could, but somehow the students weren't motivated to stay. Taking this protest as a cue, Ms. Nyimsava told me that she wanted me to engage them better in the subject matter, yet she didn't give me any ideas on how to do that. I thought I was doing well enough keeping them from bodily harm. She saw the wandering of the two kids as a failure on my part. I found the whole conversation very frustrating but thanked her for her (unhelpful - don't worry Dad, I didn't say that part) advice.

That evening, when the day had wrapped up and I returned to my bunkhouse, I walked over to Beatrice who was seated at her desk, painting some bright splotches with a quality watercolor set she had brought from home. She seemed to hide what she was painting by placing it carefully under a shoebox lid as I approached, then she turned in her chair to face me fully. I thanked her for helping me. Because of her, the adult search party did not even need to disembark from their bus and could return quickly to resume their regular activities. She said she was glad to help, but some of the friendliness in her eyes had left. I asked if she was going to trivia night, but she declined.

After dinner, I went to Trivia, but Gil was nowhere to be found. My team of one placed third which wasn't terrible, but it didn't put my mind at ease like when he and I placed first together. I didn't see him every day, so I didn't know what other activities or interruptions he had.

The next morning, I showered and dressed casually because I had some time off. What Bea had done for me was incredibly helpful and there was still much about the Grand Canyon I wanted to explore by myself that I decided to hike alone. If I came across another group in distress in any way, I could lend my services just like she had. Since I was already familiar with the Hermit Trail, I decided to start again at the Hermit Trailhead, then take it all the way to Dripping Spring, about three and half miles out. The name sounded so refreshing on such a hot, dry day and I had never trekked there, so I was excited to go. According to paces I had walked previously without pausing to explain wildlife to groups of young people, I would be able to hike to Dripping Spring and back in seven hours or so. I packed a large thermos of water, some iodine water tablets for the natural water I might find there, some trail mix, a couple of apples, and a mylar blanket. I tied a sweatshirt around my waist on the off chance that if I were stuck there overnight, I would be warm enough.

Dad, hiking the trail was simply exhilarating. At several points, I stopped and stared at the breathtaking Canyon, She is so grand. I say She because if the Grand Canyon isn't a yoni symbol, then what is? Certainly, an overabundance of phallic monuments, both natural and man-made ones, have sprouted all over the world, it seems well-balanced that Mother Earth revealed this feminine one. Well, that's how I like to think of it/her. I wouldn't be surprised if I am influenced by Native American philosophies since I've lived here. As the clouds move across the sky, their shadows dapple her perpetual variegations and this Grand Dame seems to change before me, yet she is constant. I am drawn in by her warm tones, her rounded prominences, her contoured chasm, her secret crevices, her sacred moisture, her reassuring heft. A slight misstep can kill in an instant, or one can die by degrees in her wilderness. She is not a trifle, but commands respect, reminding us of forces more powerful and a time greater than those we measure.

After a few hours of hiking, I stood in the shade of a juniper tree on a large rock, near to the trail. I pulled my thermos out, uncapped it, gulped down about half of the water in it, then stood it on the rock. Since rattlesnakes and the like are abundant, I grabbed a dead branch that had fallen onto the ground from the limbs above in case I needed to ward off some creature. Sure enough, just as I sat down, I heard a rattle and saw a movement out of the corner of my eye. I moved the stick into position faster than I could swivel my head and it is a good thing I did because the snake struck very quickly. However, because I had been faster, or perhaps because it had been a little slower, it clamped its jaw around the wood, instead of my arm. I watched the venom drip down the stick to the rock, grateful I had not been on the receiving end of it. Sadly, my thermos of water rolled off the other side of the rock, spilling its precious contents into the place the snake had come from, so I didn't dare try to retrieve it because what if a nest existed on the other side? Since I had no water, I decided to return faster than I had planned, but my previous swallows and the juice from my bites of apple sustained me, so I wasn't overheated in the least.

Having returned to the campground, I headed straight to my bunkhouse. I took a long, cool shower which calmed me, then prepared to guide my afternoon group to Waldron Basin. After I finished writing out the forms of life, I felt necessary to identify to this group on an index card, my eyes caught sight of something colorful in the trash can next to Beatrice's desk. I then remembered. Beatrice hid whatever it was that she had been painting so I made my way over and fished it out. The unfinished works were some kind of wheels or flowers. I couldn't quite make out exactly what they were because they weren't finished, but I don't think they weren't anything unusual. Perhaps she hid the painting because she isn't confident in her skills. Then I sat down to write this letter to you.

That's all I have for now. Please hug and kiss Mom for me.

Love,

Mandy

Letter 4

Mr. Adam Hood to Miss Amanda Hood

(June 1996)

My Darling Daughter,

You, like most women, tend to see things that aren't there - you have romanticized the Grand Canyon. Dry, dusty, prickly, rocky, sharp-edged, teeming with venom in various forms, fickle with her moisture, and freezing at night, She (borrowing your pronoun here) is unlike any woman I have ever known, and I have known a great many. That she would murder those who adore her whether slowly or quickly unveils her as a "harsh mistress" rather than a lover. I might go there someday, but now I'm not sure I would go with you, for I'm afraid you would show me things that aren't there, rather than things that are. I can see why they hired you - you feed the visions of those impressionable young people. Someone like Gil could guide me instead because he, like most men, tends to have a more common-sense approach to Nature. And please feel free not to waste your fingers on such effusive writing, it is not to my taste, nor does it truly compensate for my time away from work.

I am so grateful you were able to avoid the worst of the rattlesnakes. Nature can be beautiful, but deadly. It is important to prepare and defend against these kinds of predators and sometimes sacrifices must be made. Instead of being so independent, you might consider not hiking alone in the future. That way, should an emergency arise, you will increase your chance of surviving it. I worry about you so much.

As for those kids wandering off, I'm not surprised - I was a pretty horny teenager. Did I ever tell you about the time I was seeing your mother and I put a ladder to her bedroom window? It was right before her eighteenth birthday, so it was okay. At one point, your grandmother knocked and entered the room to say goodnight to your mother whose torso was still clothed in her nightgown. Geegaw didn't see me on the other side of the bed, so it all went off without a hitch.

Your boss's detention of the students seems a bit harsh but not everyone is a born leader. In my day, if kids pulled a stunt like that, they would simply be paddled, but I suppose that's not politically correct now.

Your girlfriend sounds like a sneak. I wouldn't spend much time with her if I were with you. You don't need to compromise your morals with whatever she has up her sleeve. One of the things I find charming about you is how naive you are. Please never lose this, but also, try to understand that it can cost you if you're not careful.

I sincerely hope that you do not turn out like your mother. At least you know how to read a map. The other day, she and I were driving to a new park I wanted to explore, and I swear, she didn't understand how to orient herself in relation to the map. She had us so completely turned around that we wound up five miles farther from our destination, which was only ten miles away. I finally pulled the car over, demanded the map, which she was holding upside-down, and drove us to the right place. The whole time there she didn't even act like she knew she had really screwed up, just noticed things outside the window like a small child. Some days, I think if I wasn't here for her, she wouldn't make it in life. She started out fine putting herself through college, but since she had you, she has not accomplished much. Even her boss cut her hours severely the other day - she went from four days a week down to two. It's okay since we are not desperate for the money, but she just kind of roams about the house aimlessly and I constantly have to redirect her to do the dishes, or vacuum, or even cook dinner. The other night, she gave us cereal and milk when I forgot to suggest what to make. Her doctor says menopause causes a foggy brain, but your mother has a cumulus cloud for a mind at this point. I hope by the time you reach middle age; science will have improved enough to help women avoid this depressing phase.

I've got to go out of town for a work trip, so I won't be here the next time you call.

Love,

Dad

Letter 5

Miss Amanda Hood to Mr. Adam Hood

(June 1996)

Dear Dad,

Thank you for being concerned about me. I know you worry, but really, I'm fine. I would not be where I am today if I didn't already know how to look out for myself, impecuniousness notwithstanding.

Mom sounds like she is in rough shape, both from your description as well as my last phone call. Speaking with her was initially difficult because not only did it take her longer than normal to understand what I was telling her; her reactions were weird. While she laughed at nearly every funny story, she laughed at other stuff that wasn't, which was kind of rude. When we moved on to remembering that trip, we all took to England back in '85, she was her old self and laughed in only the right places. She even remembered the night at that fancy restaurant in London that we heard a loud crash in the kitchen, the dogs barked, and the staff told us our dinner was "delayed," which I had totally forgotten about until she reminded me. We both laughed over that one, so the call ended on a good note, but it was difficult up to that point.

I am glad that you are there for her though. I think it's beautiful that your marriage has lasted over twenty-five years when so many of your peers ended theirs in divorce. And you don't fool me for a minute. I know it's common for men to brag about their conquests, but the few relationships you had prior to dating Mom could hardly be described as "many women."

Dad, you were right about Beatrice. She went down in flames, totally disgraced. It all started last week when the counselors and kids embarked on a three-day commercial paddle-rafting and camping trip with the Fiddle Faddle Paddle (FFP) group. FFP has been guiding rafting tours for Grand Canyon Youth Campgrounds for over twenty years, so they know exactly what they're doing. All their guides even play the fiddle at the campsites, and they take requests which can be surreal. Have you ever heard "Pour Some Sugar on Me" by Def Leppard played on a fiddle? No? Well, I have. Actually, "Never Tear Us Apart" by INXS on a stringed instrument turned out pretty well, but that's the rare exception.

Even though FFP has taken the kids on one- and two-day rafting trips each week since the beginning of camp, putting in farther upstream at Petroglyph and Kayak beaches, kids don't always have full control over themselves, nor do they have the necessary strength for rip-roaring rapids, so we don't take the more challenging stretches, but they do have to paddle. They complain a lot about it, but they don't cry because the peer pressure to pull one's weight is intense. They learn early on that they can't escape the boat or the glares which is funny, though I don't smile. I don't want to embarrass them, and they all learn the lesson, even vicariously.

On the first day, the FFP guides re-familiarized everyone with paddling technique, including Gil, who was substituting for a counselor who had fallen ill. Since we're used to teaming up, he and I decided to be the co-counselors in our seven-person raft, which meant there were four students in addition to the FFP guide. Bea and Tyler accompanied kids in another raft and a third smaller raft with a guide and two students carried most of the supplies we'd need for the trip. We put in at Lee's Ferry, then paddled down the Colorado River at a good pace, but after a few hours, the kids were visibly tired, so we beached the raft near Ten Mile Rock and set up the brown bagged lunch. Gil disappeared for a while, but the lunch was easy enough to manage. When he did reappear, he was holding his left hand with his right hand quite tenderly.

"Did you break your fingers again?" I asked.

"No," he answered. "I found some cool rocks to construct a cairn, but I didn't balance them correctly and they came crashing down."

"Oh wow," I said, looking over his bloody wounded hands. There was a particular abrasion that looked more serious than the others.

"Do you need me to treat your wounds or anything?" I asked him, unsure of how he'd want help.

"Actually, it's not as bad as it looks," he assured me. "All I really want is to keep it dipped in the water which I think will feel really good." I wasn't going to argue with Gil - he's a grown man and usually smart - so I didn't press him further. If he felt a dip in the river would heal him, then he could deal with the consequence of being wrong, though my mind mutely raised the possibility of infection.

We cleaned up our lunch, then climbed back into the raft for another calm, but tiring ten-mile stretch. This time we beached the rafts at Marble Canyon, whose grooved and swirling rock formations make one feel as if we are imperfect needles playing a warped record of a song that never ends. If we could roll bowling balls along "The Wave" it would make for the most mesmerizing marble track ever, but I guess that would be sacrosanct to this area that used to be part of the Navajo territory. I'm still waiting for the enchantment of the place to temper a little, but it hasn't. Mother Nature is quite perfect here, balancing beauty and brutality.

After dinner, we sat around the campfire and the kids requested songs on the fiddle which the guide played to our utter amusement. Later, he played songs of his own choosing, ones that matched the mood of the darkening sky and the realization that though we were all together around a bright and cozy fire, we were quite isolated from our usual civilization. Maybe that's why I gravitate to anthropomorphizing the area - I don't want to feel so alone and I want the boundless space to have a purpose of being. After an hour of this mournful music, I sent the kids to their tents, crawled into mine, and drifted off to sleep.

The next morning, I woke up before anyone else in order to relieve myself and to brush my teeth which I had forgotten to do the night before. I had just quietly unzipped and peeled back part of my tent flap, having bent low since it had stuck at one point, and it was then that I sensed Beatrice leaving Gil's tent. That is, she had walked several feet in a direction exactly away from his tent door and the flap was moving so I couldn't be one hundred percent sure, but it seemed so. I don't think she saw me at all. It's none of my business, so I wouldn't pry, but if either of them had confided in me, I wouldn't have been surprised. If they were up to something, it was best kept under wraps because kids are even more merciless than the rangers when they discover counselor relationships or breakups, so I said nothing as well.

After breakfast, we put in again, and had paddled for about five miles when something weird happened. As the rapids began to pick up a little speed, we were required to balance ourselves, not a lot, just a little. Gil, who didn't speak much, had been paddling with the rest of us, but also leaning to the side a bit to keep his hand in the cool waters when the pace slackened. However, at one point, he just sort of fell over the side. He came up sputtering and clambered back into the raft, apologizing sheepishly, but he gave no reason for having gone over. The guide asked him if he was all right, which Gil said he was, so we paddled on, including Gil, but we were all shaken by it. We set up camp for lunch at Redwall Cavern which we explored less than would have suited me. This was because the guide started asking Gil some questions that I couldn't hear, but apparently the answers were unsatisfactory. He loaded everyone and everything back into the rafts. Even though this was a paddle-only excursion, the guide pulled motors out of the supply raft and attached them onto all our rafts. Not one person complained. He then radioed his team to meet us at Nankoweap granaries where we had been scheduled to camp the next day but would arrive by early evening since we were traveling at a much faster rate of speed. As soon as we arrived, other FFP members met us. They asked for another counselor to accompany them and Gil, who seemed feverish, on the night trek, doling out headlamps to have a safer journey. Bea volunteered, which left us short two counselors, but two new FFP staff joined, so we maintained the same number of adults, plus they had packed some extra supplies to make the disruption worthwhile. Fresh mangoes along the Colorado River? Don't mind if I do!

The rest of the rafting trip went without a hitch, we landed at Phantom Ranch incident-free, but I was eager to get back and find out what had happened. Sure enough, as soon as the bus rolled into the Campground, Bea was there to help unload and tell me everything. Gil had definitely come down with an infection because...his rock cairn had fallen onto his hand and momentarily trapped it with a snake who had been hiding nearby. It was one of those Sonoran Lyre snakes. Again, they don't bite, but they do chew their victims. That's why that one wound had looked so bad. Gil had been hiding that he had been attacked by a snake, but that's the crazy thing. Sonoran Lyre snakes aren't that poisonous. However, when Gil's rock cairn tumbled, it stirred up dust which had a fungus he inhaled, and some spores also landed in his wound. Therefore, Gil suffered from Valley Fever which caused his collapse. On the trek back to civilization along the Nankoweap Trail, which is historically the most difficult one at the Canyon, he fell a few times, so someone had to keep holding onto him the whole way back. Bea said the climb took hours, but they finally made it to the FFP vehicles, instead of having to call in a helicopter rescue. Then they drove straight to the emergency room at Flagstaff Medical Center where he was rigorously evaluated. The doctors treated him with antifungals and supportive care right away, keeping him there for observation overnight. Because Gil is young and healthy, he rebounded enough to be discharged the next morning, so Bea picked him up. He was fine to return to camp and rest a bit before Ms. Nyimsava gave him permission to resume arts and crafts with the kids again, which he did.

That night, I caught up with Gil before we engaged in our trivia tournament.

"How are you feeling?" I asked him directly.

"I'm fine. It's fine." he answered.

"I had no idea that you had been attacked by a snake and a fungus," I said.

"Yeah well, I couldn't be sure, because I couldn't see my trapped hand until I was able to move the rocks off, but I did hear a rattle and see a snake slither away. I didn't want to raise any false alarms about a rattlesnake since I didn't have puncture wounds or symptoms. At least, early on I didn't."

"I can understand that." I tried to think of something positive. "Bea was helpful. I'm glad she was able to look out for you." Would he confess that they were dating on some level? I wondered.

"She was helpful, but since then, she's been blabbing to everyone what happened. I wish she wouldn't do that. She needs to respect my privacy when it comes to my health information." Always more informed than me about current events he added, "Congress will be passing this law called [hip-something, I don't quite remember what he said] soon, and in the next few years, it will be totally against the law to share people's private medical information. I look forward to that." he finished with a scowl.

"I guess it's not right for her to talk about you without your agreement, but I appreciate that she shared the truth of what happened. It's a great lesson about not building unauthorized rock cairns, for instance," I finished with a smile. He didn't respond, so I left it at that. We entered the bunkhouse and carried out the usual bloodbath. This time, Tyler took a Polaroid of us with our trophy, which I'm enclosing. If you look hard enough, you can almost see a smile on Gil's lips, hahaha. Do you see how muscular he is though? I will never challenge him to arm-wrestle, even with his bad hand.

The next day, the groups who had rafted together sat down in the arts and crafts room to view a slide show of our recent trip. It's always fun for me to look at the slides from our adventures because I often miss expressions of people enjoying themselves at the time when I am so preoccupied with responsibilities. Even Ms. Nyimsava joined us, having poured some freshly popped popcorn into paper bags for the kids and counselors to enjoy while we watched the slide show. We settled in, munching loudly. Tyler darkened the lights and turned the projector on.

The first few slides showed us on the bus going there, you know, the usual goofy, silly expressions of kids hanging out of windows, standing in their seats. Ms. Nyimsava looked at everyone with a fake stern expression which made the kids snicker in their chairs. We were all kind of chuckling when it happened. The next slide was not of the kids or the bus, but there was Beatrice, absolutely starkers, kneeling on the ground, with a male person's most prominent and very straight member in her mouth. I'd say her lips were wrapped around it, but it was clear that she was smiling and quite pleased. It made me think she had posed for the picture, but now, looking at her in the audience, with her mouth equally open, this time in horror, she was definitely not in agreement to the photo being shared. As the content of the image dawned on the teenagers, they became wild with whooping and hollering. Ms. Nyimsava got really still for a moment, then demanded that Tyler shut off the machine and turn the lights back on. I looked harder at it, trying to figure out who the guy was, but of course, I don't know anyone in that way.

Remembering how close Gil and Bea had been in the past week, I blurted out to him, "Is that you?".

He looked thunderclouds at me and said, "No, of course not." I was really embarrassed that I even said anything, so I tried to think of who else it could be. I saw Tyler smiling, and, knowing that guy's shameless history, suggested it might be him.

Gil said, "Who knows?" and I thought, "yeah, how could anyone know except the people directly involved?" I couldn't even figure out how the image was made into a slide, unnoticed by the developers in town. Surely, they wouldn't have released such a pornographic image. Ms. Nyimsava demanded how Tyler could have even thought of putting such a slide into the carousel, but he swore he didn't. He pulled it out, then said it wasn't like a regular slide. Upon closer inspection, he thought that someone lifted some kind of film, like off of a picture or Polaroid, then stuck it to a piece of glass and fitted that into a homemade cardboard surround. By this point, Bea had run off crying, so no one knew who did it, or who else was in the picture. Ms. Nyimsava took the slide out of the room. Having nothing else to do, Tyler inspected the rest of the slides, then we resumed the show, but it wasn't nearly as interesting.

About an hour later, when I was setting out for a short hike with the kids, we saw Bea walk out of our bunkhouse with her heavy duffle bag and climb into a taxi. That was the last I saw of her.

As I hiked with the kids, I thought about all she had done for people, yet it was all for naught. I guess the bigger they are, the harder they fall. I miss her, but I don't miss what she is associated with at the end, so I don't bring her up to anyone else. No one talks about her either, not even Gil, even though I think she helped him the most. He was very put off by her behavior in the photo. Not too many days later, he left, embarking on some internship in Greece, so I don't know when I'll see him again, but we promised each other that we would write. He said I could always send letters to his parents' house, who moved to Pittsburgh last year, even when he's not there, as he would receive them.

I should stop now and get some sleep. In a week and a half, I'll have a new adventure- riding on mules! Please give a hug and kiss to Mom from me.

Love,

Mandy

Letter 6

Mr. Adam Hood to Miss Amanda Hood

(July 1996)

My Dear Mandy,

I know you have been trying to reach us by phone, but I just can't bring myself to speak directly to you yet. However, it is important that you know what is going on with your mother.

As you noted before, she has acted unnaturally in conversations and I think you're aware she has broken a few things, including several coffee carafes, whose frequency of crashes aren't readily explained by the normal slips and falls of washing them periodically. The fact is your mother has syphilis. Or had it. She is on antibiotics right now, specifically a certain course of penicillin. Even though she has had courses of antibiotics in the past, none of them were targeted to this disease so it progressed. It pains me to write this. This disease, of which I can hardly bring myself to print the name again, has existed in her body, undetected for the past twenty years or so. I don't quite understand how it was undetected, one would think she would have alerted someone if she had the dreadful chancres, but that didn't happen. What did happen is that she crashed the car three days ago. No, she wasn't hurt, thank God, nor was the driver whom she t-boned in running the red light, but because she has been sick for so long, it has caused her brain to atrophy. When she was taken to the hospital as a precaution, they ran an MRI to look for brain damage.

My Darling Daughter, I hope you never have to see the brain scans of your dear mother. There is literally an inch of space between her brain and her skull in all directions. This condition prompted the doctors to run a battery of blood tests, one of which signaled the disease. They performed a spinal tap to confirm the diagnosis, then delivered the penicillin intravenously until they released her from the hospital. The doctor emphasized that the atrophy cannot be reversed and that it will continue, though at a slower rate, even though the disease itself will be cured. She will become increasingly dependent on others until her death, which he measures at a year out or so. I am deeply aggrieved.

I know you will help me as your mother and I will need it, but for now, I can deal with her alone while you finish out your experience. She is embarrassed to have carried this "social disease" and distressed that she is no longer allowed to drive, but I am profoundly grateful to the Powers That Be that nothing worse happened. Naturally, we are not sharing this news with anyone else, and we ask you to keep it please also to yourself. If you need to say something at some point, "progressive dementia" will convey what is most important for others to know.

Much love,

Dad

P.S. Because the doctor can't nail down the exact time of your mother's infection, it is possible that she has been carrying it for decades. Furthermore, she could have passed it to you in some innocent way, like if a wound of hers touched a wound of yours. Please get yourself tested. Let me know if you need me to call up a testing site for you. I couldn't bear it if you both suffered this nightmare.

Letter 7

Miss Amanda Hood to Mr. Adam Hood

(July 1996)

Dear Dad,

I have just received your letter and I am genuinely heartbroken. I can't believe this is happening to Mom. She doesn't deserve this. She has been so generous and wonderful all my life and to die this young isn't justified. Why? Why? How? And how did she acquire it? The implications are just staggering. Even "decades" ago puts you two at "well-married." That would mean she had an affair and that just doesn't seem likely. Could the doctor be off in his timeline? Could it have been a former lover of hers prior to marriage? Maybe she had been with someone else before you but was too shy to tell you? Please don't hold that against her if it was so, but that would be much better to consider than the alternative theory of her cheating on you.

Since counselors are often young people, there is literature available on various health clinics throughout the campground. I think if I go alone, then no one else will know. Gil said something about a "hip" law that will go into effect and that medical privacy was going to be a part of it at some point, so perhaps that will protect me from clinic staff blabbing to others. I certainly see his point now. I hope no one thinks ill of me for testing for syphilis. This is extremely upsetting. I will leave a message on your answering machine; you don't have to pick up. I just want Mom to know how much I love, support, and miss her. And thank you for suggesting that I get checked out. I expect you should also do the same if you haven't already.

Much love,

Mandy

Letter 8

Mrs. Amy Hood to Miss Amanda Hood

(July 1996)

Dear Mandy,

Dad says to write you a letter. I am fine. Someti[mes] I don't remember, but I am okay. Please don't worry. You will always be my busy bee.
Love,
Mom

Letter 9

Ms. Evette Nyimsava to Mr. George Collins

(July 1996)

Evette Nyimsava

Assistant Director

Grand Canyon Youth Campground

243 South Rim Drive

Grand Canyon Village, Arizona 86023

July 10th, 1996

George Collins

Director

Grand Canyon Youth Campground

243 South Rim Drive

Grand Canyon Village, Arizona 86023

Dear Director Collins,

I, Evette Nyimsava, do hereby tender my letter of resignation as Assistant Director, to be effective immediately, this 10th day of July 1996. I recognize that while the horrific actions of a few minors and Counselor Amanda Hood are not directly my responsibility, I had not performed in my role sufficiently in the past to have prevented them. In hindsight, I regret not having expelled the minors when they first broke the rules of our organization by wandering off on a hike away from Counselor Hood, who had managed the hike. I also accept that I did not provide enough support to Counselor Hood when she described the various ways these students tested her, nor did I reaffirm the wealth of knowledge she brought to the students every day. Furthermore, I should have created a more open and sympathetic presence in which Counselor Hood could have relayed to me some of the upheaval she has been suffering in her personal life. The loss of Counselor Hood's company, as well as the innocence of our camp is forever changed for the worse. The best I can do is to remove myself from the organization so that my ineffectual norms and practices do not further damage it.

I would like to express my sincerest gratitude to Grand Canyon Youth Campground for the rich life experiences I have had on its grounds and with its people. From the education about the Grand Canyon itself, the artwork it inspired, the survival skills it conveyed, to the nurturing of its community, I have learned more about myself and others, than I believe I would have through any other group or setting. I have truly cherished holding all the positions with Grand Canyon Youth Campground such as Counselor, Head Counselor, Activities Manager, Registration Administrator, and Assistant Director, so that leaving this organization translates to a temporary loss of my own identity.

In the future, I will seek employment with a different organization, though not immediately, as I will use this time for a period of deep introspection, in order to avoid repetition of my mistakes. I wish Grand Canyon Youth Campground great success in all its endeavors.

Respectfully,

Evette Nyimsava

Letter 10

Miss Amanda Hood to Mr. Gilbert DeRoquedu

(October 1996)

Dear Gil,

I hope this letter finds you well. I don't know if your parents will forward it to you while you are in Greece or whether you'll read it when you return home, but I suppose it doesn't matter. I'm guessing that you are very preoccupied with your research, and I don't remember who else you were close to, except me, so it is a strong possibility you haven't heard. I was let go by Grand Canyon Youth Campground back in July and I will never be recommended to any other job by them.

Please know that I don't regret my actions. I honestly don't think I would have behaved differently if I were older or more experienced with kids, but I now know that I was not designed to prevent or oversee the frequent poor choices that teenagers often make. What I do regret is that I didn't leave earlier when I could have done so under my own power. While not all of these kids were disrespectful, enough were that most days I woke up with a feeling of dread. I only felt joy when I was off the clock and winning trivia with you. That's the truth of the matter. Our camaraderie was my terra firma. You didn't question my knowledge, but treated me with respect, and together we built something solid. The same cannot be said of my experiences with the teenagers.

Due to my actions, I have also been barred from seeking employment under The National Park Service or any of its affiliated institutions. This has left me stewing as to what I can do with my degree because nothing comes close to the intimate teaching of people about our great land or learning more from Native Americans. For now, I have chosen a job as a customer service representative with a credit card company, so I am currently employed.

To help my father manage my mother's progressive dementia, I continue to live at home with my parents. Some days are easier than others, but I am glad to spend what time

I can with my mom and reminisce with her in ways that give her pleasure. I love her laugh and never want to lose it. She listens to me complain about work sometimes, like she used to listen to all of my problems when I was a kid, so she's there in certain ways for me too, though she doesn't always understand the complexities of what I describe. Her Oh's and her murmurs still reassure me though. And this part of my adulthood isn't quite as scary as it would be if Dad weren't ultimately managing her care too. It's like when he put training wheels on my bike. In the future, I'll interview some visiting nurses, some adult daycares, but I can take it slowly and each decision that I make for her ongoing care will be run by him. I scarcely see him, but I think that it's also heartbreaking for him how mentally unwell my mom is. I'm sorry to dump on you, you're probably busy, but this is what is going on with me. However, I still want to tell you what happened at camp because I hope you never experience it if you return as a counselor there.

After you left, I carried on our trivia team just as you had without me - second or third place mostly - which really underscores how well we worked together, but that's beside the point. We made too many enemies out of our competitors, so no one else joined me, but the people I knew best anyway were gone, so it didn't really matter. The next week, we started the Mule Adventures.

My group and I were assigned to Apa Aha, a Havasupai guide from Fiddle Faddle Saddle (FFS) who oversaw our mountings and told us Jessica's mule was born without a voice box, so we needed to be extra sensitive if it seemed off in any way, like headshakes or such to indicate a problem. Then he led us down the trail from the Livery Barn. With Apa Aha taking the lead and me following the group at the rear, we traveled along the Bright Angel Trail whose majestic views were only slightly hampered by the smell of mule deposits every hundred feet or so. Apparently, the NPS does clean up after the mules, but they must not have done so for some time prior to the day we rode. The canyon was gorgeous as always.

Though the air was thick and hot, we moved along at a good pace, stopping here and there to listen to Apa Aha explain the geological formations or tell a Havasupai legend. The third time we stopped, I noticed that Jessica, Chris, Rob, Jason, and Chad had hung back a bit and were talking to each other quietly while the guide was speaking. I couldn't easily maneuver my mule over to them, nor did I want to dismount because it might be difficult to climb back on, so I settled for looking at them sternly, but they completely ignored me. Apa Aha didn't seem to notice, or maybe he was used to it, but I was irritated. Miles later, at the next informational stop that was beyond two blind corners, other kids moved their mules past them to be closer to the guide and the guide assumed that the kids who were missing would come through when the first group had cleared. I knew none of this until I approached, but when I rounded the first corner and happened upon the group, that's when I saw their cruelty.

Apparently, the voiceless mule had stepped into a hole, twisted his ankle, and lay down lame on the ground. The stupid kids in some misguided attempt to bring it to its feet had dismounted and were poking the poor animal with sticks, while their mules started to wander back down the trail toward me. I grabbed my walkie talkie, then realized I had stupidly forgotten to synchronize frequencies with the guide. I was afraid of spooking the loose mules, so I didn't yell for the kids to get them, but I waved my hands furiously trying to get their attention. They didn't notice me at all. I tied my mule to a sturdy ponderosa pine and dismounted. By this point, the tormented animal was writhing in mute pain. The kids were so engrossed in what amounted to torture, they didn't see me advance, but I was too late. One of the sadists had literally, but somewhat accidentally, stabbed the animal in the eye. A gush of liquid and blood flew out, but I barely focused I was so fucking angry. I grabbed two kids by the back of their hair and yanked them to the ground, then slapped the face of the stabber HARD. My hands were flying between heads, I hated them all so much at that moment. I'm shaking just writing this down for you. The kids moved away as soon as their initial shock wore off. It's weird that they didn't retaliate, but I'm guessing they knew they had done something wrong. Only one kid pierced the eye of the beast, but since they had all participated in some way, it was as if they were all guilty of having perpetrated the crime. While they muddled in their stupors, I quickly and carefully approached the other mules and tied them to other ponderosa pines, having urinated my own pants under such duress.

Seconds later, Apa Aha appeared around the other corner, coming back from his lecture since he realized that six people, including the other adult, had taken longer than expected. When he saw that the mute animal writhing in pain from a stabbed eyeball, he did the only humane thing one could do - he finished it off by shooting it in the head. The shot echoed around the canyon and then his radio crackled to life. He explained the situation to his fellow guides, and they came on their own mules within forty-five minutes. I sat down on the ground and tried to calm myself through breathing exercises. The rotten kids just sat off on one side. No one else spoke.

When the other guides arrived, they and Apa Aha dug a hole in the soil several feet away from the trail. Then they dragged the dead mule over to the hole, shoved it in, and completed the burial. The guides then untied the riderless mules, helped the kids mount them, helped me to mount mine, and we proceeded back up the trail in complete silence. When we reached the Livery Barn, I radioed Ms. Nyimsava in my very shaky voice to meet us, which she did immediately. She and the guides walked the sadists back to the campgrounds while FFS supplied the kids who hadn't been involved in any way with roasted pinyon nuts and a sweet drink called "Pumpkin Spring Juice" (which doesn't have any water from Pumpkin Spring Pool because that would be lethal) but is the usual artificially-orange "bug juice" the kids drink everywhere. I stayed with those kids until I realized that I had wet my pants. I don't think anyone noticed because I had a sweatshirt tied around my waist, but then Serena came down to the Barn, telling me that Ms. Nyimsava had sent for me.

I walked back to the campground to her air-conditioned office which left me feeling very, very cold. I was glad she didn't have the teens there, but she bade me to sit in one of the chairs across the desk from her. I sat down and told her everything I knew, but I cried at times because it was so horrible. This woman has never listened to me about how difficult the children were, just told me to "pick your battles" and never gave me genuine advice. I also told her a little about having just received a letter from my mom which upset me a lot. Ms. Nyimsava recently lost a parent to Alzheimer's disease, so she understood on some level where I was coming from. However, she said because I had struck the children, even though she understood how wrong they were, the parents could sue the organization if she didn't let me go. In fact, they still might try to sue Grand Canyon Youth Campground, but it would be more like "beating a dead horse" which she had the gall to utter in my presence. She apologized for that once she realized the foolishness of her words. Then she made arrangements for my dismissal, having me write and sign a statement of resignation, effective immediately, and that I would agree not to seek employment with the NPS or its affiliates. I know it's small, but she made a point that I couldn't participate in the championship trivia game either. Somehow that stung the most in that moment. She reserved a hotel room nearby so I could plan to go home, but not remain on the campground while doing so. Last, she hugged me goodbye, which was super weird because we were never that close. I guess it made her feel better though she looked super sad.

I packed my stuff and drove off the campground. When I arrived at the hotel, I called my dad and let him know what happened. He was upset but recommended that I return as soon as possible in order to look for a new job. I drove back home along the route I took out, though I missed staying at this really cool hotel that I once lodged at in Amarillo. I hope to return to the Grand Canyon someday, maybe when I'm married and have children. Hopefully, I'll remember enough to teach them.

Sincerely,

Mandy

Letter 11

Mr. Gilbert DeRoquedu to Miss Amanda Hood

(December 1996)

Dear Mandy,

Merry Christmas! I have just returned home for a brief holiday from my internship in Greece and was delighted to receive your letter, though I'm sorry to read how things ended for you at Camp. In fact, I paused to add the exclamation point for its inappropriate cheer, considering what you wrote, but I hope enough time has passed to assuage some of those harsher feelings. I empathize with everything you described, from the regular difficult teenager behavior to their blood sport. You are completely blameless in striking those tormentors. I cringe to imagine how they might have continued to abuse the animal had you not intervened. And Apa Aha's humane killing was the only decent thing left to do. Frankly, I am relieved that you are no longer with the group, for I fear what these vicious teens would have done had they decided to target you instead. If it's any consolation, they rarely ever listened to me either.

Your job with the credit card company sounds intriguing. Do you grant credit cards to new customers, review their credit files, check their scores? I imagine you have interesting conversations if that is the type of position you hold. I currently possess two credit cards, but I try not to use them because I heard that credit bureaus and credit card companies perceive a customer as riskier if they have a balance. However, one of the cards earns frequent flyer miles so I use it for large purchases even though I have the cash. Most recently, I did use one to pay for my round trip to the United States and back to Greece. Do you have any special plans for Christmas or New Year's Eve? Please write when you can.

Cordially,

Gil

Letter 12

Miss Amanda Hood to Mr. Gilbert DeRoquedu

(January 1997)

Dear Gil,

Happy New Year! Thank you so much for your warm letter. I had a quiet New Year's Eve with just my parents. They still don't approve of me having alcohol, even though I am a grown woman, so I had sparkling grape juice, but I watched the ball drop in New York City on the television. I daydreamed a little about being there, in the crowds, slightly buzzed, toes numbed by the cold, and a handsome stranger taking me in his arms for a New Year's embrace, with the colorful holiday confetti swirling all around us. I will venture to New York at some later date, but for now, I need to be home. I am sorry to report that my mother's dementia is progressing, so I may be more involved in her care in the next few weeks. One of the perks of my new job is that I can work ten-hour shifts, four days a week, so I am free one weekday a week to take her to appointments and such, which does make things a little easier. I have taken over much of the cooking now, but that is for the best because when I move out, I will need to cook for myself. I am grateful that my mom wrote down her most important recipes. While my dishes don't taste exactly like hers, I'm happy to bring familiarity to our dinner table. My dad is often preoccupied with his work, so he doesn't always notice, but when he does, he really sings my praises. His compliments on my cooking give me the lift I didn't know I needed and inspire me to do more. I hope he likes the onion tart I'm trying tonight.

You kindly asked about some parts of my job, so I will try to be as succinct as possible, though I really appreciate the chance to write about something that isn't on the home front. Your card with the frequent flyer miles program sounds fantastic. However, I do want to address your understanding of how credit bureaus perceive you. I believe you, as well as many other Americans, are often victims of misinformation. While no credit bureau has spoken to me directly, my new position has provided me a unique perspective into their world.

I guess the best way to begin this is to describe financial credit not as its own beast, but simply as a form of trust. Trust is something we want others to have, and so, we establish our trust in a few unchanging ways which I will detail below, then relate them to the credit industry.

- First, we establish trust by holding trustworthy relationships with other people. For future creditors, you want to show that other creditors trust you with a variety of credit relationships like those of credit cards, overdraft accounts, car loans, student loans, and mortgages. When you show that you are entrusted by a wide variety of creditors, you show that you are a lower credit risk, therefore, this contributes positively to your score.

- Second, we establish trust by demonstrating that we have been entrusted by other people for as long a time as possible. Therefore, I recommend opening as many credit cards as you are comfortable owning, the earlier, the better. I'm not saying open them all at once, nor am I saying use them all at once, but use them to the point they don't get canceled for inactivity and don't close them yourself. This way, you demonstrate your creditworthiness for a long time, which I believe contributes positively to your credit score.

- Third, we establish trust by meeting our obligations. Therefore, I highly recommend that you make your payments on time, which I imagine you already do. It doesn't matter if you pay off your cards immediately, or pay them down gradually, just meet each minimum payment by the due date. Delinquent payments detract from your credit score and timely payments add to it.

- Fourth, we establish our trust in other people by not taking advantage of everything they have to offer. For credit cards, this translates to never using more than half of any credit line, no matter the temptation. I know this seems counterintuitive, but credit card companies don't really want you to max out the line, no matter how low the line is. Therefore, it is in your absolute best interest to have as high a credit line as possible and use the lowest fraction of it you can. So many people make the mistake of lowering their credit lines thinking the creditors will be pleased with how little there is "open to buy," when in reality, they are simply tanking their scores by showing they max out their credit cards.

- Fifth, we demonstrate our trustworthiness by exhibiting how much others entrust to us. Maybe some friends trust you to take care of their homes when they are away, but other people entrust not only their homes, but their pets and houseplants too. In the same way, large credit lines demonstrate how much creditors entrust you with borrowing, so ask for credit line increases as often as you can. Yes, your score will drop a few points for six months or so from the time of application, but it will bounce back if you are following my previous points of advice.

- Sixth, (and this is specific to financial credit) credit card companies don't really count it against you to pay your balance in full, so do that when you can. Bonus: you'll save interest this way. In fact, if you are making small payments toward a balance, the credit card company may get nervous and lower the line, since they will perceive any more you put on the card will make it much harder to pay off. The credit bureaus won't know this, but they will know when your balance is high in relation to the lowered credit line and dock you for it.

I do hope this information helps you to improve your credit score. If you have any other questions, you are most welcome to ask me. If you have any questions about dementia, I can answer those too, ha-ha, because I am just a barrel of laughs. (Not really)

While I'd like to share fun stories of clubbing with my best friend, the truth is, I've just wrapped myself in work and home and not gone out at all. However, at one point, I did travel for work, and therein lay the drama I had been missing. Sometimes, the bank likes to send its employees to training conferences. Yours truly left for a week's training conference in the beginning of September since I had fully arranged with Dad his care for Mom. And she was as well as she could be when I returned. In the meantime, …

The bank assigned me a roommate, which presented no issue since Grand Canyon Youth Campground had habituated me to sharing sleeping spaces and bathrooms. The rule there, like everywhere, is...no hanky panky. However, this respect was lost on my roommate, Gerta, a woman a few years older than me, but clearly unhappily married. It wasn't that she spoke ill of her husband, but my heavens how she fawned over some single sales guy from another region. She sat next to him at every meeting, constantly engaging him in jokes and high school-type secrets. She even hung out with him in their free time, instead of with me. He's clean-cut, tan, and handsome in a traditional sales guy kind of way, but too fake to impress me. Also, he wears V-neck undershirts and boxer briefs. I hate having this knowledge.

Hours after I had fallen asleep in my twin bed one evening, Gerta and Studley Do-Wrong stumbled into the room. I woke up, but decided not to say anything when Gerta asked, "Mandy? Mandy, are you awake?" Then she said to him, "She's asleep." They made their way farther into the room, making kissing sounds. I heard a zipper unzip, then a frenzy of fabric noises as they quickly undressed. They climbed into her bed so carefully and that's when I heard her say, "Don't you know I'm married?" I didn't know what to make of such a ridiculous statement. Did she not just undress herself and invite him into her bed by her actions? And why on Earth would she appeal to his sense of morality when he's not even married, but she swore the vows? It was like the last-ditch effort of a desperate person, losing their battle. What a dumb thing for her to say. He didn't even answer her, but shortly thereafter, the bed creaked, and I heard her ridiculous moaning. I decided to give her one more chance and rolled over. They totally froze for a few seconds. I pretended to snore lightly which prompted them to shake the bed. It was over in about a minute. All I could think was what a lousy price she paid to be unfaithful. She didn't even get any foreplay, ha-ha. And I don't think anything else happened because I'm a light sleeper. In the morning, he was still there. I just said "hi" to him on my way to the bathroom while he was standing in his stupid underwear. He just grinned at me. I didn't even look at her. Later, she told me that he just stayed over because they had drunk too much to send him back to his room, but that nothing happened. I said I didn't care, and it wasn't my business. Gert must have felt guilty because she was much nicer to me after that. When we see each other in the hallways at work, she gives me this knowing smile like I'm this great protectress of her secret. I hate it. I grimace and move on, but I did put in a request to not room with her for any future trips.

Would you please tell me about your adventures in Greece? I know we could call each other, but I would prefer to read about sun-drenched vistas, crystal-blue waters, juicy pomegranates, and anything else you would like to share. Of course, I am most interested in your progress in your career, but whatever you write about would lift me during these dreary winter days. And isn't letter-writing a charming activity? I've started to use emails at work, but I'm thrilled to scratch my pen on paper - it feels like more of an artistic creation than simply a form of communication. Is that your take as well, or do you feel differently?

Sincerely,

Mandy

Letter 13

Mr. Gilbert DeRoquedu to Miss Amanda Hood

(January 1997)

Dear Mandy,

It is a pleasure for me to both write letters to you and receive letters from you, as well as something we can continue no matter how far apart we are. Though I am no stranger to the telephone, I am glad not to interrupt you in your family obligations or your work routine. I also benefit from subsequent rereadings of your letters when you send me such detailed information as you included in your last letter. Thank you for your credit card advice, for example. I may use it when I return to the United States from Turkey, where I plan to live for a period of eight months, starting next week. When I come back, I will need to fully establish my American life, and credit will be a part of that.

I wish I could write to you of crystal-blue waters, and I suppose there were some sun-drenched vistas, but I spent a large part of my days in an Athenian office in the dark, with several hairy men, some friendly department cats, a temperamental fan, and no air conditioning. My internship for the Society for the Promotion of Hellenic Studies was a deep dive into the x-rays of the Serpentine Column, also known as the Delphi Tripod, that denoted Greek victory at the Battle of Plataea. The column, which consisted of three bronze serpents, had once been located at Delphi and adorned with a golden tripod. The golden tripod was stolen, the heads of the serpents broke off, but the bronze coils of the column remain, though they are currently located in Constantinople, hence my next trip. The x-rays show very scratched coils of the column and are theorized to originate from the melted shields of the defeated Persians. With much diligence and discussion, the Society believes it has discovered the names of Greek military leaders etched therein. It is terribly slow, exceedingly demanding work to account for every mark, and most of my time was spent on a three-foot-tall section of the column. When I live in Constantinople, I will inspect the column itself, as well as help some other researchers capture newer images, magnified to a greater degree. The work that I've already done will aid us to focus on important markings while more easily disregarding extraneous ones in order to discover any information that earlier, less precise technology, may have missed.

At one point, I ventured to the Delphi oracle, to see the original base of the column. It was a three-hour trip by car, so I did a bit of sight-seeing out of the window. We passed many beautiful hills and valleys, dotted with Cyprus trees and limestone outcroppings. This landscape is different from that of The Grand Canyon, but equally hot and dusty. At Delphi, there are many remnants of ancient buildings to which our group has full access, so I picked my way through overgrown grasses, around various piles of limestone blocks. I mostly focused on the base of the Victory Monument that was erected after the Persian War. In the centuries since Delphi has been abandoned as an oracle, no treasures seem to have been left behind, but the limestone bases remain and with a bit of imagination, as well as imagery from a few fragments of artistic renderings, one can mentally reconstruct how grand it once was. It was so easy to visualize the majesty of Delphi, that I felt sacrilegious sitting down in one corner, eating my lunch there. However, even the Pythia, the chief priestesses, needed to consume food, so it was probably not an unknown activity in that area. After lunch, we exchanged some information with representatives of the Delphi Archeological Museum where some of the more precious statuary is preserved.

While we had no ostensible reason to drive to Thermopylae, after finishing at Delphi my colleagues and I drove an hour north to the site of that famous battle. If you don't know it, three hundred Greeks, under the leadership of King Leonides, held off thousands of Persians until the Persians snuck up a shepherd's path and overpowered them. The Greeks were so strong up until that point, that legend has it that the ground was thick with dead Persians. This battle was so famous, it has been studied by military strategists for centuries. Many people are under the mistaken impression that the area is simply a narrow opening between two large rocks, but the truth is that the fighting ground was a small strip of beach sandwiched between the water of the Gulf of Malia and the hot springs that run by the feet of the mountains. At this point, the beach is far wider than the three hundred feet it was at the time of the battle, as the gulf has deposited sediments over the millennia, so it's a little more difficult to conjure up, but there is a dirt road that runs along it, across from the monument of Leonides. To walk where the brave Spartans held off the Persians until they were decimated is to tread through a somber history. It's quiet along the path, which makes the clashing of swords and shields easier to hear in my musings. We didn't have time this last trip, but next time, I plan to walk to the water's edge of the Gulf, to better immerse myself in the experience. One of my colleagues looked for the legendary shepherd's path but couldn't find it. Then we piled into the car and headed back to Athens.

As we drove away, I again thought of you. I hope it's not weird, but as I looked at the scenery flying by, I wondered how you might compare this part of the Earth to the corner that we explored this summer. I remember how adept at identifying the vegetation and wildlife you were at the Grand Canyon. I would like to hike these rocky hillsides with you, seeing it through your mind's index. I think you would keep me safer too, pointing out dangerous snakes or slippery inclines, or advise me not to build unauthorized rock cairns. I was more sure-footed when we were together, even in our esoteric world of trivia.

If you wouldn't find me indecorous, would you be amenable to going out to lunch sometime after I return? It could be anywhere, I'm not picky, though I've certainly developed a fondness for Greek food. I recommend stifado if you haven't had it yet. It's a hearty meat stew flavored with wine and a little cinnamon, though I'm not sure how available it is in East Coast Greek American restaurants. When it's well-prepared the taste is divine. Again, the food, or the entertainment, like a movie, doesn't really matter, I would just like to spend some time with you. Whatever your answer, I look forward to hearing from you, though I understand our letters may be delayed as I'll be in Turkey. Please write back when you can. In my next letter, I'll try to include some Polaroids so you can get more of a feel of my surroundings.

Cordially,

Gil

Letter 14

Miss Amanda Hood to Mr. Gilbert DeRoquedu

(January 1997)

Dear Gil,

Thank you so much for letting me know of your travels. Eight months sounds like a long time to be away, but I wouldn't mind meeting up with you for a meal or something when you return. Lately, I've discovered a new food that I am crazy about - sushi! When I was growing up, one of my grandmothers asked me, "Do you know what the Japanese eat?"

"No," I answered because I was less worldly then than I am now.

"Raw fish," she told me, and made a disgusted face to go with it.

"Ewww," I said, because all I could imagine was the raw middle of frozen fish filets when they failed to fully cook in the oven. Have you ever had that? Cold, slimy, minced fish where you least expect it is very unpleasant, let me tell you. However, last weekend, my friend Bex, took me to an historic bar in Philadelphia that served sushi. Well, "served" isn't quite the word because the only way to obtain this raw delicacy was to order it from this large woman who sweated inside a cubicle where she made it. The star of the establishment, she formed my Philadelphia and Spicy Tuna rolls with gusto, while the other patrons and I leered over the fabric-covered partitions, spewing whatever germs weren't disinfected by our beers. I paid and tipped her for the food, then wandered over to a less-crowded spot with Bex to eat it. As I downed the incredibly delicious, slippery fish, dunked in a rich soy sauce I thought, "If this doesn't kill me, then nothing will." And now, several days later, I am writing to you about it, having suffered no ill effects. It turns out, I am madly in love with sushi.

Thank you for telling me about your interesting work. Yes, I would very much like to visit that part of the world, though I would not spend as much time interested in the flora and fauna as you might think. I, too, am fascinated by the ruins you described. I had actually read an account of the Battle of Thermopylae by Herodotus in his "Histories" (I forget who translated) in a Humanities class in our high school. I sweated the events of the battle when I read it then, so your description of the location has sent shivers up my spine. These men were so brave to face their impending death. And the betrayal by Ephialtes via the Anopaian path? What a story! I don't know if I'd be such a good and studious companion to your wanderings, I'd be so caught up in the awe and heartbreak of it all. Maybe some of that Greek wine and stew would calm me down at the end of such an emotional day, but not until that point.

To be in Greece would also mean a time away from my family, which in certain ways I would like, but in many ways, I can't truly indulge. My mom needs me more than ever. You referred to my family "obligations", but I am only obliged by my heart, not a strict sense of duty, though I think my dad would somehow prefer that - he likes titles and such. I'm always supposed to remember to call him "Dad," I can never joke around and call him "Adam," for example. His brother is the same way, always demanding that I refer to him as "Uncle Bob," and not simply "Bob," even though I'm an adult. But with my mom, I feel a kinship. I don't know if it's just the leveling of womanhood, but I see her humanity now more than I ever did before.

She is weak, therefore I am acutely aware of the strengths she used to exhibit - sophisticated political musings, her deep religious devotion, her remarkable consistency to be on-time to any event, and her constancy of provisions, whether foods or cleanliness. I cook, but not creatively. I clean, but I don't feel the sense of purpose that

I think she did. She used to hum along to the radio, for instance, and I never feel that way when I'm scrubbing the grout.

I miss her as she dies a little each day, yet at the same time, I'm grateful to know what I am missing. I hope that grief won't hit me all at once when she truly passes. Sometimes, I try to draw her old ways out of her, so that I can recapture them. She doesn't always remember why she did certain things in the past, but every once in a while, she does. Yesterday, I asked her why she used to bake chocolate chip cookies more than any other type for my after-school snack and she couldn't recall. Yet, later that afternoon, she saw me striving to wipe down the toilet after I had sprayed the paper towel with disinfectant, and she suggested I spray the toilet instead of the cloth because the power of the spray would drive germs out of the nooks and crannies around the hinges so the hinges wouldn't stink. I really appreciated that advice. I'm also nervous I'm not going to get many more of her insights in the future. Just last week, I heard her snorts of frustration and when I looked over, she was struggling to place her glasses case in a handbag that closed at the top, but whose handles had crossed over, blocking the opening. It took her actual minutes to figure out that she had to uncross the handles before she could open the bag. And she always follows me whenever we walk anywhere from the car, instead of walking beside me even though she's walked into these same stores several hundred times in my life. She's like a little kid who doesn't know the way but knows enough to trail the adult in charge. I guess that's me. She does eat her vegetables when she is supposed to, unlike most little kids I've babysat. She is the closest thing I've ever had to an actual child, which is a strange sensation when one is not officially a parent. I don't expect you to understand all of what I am telling you here, your parents are still neurotypical and without urgent needs, but writing to you is helping me parse my feelings and I definitely wouldn't do this over the telephone, so...thank you.

I should end this and make some dinner, but when I get a chance, I will head to the library to borrow the Histories of Herodotus and reread them so I can feel even more about what you have written to me. I hope you have a good flight back to Greece and I look forward to your next letter.

Sincerely,

Mandy

P.S. I have just returned from the library with the Histories of Herodotus, translated by Aubrey de Selincourt, which I am excited to read. However, before I get to it, I must address something from your previous letter. You referred to your destination as "Constantinople" instead of naming it "Istanbul," which is its current name. I was reminded of this because while I was in the library, I decided to look at a globe to better understand where you would be and when I looked at Turkey, I saw no Constantinople. I asked the librarian who told me about the name-change, so I thought I'd pass it on to you. I hope the information helps.

P.P.S. I am enclosing a Polaroid of the 1972 edition I found as it looks old and interesting.

Letter 15

Mr. Gilbert DeRoquedu to Miss Amanda Hood

(February 1997)

Dear Mandy,

Your 1972 edition, revised by John Marincola, is exactly the one of which I have a copy sitting on one of my shelves in the office here. Obviously, I recommend it, but also, you might want to read Paul Cartledge's <u>Battle of Thermopylae: The Battle That Changed the World</u> for its terrific narrative. I have also heard that Steven Pressfield's next published work will be about The Battle of Thermopylae, but that's just a rumor at this point.

"Here" is officially Istanbul, but for those who practice Greek Orthodoxy, it is still known as Constantinople. You may not know it, but I come from a Catholic background yet in Greece, converted to Greek Orthodoxy. While I've always been a faithful follower of Jesus the Christ, I have often struggled with some of the tenets of Catholicism like Mary's sinless origin or the concept of Purgatory. I see Mary as a simple Jewish woman, not someone whom I need to venerate like I do Christ, nor do I believe Purgatory exists like the Catholics claim, though I honestly haven't given the idea of Hell too much thought beyond existence. I also never regarded the Pope as anything more than another man, though I'm not overfond of the Patriarchate of Constantinople either. Mostly, I try to live out Christ's teachings every day, which comes with its own share of joy and heartache.

Though I can't be of much help, I admire the way you are tending to your mother, and I am sorry for the anguish you suffer. At the risk of sounding patronizing, I do recommend turning to God for all that you are going through, though I am perfectly willing to receive your thoughts about situations. I just know that I can't fix any of it, and I wouldn't want you to forfeit any opportunities for prayer, if you are so inclined. If you already pray, or this is not something you want to discuss or pursue, please disregard this advice. I can only summarize that prayer helps me in my darkest times.

In Constantinople, I have found a small Eastern Orthodox church to attend for services. It is an ancient building, complete with a flagged stone floor, and window holes a foot thick! The sanctuary and congregation are small, but on my wobbly, wooden chair, I often feel the expansive presence of God. I have met a few other congregants, though the social scene doesn't begin to approach the cliques of my Catholic youth. However, the people are pleasant, and once a month, they hold a potluck lunch after church, inviting anyone of any faith to join. I've met some retired American professors of antiquity as well as some French soccer players. This socialization keeps me from sheer isolation because much of my work is solitary. I don't mind being alone too often, but then after days of losing myself in the stacks of the Imperial Library of Constantinople, or at the Serpentine Column in Sultanahmet Square, I begin to feel a little anxious. Your letters relieve some of the anxiety too.

Thank you for agreeing in principle to meet for a meal. If you are bound by too many familial constraints we can plan for another time, but a sushi date sounds compelling. I haven't tried it yet, so it will be an adventure! I am curious though - from your previous letter, I gathered that your parents don't approve of you having alcohol, so how did you get around that and go to a bar? If you don't mind my asking. We don't have to go to a place that serves alcohol if you are against the idea, but it would be ideal to have our options open.

I have enclosed a few Polaroids of my surroundings - the Serpentine Column, a few scenes from Sultanahmet Square, the outside of my little church, a potluck table so you can see some of the delicious food, and a picture of me, a little heavier, probably from too many potlucks.

Cordially,

Gil

Letter 16

Miss Amanda Hood to Mr. Gilbert DeRoqueDu

(March 1997)

Dear Gil,

Thank you so much for including the Polaroids in your last letter. Intellectually, I was aware you are in Turkey, but these pictures really round out that understanding. The square is utterly beautiful! If I were there, I would take thousands of pictures. And that church, Wow! It just screams antiquity. I don't know how you take yourself away from such a place. In my encyclopedia, there's an overhead picture of the Square showing cargo ships on the water. Have you been to that port or beach? Again, it looks amazing there.

Yes, I do pray from time to time, but I could do it more often, I think. My mom spearheaded my religious upbringing, not steeped in dogma or rules, but simply taking me to church on a regular basis and identifying for me the diverse ways people in our lives lived out Christ's teachings. She also pointed out self-proclaimed Christians who wrapped themselves up in His words, but by their actions embraced ways contrary to His. For example, she's spoken out against Christians demonstrating on street corners about homosexuality being a sin. It's like, why would these so-called followers of Christ be so concerned about what other people do in their bedrooms, which is a kind of love, instead of focusing on their own divorces, infidelity, or not keeping the Sabbath? and those things are against love, both of man, and God. Shouldn't Christians just be trying to "Love one another" as He commanded us to? Mercifully, the leaders of my church have listened to her and not joined in those demonstrations. They do, however, protest in front of abortion clinics. This isn't great either, especially since they seem so angry, but I can see their point better of loving unborn babies rather than railing against homosexual practices. Nonetheless, I'm not sure what they would do with all those unborn babies - I never met an unmarried mother in this church and no one seems to have adopted any. What I do believe is that the congregants would do best by single young people to provide a great sex ed instead of preaching "purity" (to the girls) and no masturbation (to the boys). However, teaching sex ed in Sunday School won't arrive until a cold day in Hell does, hahaha.

Lately, I haven't been attending church because Mom was really the connection and she's not in a good position to go. The pastor understands and there are "prayer warriors" praying on our behalf, but she doesn't pay attention to what people are saying unless the people speak to her directly. Also, she falls asleep easily, even when sitting up. There's less and less of her sparkling personality now. Writing to you reminds me of who she used to be and how much I had tied my religious practices to her. I think I'll look at some photos of her from years ago after I finish this letter because I've been too long with someone who is dying, and I want to remember how she used to live. It will also help me to think about how I will continue my religious journey without her further guidance.

You asked about how I went to a bar when my parents don't approve of my drinking alcohol. Mostly, it's my dad who worries about it. Since his mom drank to excess when he was growing up, he's temperate, but also, he still thinks of me as his "Little Girl." Living at home with him and Mom, even though I do many adult things, blurs my real adulthood to him too. Basically, I told him and Mom that I was going out with Bex and that we might try some sushi at a restaurant. It's technically true that the bar could be considered a restaurant because they do serve some food, but

I just omitted the name of the place as well as the fact that I had any alcohol when I told them. Dad takes after his mom regarding "raw fish," so I didn't worry that he would press me for details.

Frankly, my dad is the way he is primarily because of his mother. He doesn't speak to her much anymore, but he internalized her snobbery. She is in a nursing home now, but when she lived independently, she was the matriarch of our family. Dedicated to class distinction, she registered her family in the local WASP book, announcing my aunts as "debutantes" in their youth, and sent my dad and uncle in tuxedos to other WASP kid birthday parties. By the time I came along, we typically spent every other Sunday night having dinner at her house, where she held court. This meant we all sat around the dining room table, eating off of real China plates, using actual silver utensils, and trading observations about how people of other classes, races, religions, and ethnicities "proved" why their statuses should always be lower than those of WASPS. I know now that it was terrible. My dad tried to fight some of it when he was younger by sneaking a Black friend into his childhood home to eat off of the silverware in the middle of the night, but currently, he's as bad as she is. I stopped contributing to these misinformed discussions when I realized the real hypocrisy of my grandmother. She had been a reading specialist when she was younger, but she didn't teach me how to read and write, my Black first grade teacher did. My grandmother is really wrong about Black people. And if she's wrong about them, how right could she be to say that the Jewish people in her school "loved" singing Christmas carols? Did they even have a choice? Grandmama who only attends church for Easter (she wears a special hat), or Christmas Eve service (she likes the music) never speaks about God, nor expresses people as "God's children," she just wears her Christianity as a brand.

I also saw how she treated my mom, whose family wasn't in the stupid society book, but who raised me with a lot of realism. Mom worked very respectfully for a living and celebrated many of my accomplishments like graduating from college. I can't think of a time when Grandmama ever spoke positively about another grown woman without a backhanded compliment. Even when talking about her friend last week she said, "Emily is a dear friend, but she is so homely." She's never complimented Mom's cooking, or the fact that Mom mostly raised me, but she did sometimes speak wistfully of a girl (from the society book, of course) my dad dated in high school. That always seemed really mean to me, but Mom didn't say anything whenever it came up, just looked down at her plate and stabbed her potatoes. Dad didn't say anything either, then someone else usually talked about how they didn't like the current popular phrase originating in the African American community they had been hearing and the conversation moved on. I'm grateful those awful dinners are over now, but their nastiness still plays in my head.

I should probably go. Dad has been away for work this week, so I've been solely responsible for Mom who will probably wake up from her nap soon and request dinner. Tonight, I'm making her all-time favorite - lasagna! She likes it this special way that an Italian lady once taught her - to put chunks of pasta, meat, cheese, and sauce in the pan in no particular order, nor in layers, but to spoon the contents as her heart and her family direct. It's like a dish of unity, and right now, I'm going to do it with my mother before she is unable to participate like this. I think I'll take a few pictures of us too because I know I will always treasure moments like these. Write soon!

Affectionately,

Mandy

Letter 17

Mrs. Claire Haskins[sic] to Miss Amanda Hood

(April 1997)

Dear Mandy,

I barely know how to begin this letter, but I have a responsibility to tell you a few things now that your father has passed away. You see, your father and I were lovers for many years. We had met in high school and fell in love right away. Adam was a complete gentleman, but more importantly, warm, open, honest, and affectionate. He took me on dates to the roller rink, or out for a soda, and often to the movies. The movie theater was our favorite place because we could spend time together in the dark without prying eyes. Your father loved me just as much as I loved him, but the unfortunate truth is that his mother would not welcome me in their home because I am Jewish. I am not ashamed of my heritage, I love my family, but I also know what a difficult marriage we would have had with the constant disapproval of your grandmother. At one point we tried to break it off. He even met other women, including your mother, at that time. I also met my husband during those difficult years, but we could not stay separated. We missed each other terribly. Though we loved our spouses, we needed to continue to see one another.

And so, I knew all about your mother's pregnancy with you, your birth, and I watched you grow up through all of the pictures Adam shared with me. He also told me lots of stories about you, he loved you so much. And when my husband left me for a time for another woman, your father was my source of comfort, my sanity, as I juggled work and caring for my sons. When my husband returned, I forgave him, and we worked through some conflicts, but since he didn't realize he had contracted syphilis, he passed it on to me, I gave it to your father, and now, your mother is currently suffering from its effects. I am so deeply sorry. I thought that Adam would have said something to your mom, but I know now that she didn't present any obvious symptoms decades ago, so your dad didn't think she had it. Your father did take the full course of medicine, so he was cleared, but he realized his mistake in not confessing to your mother last summer. Please know that he had tremendous guilt over his inaction and was further ashamed to tell you that we were to blame. He spent many, many afternoons crying in my arms over your mother's deterioration. It is my belief that his guilt consumed him and contributed significantly to the heart attack which killed him.

Though you probably wouldn't ask this, I am also writing to tell you that he died in my arms after we had just made love. I know you don't really need the details, but I want you to know that he passed away, not in an unfamiliar hotel room as may have been reported, but in our favorite getaway hotel in Amarillo (one I think you know about) with someone who loved him deeply, holding him tenderly. I ask nothing of you, but I wanted you to know everything before my life changes ever more and I lose the reasons, connection, and courage to write to you.

Adieu,

Claire Haskins (not my real name)

Letter 18

Mr. Gilbert DeRoquedu to Miss Amanda Hood

(April 1997)

Dear Mandy,

My parents have just informed me of the death of your father. I am so sorry to hear of his passing, especially considering the burdens you were already bearing. I pray God holds you in the hollow of His hand, His presence strengthens you, He carries you through this Valley of the Shadow of Death, and His love shields you from the greatest depths of grief.

I don't expect you to write to me anytime soon, there is certainly no pressure, but if you are inclined, you are welcome to share such sorrows or reflections as bereavement often brings. If you are not so inclined, I offer to you a practice I use when I am my most melancholy and prayer is not enough - I write letters to Our Heavenly Father. This unsent correspondence helped me to process the grief of my grandfather's death many years ago. Please write to me whenever you are comfortable doing so.

In sympathy,

Gil

Letter 19

Mr. Gilbert DeRoquedu to Miss Amanda Hood

(July 1997)

Dear Mandy,

How are you? It's been months since I've heard from you, but I want you to know I still think about you, quite often, actually. I hope you are well. If there's anything I can do for you, please don't hesitate to write or even call me. I don't know if you can make international calls, but if you can, my parents will gladly give my number here to you.

Even if you can't take the time to write, I hope you can take the time to read my letter. I'll make this my last letter until I hear from you because I don't want you to feel pressured to write back. Besides, very little has changed since I last wrote to you. The research plods on, the sermons enlighten me, and I try new foods at the potlucks. Okay, actually I have added something to my life - I've joined a local soccer club! While it's not terribly competitive, what games we play and practice we do force me to exercise, all the merits of which are completely undone by the alcohol we drink afterwards, whether we practice, win, or lose.

Raki, known as "lion's milk," is the national anise-flavored drink which is quite delicious if one relishes great draughts of licorice spirits and quite awful if one does not. At first, I didn't like it, but it's grown on me, especially when paired with mezeh, which are tapas here. (Mom says tapas are all the rage there, so I'm guessing you've had them since you are already so adventurous food-wise.) Sometimes we walk to Yusef's family home and drink and eat there. Yusef is a subpar soccer player but watching him play backgammon is like watching a master at his craft. We all take turns trying to beat him, but the best any of us can do is to lose to him by the fewest points. Not only is he fascinating, but so is the ancient family board with which he plays - the tiny ivory dice look like baby teeth tossed upon the board, their corners are so worn down, and the engraved wood with its ebony and mother of pearl inlays just mesmerizes. Months ago, Yusef's mom used her daughters to offer the food and drink, but she gave it up when no one really paid attention to any of them. Now she just bustles around us, refilling our drinks and filling our plates with tasty mezeh of falafel and shawarma. I have no idea how dating works here, now that I think of it, but it didn't work that way in his home. I'm glad I have you to think about though. In fact, I not only think of you, but I also dream of you. Tonight, I will dream that your heart is lighter, your mother is in fine spirits, you have suddenly won the state lottery, and you are on the next flight to see me. In my dreams I will see you soon.

Affectionately,

Gil

Letter 20

Mrs. Amy Hood to Miss Amanda Hood

(Written October 1995, Received July 1997)

My Darling Daughter Mandy,

If you are reading this letter, it means that I am no longer with you. I'm sorry I can't be there to help you. Depending on how far into the future this is, I'm assuming that Dad isn't still around to help run things, but if he is, I hope that he, in addition to my words, can give you some comfort. It may seem odd to find such a letter when we have just been living our day-to-day lives with no drama, but I felt compelled to share with you my heart because life can change in an instant. Just an hour ago, I ran a stop-sign with no consequences, but the honk of an irritated driver jolted me to my brush with Fate. I've never had a traffic violation of any kind, and the brief lapse of careful driving shocked me. I don't know why I was so careless, but then, I was reminded of my own mortality. Perhaps I'll write more up-to-date letters in the future, after you have some other life events, but I am writing this one while you are in your junior year of college. The point is, I never want you to wonder how I've felt about you. Even though I've hugged you every day of your life with us, you are so much more than your physical presence. I could not be more honored to be your mother.

Now that you have almost finished college, I know the woman you are, and you fill me with awe. Your keen observations, prudence, persistence, energy, and commitment are like nothing I've ever seen in my family, nor in that of your father. I think I first noticed these in your babyhood.

I have never known a baby like you. While it's true that you are the baby, I was closest to in my life, certain traits of yours stood out. You did not crawl fast to the newest toy put on the scene, you observed me first, as if to check that it was okay. After I reassured you with words and a smile, you took in your surroundings and when you were perfectly ready, you approached it, deftly navigating obstacles in your path. Upon reaching the novelty, you inspected it from all sides, then you touched it gingerly. Slowly, you would bring the toy to your mouth for greater inspection, grazing it gently with your lips, certainly not glomming onto it in the ways of other babies. No electronic noise, no funny pop-ups would take you by complete surprise, for you had studied your playthings carefully. It was for this that we called you "Our Careful Girl." You have always checked your steps, not in a worrisome way, but in a surefooted one. This was the early indicator of how solid your reasoning was, and it floored me. So, opposite the rashness of your foolish mother. This, My Darling Daughter, will serve you in life so very, very well. I'm excited (as I always am) to see how it all plays out and the wonderful things you will do.

BUT a very big but here, you are not without your incredible creativity, and this will serve you equally well. As you know, I have always been a fan of the short story "The

Purloined Letter," but what you may not know is that in you I see the brilliance, as Edgar Allan Poe so aptly described in reasoning, as both a "poet and mathematician." You are not a simpering, boring person who reasons yourself out of life's experiences, you flood me with your ability to create things that are at once practical and fascinating. You take something and greatly develop it. A perfect example is when you made your Halloween costume at ten years old.

First, you sketched your heart's desire - a sparkly, poofy, frou-frou of a skirt. It was so over-the-top fluffy, I nearly laughed, but you won me over completely. Using yarn in the place of strips of tulle, you practiced a looping technique around a belt so you could perfect it, as well as give me the visual I needed to confidently invest in the tulle. And the result? Your beautiful, multi-colored full skirt won the admiration of every house we trick-or-treated at that year, as well as the First-Place prize in our church parade. It was the frou-frou skirt of dreams, but one that did not fall apart like so many cheaply made costumes today. In fact, I have safely stored it in the attic so that you may give it to your own little girl, if she should want to wear something like that one day.

Unsurprisingly, you have applied these traits of yours with greater and greater success in school projects and extracurricular activities. In addition to being Our Careful Girl, you have also been My Busy Bee because your level of activity seems almost limitless and makes my days sweeter than any honey I've ever tasted. I expect you'll sprout wings and fly away one day, but happily, today is not that day. You did not know, but when the principal announced your scholarship at your graduation from your trivia participation, I cried. Right there in row E, seat 5, I literally dropped tears onto the floor, I was, and am, so proud of you. It was the culmination of so many Saturday morning meets, weekday practices, and regional trips. Your commitment to your teammates, your school, but most of all to yourself literally paid off. Now, you are in college, pursuing your interests, but also earning good grades, looking after yourself responsibly, substantiating the investment that others made in you. You never cease to amaze me.

Mandy, there is nothing you aren't capable of, and that includes solid relationships. While you may fall very hard for a romantic person, I have every belief that your marriage will satisfy in ways mine didn't. Since this letter will be released in the event of my death, I'm not worried about repercussions here.

The fact is, I married your father when I was entirely too young and inexperienced. He was my first sexual partner and so a part of me felt strongly, probably due to my upbringing, that I should marry him. This could not be farther from the truth. I see that now, but it is too late to try with someone new. I've invested my life with Adam in you and I won't do anything to compromise that, no matter what he does.

Don't think that I don't know about his out-of-town relationships. While I do believe he works during those trips, I also think there is someone, or someones, on the side. I don't have any proof, mostly gut feeling. Sometimes, I smell a different scent from his clothes. I know it's not our brand of laundry detergent or fabric softener because the perfume is exotic like that of patchouli. Moreover, he always seems a bit down when he returns. He puts on a smile, but it's his sad one and he doesn't want anything from me but retires to his office for long solitary periods. I've learned not to bother him during these times. I wonder sometimes if he's crying. But it doesn't matter. The point is: your father always comes home to me and that is enough in my little world.

However, I don't want that for you.

You deserve a man who is head-over-heels only in love with you, practically worships the ground you walk on. They are out there. I never strayed from our marriage officially, but my heart did once long ago. It isn't of much importance; nothing could be done. He and I met in a Bible-study group. Talking with him over passages we read and how they related to our lives, I learned a lot about this man. As I listened, I realized what it would be like to marry such a person - one whose life I never questioned, one who was entirely open with me, one who respected my mind and accepted my heart. He always asked me what I thought or felt about our assorted topics, often crediting my words and ideas before he added his own. He also did the little things - made sure I had a comfortable seat, walked me out to the car under his umbrella (I always forgot mine), and even bought a fancy creamer I once mentioned I liked for our coffees. He wasn't flirtatious, just kind, straightforward, and treated my mind and body with incredible respect. When he moved away, my world was less gentle. He was married, I don't know if happily, but that is okay. His very existence, albeit fleeting, was enough for me to feel balanced on this Earth and I treasure that time together we had.

I'm not saying your father doesn't love me, I think he is naturally fond of me, but there is an intimacy I don't feel I have with him, and I think I never will. I have accepted this, but I want more for you. I can't quite counter it in our home life and sometimes I worry about the example I put before you, as well as what he demonstrates in a relationship. However, when you live separately from us permanently among a wider variety of people, unlike I did, you will have more success choosing the right person.

You will love deeply, but also smartly. I will help you do this as long as you have me in your life and I hope you will see this fulfilled by the end of mine. Even if I did not have the right answers to all of your important questions,

I hope that you will have considered me worthy of your womanly friendship. I will be equally honored to have been your friend as I have been as your mother. I have loved you like I have loved no one else.

From the bottom of my heart, thank you for having been my daughter.

Much love,

Mom

PART TWO: CYBERSPACE

Email 1

From Blaise Ayers to Amanda Vero

(September 2019)

Dear Mandy,

Welcome to We Raise Up Moms in Real Solidarity (WRUMIRS)!

We are excited to get to know you and your family. With WRUMIRS, you'll find lots of activities for you and your little one(s) to engage both socially and politically. We pride ourselves in our activism, as well as our support of moms. Whatever you need, there is probably already a subgroup available to help you. You may join as many or as few subgroups as you prefer - there is no requirement. All we ask is that if you join a subgroup, please add activities for it on our calendar according to its color code, given in the key. There is no attendance requirement either.

Because WRUMIRS is a public, non-profit organization, we do not discriminate against any parents, for any reason, and this includes all parenting philosophies. This means if you breast-feed exclusively (we have a group called Nips & Blips for that too, lol) you don't badmouth bottle-feeding. No one set of parents raises their children the same way as another, we are all unique, stemming from a wide variety of circumstances, so we show respect to those whose ideals differ from ours. Some other parenting philosophies that you might perceive differences about within our group are screen time, baby-wearing, vaccination, working versus stay-at-home moms, daycare, organic food versus processed food, home-school versus traditional school, and religious education. However, WRUMIRS is very united politically, having formed the day after Trumpty Dumpty was elected in 2016. If you are with us, you know the current POTUS is trash. Feel free to criticize him all you like; you will find much solidarity for that among your fellow WRUMIRS moms.

Some of our subgroups are as follows:

Activists Are Us - Meeting times vary depending on the current political issues which can change frequently. All ages welcome. Stay tuned and stay active!

Babysitting Club - A weekly group of moms dedicated to taking turns watching each other's children who are five or younger.

Climbing the Walls - Sometimes, moms need to get away from their families. Join other moms twice a month for cocktails, movies, bowling, bus trips, or anything else that doesn't involve the kids or the husbands.

Little Tourists - Explore the rich cultural heritage of Adams County, PA and surrounding areas from Civil War Battlefields, to museums, apple orchards, local zoos, and more! All ages welcome. Trips vary according to the seasons.

Nips & Blips - A support group that meets weekly for moms who exclusively breastfeed. Extended breast feeders are also welcome. Don't forget to bring your baby and/or toddler(s)! Snacks provided.

Playground Pals - A group that meets bi-weekly after school at playgrounds in both Lippincott and Gettysburg. All ages welcome. Bring your own snacks.

Wines and Lines - Moms agree to read assigned books, then meet for a playdate and a little wine (not too much!) and discuss them. Snacks for moms included, bring your own for your kids.

Because the town and former farmland of Lippincott has the great distinction of being the only battlefield north of the Mason-Dixon line where Confederate forces won, this town, much like our neighbor Gettysburg (five miles to the west of us), is heavily dependent on tourism. On any given day, one can find large groups of people, often in Civil War period dress, touring Lippincott, and The Battlefield. The Battlefield is considered "sacred ground" due to the men who died there, so we don't hold events like our potlucks or birthday parties on that land. We do, however, encourage field trips in and around the National Military Park of Lippincott as well as that of Gettysburg for the children to learn as much as they can. Bonus: climbing the rocks at Devil's Den is loads of free fun.

After we receive your membership fee, we'll send you a link to the Calendar where you can see many activities listed. We thank you for joining us and we hope you find the solidarity you seek!

Warmest regards,

Blaise Ayers,

President of WRUMIRS

Email 2

Blaise Ayers to WRUMIRS Members

(September 2019)

Dear Fellow Moms,

WRUMIRS is delighted to welcome our newest member, Amanda Vero (preferred name Mandy), to our fabulous group! Mandy and her husband, Peter Vero, recently moved to Lippincott from Baltimore, Maryland for Peter's job as a Graduate Professor of Biology at Battlefield

University. Mandy is a new stay-at-home mom to baby boy Teddy, taking a break from her career as a credit analyst with Bankmart. In addition to Teddy, Mandy and Peter have two fur babies, both Chihuahuas, named Taco and Pita. In her free-time, Mandy likes to scrapbook, bake cakes, and read books. Currently, Mandy is nursing Teddy (hint, hint Nips and Blips). They have no allergies and look forward to many events with our group. Please reach out to Mandy if you have an upcoming event to invite her to, or just to say hello.

Warmest regards,

Blaise Ayers,

President

Email 3

Eliza Dupont to Amanda Vero

(September 2019)

Hi Mandy!

My name is Eliza, and I am so glad that you have found our group. I have a five-year-old daughter named Danielle and a ten-month-old son named Lawrence, but I remember what it was to be a new mom. My husband is also a professor at the University, but for Undergraduate French in the Modern Languages Department, so we might see each other at family University events.

WRUMIRS, however, has been my saving grace as a mom, especially the Nips and Blips group. Since you breastfeed, you might want to consider attending. It is one of the few places I initially felt as comfortable breastfeeding among other people as I feel at home. Now, I'll breastfeed anywhere, including nurse-ins. (A nurse-in is a political demonstration that nursing moms deploy when a fellow mom has been discriminated against at a business for simply feeding her child in the way Nature intended. We've held nurse-ins at restaurants, grocery stores, football stadiums, and church services. Those foolish businesses often cave because if there's one thing, they don't want to see more of it is my exceptionally large breasts tandem nursing my five-year-old and my baby, LOL. That's probably TMI for a new mom such as yourself, but that's who I am. Okay, back to Nips and Blips.)

We usually meet in the nursery of Lippincott Lutheran on Tuesday mornings at nine, but we can meet anywhere, including each other's houses. Over the years, I've received a lot of great advice, but at this point, I am very glad to share all that I know in order to make it easier for fellow moms. The other thing I really like about WRUMIRS is the potlucks. I don't know about you, but since we don't have family in the area, having other people whom I know cook for us is very charming and homey. (I tend to avoid Marisol's gelatin dishes though, which is nothing about her, but more about savory, natural, gelatins that still surprise me. I expect my gelatins to be full of sugar and artificial dyes, surrounded by canned fruit and whipped topping, as the bases for desserts because I've never escaped my childhood of the seventies.)

Anyway, welcome to our group, and if you need anything, even some silly stories of when I was an au pair in France, please don't hesitate to call me, or any other mom listed in the directory.

See you soon,

Eliza

Email 4

Amanda Vero to Eliza Dupont

(September 2019)

Dear Eliza,

Thank you so very much for your warm email! I really appreciate that you took the time to tell me about so many things. I had no idea about family events at the University, but now that you've told me about it, I'm excited to go. Well, not Peter, socializing isn't really his thing, but maybe he'll find someone he can talk science fiction with, which is totally not my thing.

I too am a child of the seventies! And gelatin with canned fruit and whipped topping is EXACTLY what I think of when I think of potluck desserts. Do you have a cookbook from the seventies? I do and that's what's in it, plus some recipes for tomato aspic, LOL. Do you remember tomato aspic? I don't think I could get used to savory gelatins either, that's what they make me think of.

Since I'm sharing that I'm a child of the seventies and a new mom, I might as well share further that I am only just now a mom because we married later in life, then had fertility issues leading up to Teddy. We named him Theodore because after so much bad luck, he is our Gift from God, which is what his name means. I hope this isn't TMI. All I know is that I am deeply relieved not to receive any more shots in the butt from Peter just to make this happen. Okay, that's probably TMI now, LOL.

I would very much appreciate any advice you have on nursing because I still use the nipple shield and hope to just nurse Teddy without it one day. He was born a month early, so it's understandable that he needs it, but I don't know when he'll just revert to the nipple. He just doesn't always grasp it like I think he should. Luckily, I don't seem to have a problem with volume. The breasts work like they're supposed to - they supply more milk when Teddy nurses more and less when he nurses less. I think I'm lucky in this regard.

I would LOVE to hear of any stories of your time in France. Is that how you met your husband? I have been to Paris, but only as a tourist on my honeymoon, so I feel like I missed out on authentic French life. Your stories would really fill me in, I think.

I've got to go walk Taco and Pita. I hope you and your little ones are well.

Sincerely,

Mandy

Email 5

Eliza Dupont to Amanda Vero

(September 2019)

Dear Mandy,

Our Nips and Blips group is perfect for discussing any breastfeeding concerns like your artificial nipple issue. Our next meeting is scheduled for next Tuesday at nine. Can you make that one? No rush to answer, just let us know ahead of time.

See you soon,

Eliza

Email 6

Amanda Vero to Eliza Dupont

(September 2019)

Dear Eliza,

I can totally make that one, thank you so much for inviting me. Is there anything I should bring?

Sincerely,

Mandy

Email 7

Eliza Dupont to Amanda Vero

(September 2019)

Nope, just bring yourself and anything you might need for yourself and Teddy. Oh, and Teddy too, LoL.

Email 8

Amanda Vero to Eliza Dupont

(September 2019)

Dear Eliza,

Thank you so much for bringing me into Nips and Blips! You wouldn't believe it, but I tried what you said, and it totally worked! For the past few days, Teddy has been able to take my real nipple instead of the artificial one.

I can't tell you how relieved I am. I was so afraid that I had been breastfeeding wrong and maybe ruining him a little in the process. I was really worried that his little palate was going to be misshapen, and he would have severe malocclusion, requiring years of orthodontia like I did because my mom didn't breastfeed me. As a kid with very bucked teeth, I was bullied a lot until my braces fixed the problem. Even so, I remember one of my friends literally teasing me because my retainer showed an exceedingly high and narrow roof to my mouth. It was a stupid thing to be teased about, but I really wanted Teddy to avoid it. Thank you, thank you. I can't wait to see you all at the other events. I am super glad I found this group.

Sincerely,

Mandy

P.S. Okay, I did have a moment of awkwardness with Bela. I didn't expect anyone to use our subgroup to sell me something. I bought a ten-dollar bottle of oil, but only out of guilt. I don't usually use stuff like that. Is this a usual occurrence?

Email 9

Eliza Dupont to Amanda Vero

(September 2019)

Dear Mandy,

No problem! I know what a lifesaver WRUMIRS is, having been in it for several years. Some of the info I passed on to you came from other moms when I first joined while Danielle was still a baby. I learned so much from those "old heads." Sadly, a lot of them aged out of the group because kids only grow up, and then, from what I've seen, other social groups become more important like youth soccer, and school activities, and Scouts, etc. so the mommy stuff takes a backseat. But, oh man, in those early days, a moms group is exactly what's needed. No one else seems to understand first time motherhood like a moms group. And WRUMIRS is especially good because it's not just about the kids, but there's moms-only stuff and intellectual stuff like Activists, and the BABYSITTING, which is more supportive than anything else I can think of. Not paying other people to watch your kids just to take care of doctor's appointments and things during the workweek is so incredibly convenient and empowering. Some socialist countries have municipal centers where you can leave your kid to play for a couple of hours, but all we have here is each other, especially us University folks. My family is in a different state, so my mom can't even sit for me on a whim. It's always for date night only when she visits, and it's really planned. I'm getting way off track here.

Anyway, while I'm really glad to give back, I'm still learning, whether I'm confronting new issues like new foods, speech/language delays, or having conferences with the preschool teachers. I swear, it's always something.

I also want to thank you because since you shared your adorable Teddy with Danielle, it was really helpful to remind her that babies have different developmental stages. Lawrence used to lie there and listen to her sing to him like Teddy did, but nowadays, he's more interested in crawling away and picking up toys. His favorite thing to do right now is chase after a duck she pulls on a string. He laughs and laughs over that one, but when she starts to sing, he wanders off and she pouts. Because of Teddy, I could make my point better that Lawrence didn't stop loving her singing, he's just doing different things, whereas Teddy is still staying in one place, completely entertained by her music. Your bringing Teddy was a total win-win.

I look forward to seeing you more,

Eliza

P.S. Yes, I try to avoid Bela because otherwise my interactions with her also turn into sales. Try not to hang out in the nursery after the group ends and she'll buttonhole somebody else.

Email 10

Gilbert DeRoquedu to Amanda Vero

(October 2019)

Dear Mandy,

We just parted company a few hours ago, but I couldn't wait to tell you how delighted I am that we bumped into each other! Again, I am sorry for having to leave Lippincott Coffee House so quickly. I had an obligation to attend that I just couldn't get out of. I would much rather have sat down and caught up with you, but I appreciate that you gave your email address to me instead. Normally, I am not in South Central Pennsylvania, but I needed to come to Battlefield University for some research. In fact, I live four hours away, in Pittsburgh. I do travel for work frequently, mostly to Greece, but sometimes to Egypt, Turkey, and Paris, so I expect I'll return to the area in a few months.

Do you live in Lippincott proper, or have any connection to the University? I was at the University to speak to a colleague, but prior to that, I had taken the Auto Tour of the Gettysburg Battlefield. The tour wound through fields and woods until it emptied out where Pickett's Charge took place. I climbed out of the car and stood at the High-Water mark, realizing just how perilously close the Union came to losing. I found it thrilling, but also anxiety-inducing, to stand in the very spot where Confederate and US forces clashed with their greatest ferocity, decided the battle for Good, and changed the War for the better. Later, I ate "victuals" at Farnsworth House whose pickled watermelon and game pie were exactly suited to the day. The appearance of reenactors in Civil War uniforms and hoop skirts on the streets were a bit disorienting, but the pinging of their cell phones from their dress pockets and reticules transported me back to reality. Is this how you live every day? It is extraordinary.

Please, please tell me about yourself. I would very much like to know what has happened in your life since we last exchanged communication. You seem very happy now, so I hope Life has been kind to you. It was tremendously great to run into you again.

Cordially,

Gil

Email 11

Amanda Vero to Gilbert DeRoquedu

(October 2019)

Dear Gil,

It is great to receive a letter from you! It seems like ages since we last wrote to each other. Maybe thirty years? So much has changed, hasn't it? We don't use pen and paper, but email now. My hair is no longer mousy-brown, but crone-gray and I don't weigh what I used to when I hiked the Grand Canyon. For that though, I am kind of grateful, because it is a signifier of one of the most important changes in my life - my beautiful, bouncing baby boy Teddy. He probably is the reason for the gray hair too, LOL!

In 2002, I met Peter Vero. We were introduced at BankMart where I was managing a customer service team and he began to work as a customer service representative to pay his bills while he pursued a master's degree in Biology. We hit it off immediately, dated for a couple of years, then moved in together. He transitioned to becoming an Assistant Professor and we married in 2006. Soon after, we discovered the gaming world of MMO's, so we didn't get out much then.

After several years of fertility problems, we finally became pregnant with Teddy and were overjoyed at his birth. Since he might be our only one, I stopped working to soak up motherhood full-time. It is good in many ways, in others not so much. I am able to breastfeed him, so there's that, but I look forward to his toddlerhood, when he will be able to express himself better, because I don't always know what's wrong. Peter is a tremendous help, especially when I am very tired after sleepless nights due to teething, or growth spurts that require extra feedings. Recently, I found a mothers' group, which is already helping me socially as a woman, and may help me more as a mom. How about you - are you married? Do you have any children?

I did take the liberty to look you up a bit on the Internet. You are so renowned, wow! Six books on Ancient Greece are so impressive! No wonder you were at the University - they were clearly lucky to have you, whatever you were doing. I imagine you were lending them your expertise, in a lecture or something. And if I'm not mistaken, you created a set of postage stamps too? I'm also impressed by your world travels. I bet any workdays you spend in France justify those long hours in Madame DeLille's class better than my honeymoon did. Due to the baby, I don't think I will go anywhere for quite some time, but I will gladly live vicariously through your trips if you want to share them.

Since we are new to Lippincott, I haven't visited the Gettysburg or Lippincott Battlefields very much, but I have been in awe when I've gone. Pickett's Charge is exactly as you describe. The bravery of the Confederates even reminds me of Leonides and his Three Hundred. By the way, did you happen to read <u>The Gates of Fire</u> by Pressfield? I did and I even saw the movie "300", on which it was based. I don't think the movie was as good as the book though. I'm guessing you could speak pretty well on this topic.

You didn't put it out there, but I think now you might be wondering what happened to my letter-writing to you. I actually saved your last letters and I think you were expecting some kind of response, which I realize now I didn't give. Since my dad died, I was overwhelmed by not only taking over the complete care of my mom but wrapping up his affairs too. Mom died a few months later, but not before I made various arrangements for her deteriorating conditions like adult daycare, home care, and finally hospice. It was a very trying time. Okay, maybe I developed a few gray hairs prior to Teddy's birth. I hope you can understand this. Again, I'm extremely glad we've reconnected. I must put a little one down for a nap. Email anytime!

Sincerely,

Mandy

P.S. My pronouns are she/her

Email 12

Gilbert DeRoquedu to Amanda Vero

(October 2019)

Dear Mandy,

I wouldn't say renowned, but yes, my publications are cited frequently by other scholars of antiquity. Typically, Hellenic scholars publish several works each, so my amount of research still falls within the bell curve for this discipline, but it lands closer to an extreme end. Yes, my submitted artwork was approved for US Postage Stamps, as part of a series on the Grand Canyon. My point of pride, however, is still my thesis on Helen of Troy as a basis for the Virgin Mary in Christian theology for which I received my Ph.D. As for Pressfield's book, I would describe it correctly categorized as historical fiction, but the prose is riveting. The movie is pure fiction, but a good popcorn flick, nonetheless.

A hearty congratulations on your newfound motherhood. It sounds like you are well-supported by both your marriage and your social group. Is this one of those moms' clubs that drinks wine? I see it so frequently in social media memes, I'm beginning to think there is some truth to it. I drink a good Scotch after trivia tournaments on Tuesdays. Do you keep up with your trivia? If I remember correctly, you were quite the whiz.

Yes, I am married. I met my wife, Melissa, at a cafe in Constantinople in 1997, while she was studying visual arts, and I was doing research. We have one son who is a little over a year old and a golden retriever who is twelve years old. We don't vacation as a family as much as we used to before our son arrived, but I continue to travel to conferences and for research purposes. I also have a niece named Harmonia who lives near us in Pittsburgh. She is seventeen and I have doted on her as if she is my own daughter. Yesterday, we watched an episode of "Old Maids and New Laids" together as we do every week because I use it as a springboard for dating advice. At her age, most dating dramas are as trashy as reality television, so lessons from the show apply very well. Plus, it's just fun to mock the desperate contestants. As a student, Harmonia is very well-accomplished, slated to attend the University of Pennsylvania having skipped a year of college through her Forward Promotion exams. Watching tawdry television is a way for her to relax a little too. Sometimes, she gets wound a bit tight and mouths off, but mostly she is a terrific kid. If you can't tell, I am immensely proud of her.

You kept letters of mine? I don't remember everything I wrote, but I think I can recall their spirit. If you don't mind, I'd like to see them, if you'd be able to upload them. I don't know if I have any of yours. My parents died a few years ago leaving me their house so I'll look around in the attic when I have the chance, in case they kept anything. In the meantime, it is completely understandable that we lost touch. You were clearly dealing with important issues, and I met my wife soon after. What matters now is that we have reconnected and for that, I am delighted. I have a few other emails to write now so I'll wrap up. I look forward to reading more from you, whenever it is convenient for you to write back.

Cordially,

Gil

(Pronouns he/him)

Email 13

Amanda Vero to Gilbert DeRoquedu

(October 2019)

Dear Gil,

I found your thesis online and have just read it. I am tremendously impressed you defended something no one else in the history of Greek studies ever proposed before. I suppose that's the point of theses in general, but still, for someone in modernity to find something new to assert despite millennia of analyses, is quite a feat.

I translated some of The Odyssey and The Iliad from Latin to English in high school, but I don't remember much and I'm sure my translations weren't the best. I just delved into The Odyssey a few hours ago because I wanted to read about Helen's beauty again since it supposedly launched so many ships, but all I gathered is she was "white-armed" and wore "long dresses", so I hope the launching had more to do with her character? This feminist appreciates however, that her personhood is highlighted later in the Iliad, weaving a cloak that depicts those who battled in her honor, as if she was accountable in some way. There's a depth in her the likes of which are never perceived on "Old Maids and New Laids " or similar shows, lol.

You told me a lot about Harmonia, but I must admit, I am very curious about your son. What is his name please? I didn't see it in your email. Since he's twice as old as Teddy, I bet your son is doing amazing things. Is he walking yet?

Does he have any first words? What is his favorite food or toy? Teddy babbles whenever I sing to him. "Row, Row, Row Your Boat" is his new favorite, but really, he smiles as broadly for any song, that's just the one I know the words to best. Teddy is still breastfeeding, so he hasn't tried many foods, but rice cereal is definitely not what he wants. When I put the cold cereal in his mouth, his eyes watered, and his lower lip trembled so that I nursed him right away and staved off his crying. He fell asleep soon after, putting the small nightmare behind him. I'll try something sweet when I work up the courage to feed him again. Maybe I'll mash up some ripe bananas. Do you have any baby gear you swear by? I know I could ask these things to the other moms, but I would enjoy your perspective. I remember how thoughtful you always were. I can't imagine that you would recommend something that you haven't put to great use.

Speaking of my moms' group, yesterday, I brought Teddy to a little Halloween party which was adorable. All of the kids were tremendously cute in their costumes, and everyone laughed at the ridiculous bread loaf bag costume I had on Teddy. I'm so glad baby costumes are easy to put on and take off. When I had to change his diaper during the festivities, opening his costume was as simple as unzipping a sleep sack. I made sure to change him on the bathroom floor too. (I was horrified that some other mom chose to change her baby's poopy diaper on the living room floor. Some of the liquid feces even dripped onto the hardwood and I'm not confident her wipes cleaned it effectively. Some people have no idea about good manners.)

As for treats, I ate orange-frosted cupcakes topped with candy corn, so reminiscent of the ones of my youth, and listened to my new friend Eliza talk at length about her personal crusade about comprehensive sex education. Apparently, in South Central Pennsylvania, the public schools have allowed some crisis pregnancy centers to teach their idea of sex education, which is abstinence-only. What that means is that the health teachers aren't teaching and since the students aren't getting real sex education, their numbers of unplanned pregnancies per capita are higher than those of surrounding areas which means more requests for services from the crisis pregnancy centers equaling...more requests of money from them. It's a sick circle. Just when I thought I could get away from all things Eliza, because she's really intense, someone else told me she wrote a book about being an au pair in France and it starts off with a relationship with HER PROFESSOR. I don't know what to think. On one hand, I like her an awful lot and I was very taken with her political cause, on the other hand, she's a bit much and her morals may be shaky. I guess time will tell. Her daughter Danielle is sweet to Teddy though. Yesterday, she sang softly to him and well, and he just lit up like a Christmas tree. I took a picture of the two of them, which you can see if you friend me on social media [link]. BTW, I post a lot on there, so be prepared for everything if you choose to connect with me there too.

If you can't tell, I'm steeped in domesticity, so if you are uninterested in these topics, please let me know and I'll try to rocket it back, but this is where my life is right now.

I should go, but I also look forward to your next email.

Sincerely,

Mandy

[links to old letters]

Email 14

(October 2019)

Dear Mandy,

This is painful for me to address, but I can't see the sense in putting it off. When my emotions are strong, I often express myself through poetry. With respect to Samuel Taylor Coleridge, here goes:

In Melissa did Mighty Gil

A fertile feeble seed sow

Where Hope, Sweat, and Genes did distill

An inching life greater than 'nil

Yet heartbreaking to trow.

The damning ultrasound was firm,

We would bring the baby to term,

But she struggled to love our Trisomy weed,

And cursed and cried over her helpless "krill"

Plying herself with ever stronger mead

Turning   chances   of   high   function   to   swill.

And oh! That fateful seed took root,

T'was foretold he would be a boy

Whose brain her sour grapes did moot

She carried our insipid fruit

Of which no heart did partake joy.

No Fall football tackles,

No home-screened theatrical cackles,

No cleverly calculated ohms,

No bluster over erected tinker toy,

No intellect's delight in dusty tomes,

No   nuanced   arguments   would   he   employ.

But lo! Herald this Prince last crowned

For birth was his first victory

And each fresh cry streams of hope wound

This ancient of hearts to tick round

Because life's force is our glee

From other dolorous parents Gil takes heed

To be grateful for tiny steps he does see

Mighty Gil daren't sow another seed

His newfound wisdom-infertility.

Into each life, a little poo must fall, I guess, though the politest among us don't smear it onto other people's floors. Accepting Alastor's diagnosis was difficult, made worse by Melissa's drinking. I would have smashed the bottles of booze had I not been so wrapped in my own grief for a neurotypical child. I didn't know that her drinking would decrease his functionality, but I know it now. However, Alastor's limitations impart a new and profound ability in me to perceive the mundane of everyday life as nothing short of miraculous. Please write to me everything about your dear Teddy that you are comfortable sharing. While my own flesh and blood cannot achieve the same things in the same timeframe, celebrating your child's achievements on a regular timeline permits me a surrogate sense of normal progress that I would otherwise be denied.

As for sexual education, abstinence-only sounds contrary to the public health of the community, but this is far afield from my subject area. I trust the bearers of humanity such as yourself to be the arbiters of such things. I do note we are at an extraordinary level of intimacy, even greater than that of my family. You help me to relax, but if you feel uncomfortable at any point, please let me know.

Cordially,

Gil

Email 15

Amanda Vero to Gilbert DeRoquedu

(October 2019)

Dear Gil,

I'm so sorry for your heartache but admire the strength you have summoned through it. I will certainly share about Teddy since you asked me to. However, if it torments you at any point, please let me know and I'll back off.

If you don't mind this level of intimacy, then I don't. Frankly, I don't know how to be any other way, but I'll admit, you bring out a certain side of me that I don't often express with Peter. He's great, don't get me wrong, exceptionally reliable, but there is a zest for life that I feel in you, and it is refreshing. I think your research is a part of that

- you have the courage to ask the Big Questions about life, God, antiquity, and humanity. I too am on a similar journey whereas other people seem to just want to grind out an existence. Everything is a trial to them and there is no obvious joy, just escapes through video-gaming. I don't want to be a hypocrite, I've certainly engaged in the same form of escapism, but I'm past that now. There are no real goals to achieve through the virtual world. I crave real world connections and lessons. Maybe that's why I had such happiness in reconnecting with you - we met long before the Internet, though I do recognize the irony in conveying all of this through email, lol. And your poetry took me to a place, a very painful one, but one which I deeply appreciate because it is real. If at any point, you would like to bring Alastor to me, I would be honored to hold him. I would also welcome him to get to know Teddy, if you think he would be up for it, and it wouldn't be too difficult for you.

Your niece sounds fantastic, I hope that I meet her someday. Since I don't have a daughter, I can relate a bit to doting on her, but I don't have a close niece either, since I am an only child, so my Teddy is my promise of the future. Considering our ages, I doubt Peter and I will try for a second child, but it's not off the table. For now, though, we are fulfilled, but especially me because I've wanted a child for so long. Peter is supportive as always, but having a child wasn't a desire of his per se, just a way to make his wife happy. And he worried about passing his Diabetes 1 to our offspring, but mercifully that didn't happen with Teddy. I do have a niece (and a nephew) by my husband's brother, but they live in Hawaii, and we never see them except for Christmas when they fly East. We exchange gifts, but real substance to the relationships is lacking. Maybe if they moved here, we could pursue that, however, my brother-in-law's job keeps him in faraway places. I can barely imagine doing something as comfortable and casual as relaxing in recliners and watching sleazy tv with them. They're always on the go, frighteningly overscheduled since their parents try to see everyone on the East Coast every one trip. I wonder if I'll ever really know them as people.

Perhaps then, you can see why my moms group is so important to me. Do you belong to any social/sports groups?

Sincerely,

Mandy

Email 16

Gilbert DeRoquedu to Amanda Vero

(October 2019)

Dear Mandy,

As I still have much sensitivity around Alastor's issue, I think for now, I'll hold off on any playdates, but I appreciate your gesture. If I have a change of heart, I will let you know. It is enough that Melissa tries to bond with him and on her terms, with the resources she uses, especially the parents' group of Trisomy 21 kids. She clearly feels a substantial amount of guilt, but her proximity to him, her responsibility to him must be developed because we are in this for the long haul. I praise her when she cuddles and coos to him, and I am hesitant to create any absence between them, which I hope you can understand. Part of this desire of mine to foster their relationship may come from my own issues in childhood. Since we are so close, I don't mind sharing these things with you. In fact, this catharsis feels beneficial.

When I was a very little boy, about two years old, my mother left. I don't have many memories of the time, except that of my father crying when he brought me a cup of water as I yanked on the folding gate of my doorway. At a loss as to who could care for me because the seventies were not nearly as progressive a time as today, my father found the only daycare that was open for the whole workday - a Japanese daycare for kids whose first language was Japanese. According to the records I was able to obtain, I spent the entire eight months of my mother's absence failing to understand the teachers and fellow Japanese-speaking students, biting every single one of them in my own maladaptive form of communication. To this day, hearing spoken Japanese incites wildly inappropriate feelings of rage, fear, and isolation which I work to conceal. My mother returned to my father and me, they had my sister, and life moved on. But I never recaptured the warmth that I think she and I once had, nor were my parents physically affectionate in general, and because my baby sister needed much care and my parents could afford it, I was sent away to a preschool (no Japanese there), then kindergarten and boarding school through ninth grade. After a few unfortunate bouts with some bullies, the only physicality I received at the time, my undemonstrative parents pulled me out and enrolled me in advanced classes at our local high school where the older kids just ignored me and I could stretch my academic wings, though I remained sensitive to any form of criticism. Eventually, we had French class together where I noticed you right away. I joined the trivia team where I also saw you and the rest, My Dear, is history. Oh, and I also learned to touch myself which compensated for the lack of physical love anywhere else in my life at that time. Eventually, I dated women, but I admit, I overbalanced the physical side of relationships and did not invest much in the emotional side. A particularly painful rejection in Arizona didn't help either. Melissa righted a few things, but our equilibrium has been disturbed these past few years.

With no one else do I feel I could share as freely about my spouse and, I'm sorry to report, decades of marriage do not realistically incur a "happily ever after." At the end of the workday is when I feel most this nadir in our relationship. While I'm politically self-described as a "liberal," my sense of home life is more traditional - I expect to not resent my main meal and I hope to make love to my wife sometime afterward. I don't think these are extraordinary asks, but Melissa's cooking and frigidity leave me dissatisfied every evening.

I can't blame her inability to cook on her alone, her mother cooks in the same manner. It's as if they're both hellbent on extracting every pleasing color and texture of fresh vegetables, boiling each unseasoned one into a tasteless gray mush which they smother with cheese, or cheese sauce depending on the day. Half the time, I'm not sure of what plant life I'm consuming, it's so unidentifiable. Every evening at the dinner table, I spend extraordinary amounts of time trying to navigate my fork, which utensil is quite useless for the purpose of eating puddled cheese grease and these "vegetables" but should be demoted to a spoon instead. Early in our marriage, I put up with her cooking because I thought she might improve it, but I was wrong. Later, I suggested cooking classes, but she prefers the food this way since it reminds her of her mother and her childhood. On the plus side, I don't lack for calcium.

As to our issues in the bedroom, they are to the point that even my mildest suggestion of holding each other unclothed is met with a firm "No." Lately, I've taken to viewing pornographic videos, but they exude a voyeuristic feel. I don't really want to watch others having sex, especially other men. I want to make physical and emotional connections to my other half. At one point, I was so torn up over this marital crisis, I sought the advice of a psychiatrist. Now I see him regularly and take medication which subdues my anguish to a manageable level, but the need persists. Whenever I anticipate a big day for meetings or travel, I sleep in the guest room, so I don't torture myself with extra hope and ruin my next day. It is possible that my physical needs are rooted farther back than Melissa's relationship to me. This is part of what my psychiatrist sussed out not too long ago, which is why it's easier for me to share with you here. It feels good to express such things to a non-expert who isn't paid to listen to me. I do however continue to be extraordinarily sensitive to criticism. If you feel the need to judge me, please consider the softest approach because one harsh word can spike my blood pressure and send me spiraling for days.

As for distractions, I participate in trivia tournaments on Tuesdays, as noted in a prior email. Sometimes I team up with others, but mostly I play independently because I can't always predict how many hours my research will require on any given day. However, when I do attend, it relaxes me, and lately, it has taken on an extra dimension of pleasure because it reminds me of you - your fierce intellect and, if it's not too forward, your comely shape. Do you keep up with trivia?

Cordially,

Gil

Email 17

Amanda Vero to Gilbert DeRoquedu

(October 2019)

Dear Gil,

I completely understand your position regarding Alastor and will press no further, except to write how much I admire your love and thoughtfulness of your family. I suppose we all have that to certain degrees, but reading your words warms my heart. Your childhood however leaves me nearly in tears, not only from the pain you as a dear little boy experienced, but for my own perceived guilt. It helps me feel the impact of leaving my family, which I don't plan to do, but on my most difficult days, I can't say it hasn't ever crossed my mind. I definitely won't now. I wish I could hold little you and let you know it will be okay. I guess I'll just have to hug you harder the next time I see you. In the meantime, I am sending you virtual *hugs* and absolutely no harsh words.

I haven't touched trivia games in years. Maybe I'll load an app on my phone so I can shake off the rust. I'd like to live up to the idea that my intellect is fierce. I can tell you that I feel very far removed from such prowess when I'm scrubbing curdled breastmilk out of my pump, having forgotten to wash it after I had last used it.

I wasn't going to say anything, but since you mentioned your proverbial "wings", I am prompted to tell you about mine. Not imperceptible by any means but manufacturing genuine wings that people (okay just me for now) can use to fly from place to place is a real interest of mine. Last month Peter rented a garage in Nowheresville as a birthday gift to me. At first, I just spent time inside the empty space kind of panicking because it's one thing to fantasize about a momentous invention, but it's another to take steps to build it into reality. I made several trips to the bathroom those first few hours, not really accomplishing anything, but elimination of various sorts. Interestingly enough though, my mind did not release this project and so, it continues to stew in my brain. Last week, I bought some pieces from the hardware store that I plan to assemble. I must have looked crazy as I broke big sheets of lightweight material in the parking lot, then stuffed them into the passenger cabin of my sedan because that's where they would stand up the best. Yesterday, I started taping them together, but I realized I didn't have all of the hardware I needed, so I will return to the store when the Babysitting Club of the moms group watches Teddy for me. I have real theories that I want to put into practice, but finding the time is haphazard because between Teddy's teething and growth spurts, he isn't satisfied unless my nipple is in his mouth. Lately, he's taken to rejecting all artificial nipples which was good when it was the nipple shield, but he's expanded his dislike to include pacifiers and bottle nipples, which means Peter can't feed him (Ugh!). He does fall asleep at the breast, so there's that.

As for you expressing admiration for my shape, I don't mind it in the least. Honestly, since we are so close, I don't mind telling you Peter has not complimented my body since before my pregnancy. I imagine it borders on frightening to watch one's partner's form change by the growth of a mysterious creature under the skin, but I've worked hard through my calorie-counting app to reapproach my college figure, though I clearly haven't arrived. It's not perfect by any means, but I think it worthy of mention by the father of my child. Frankly, I'm not just dealing with verbal silence, but another kind as well, though I guess that's probably too much to assert here. Suffice it to say, I really thank you for the compliment.

I've been thinking about us too, especially since we didn't have that date long, long ago. If we had gone out, maybe steadily, where might we have gone? What might we have done as a couple, considering your world travels, especially?

Sorry to make this short, but Nips and Blips, my new breastfeeding subgroup I recently joined, is staging a nurse-in at a restaurant that demanded a nursing mother cover up with a napkin. Since the restaurateur didn't welcome her, he's about to get an eyeful of many, many more and much larger breasts, lol. My new friend Eliza phrases this activism as "guns out". I've never done it before, but I feel it is right to defend feeding one's baby naturally. I'll write later how it went.

Sincerely,

Mandy

Email 18

Gilbert DeRoquedu to Amanda Vero

(October 2019)

My Dear Mandy,

A nurse-in, eh? I've never heard of maternity weaponized in such a manner. Historically, some mothers have poisoned their own offspring, but it was often in secret and didn't result in societal change. Please let me know how it went.

I feel compelled to tell you - when I saw you in the coffee shop a few weeks ago, it was your figure I noticed first. Like any cis-het, red-blooded male, I blush a bit to admit this, certain thoughts raced, no, STAMPEDED, through my mind. While you covered your torso in a modest brown turtleneck and draped your beautiful tweed scarf around your shoulders, my eyes were drawn to your lower half in your long, straight, matching tweed skirt. When you turned around and I realized it was you, I almost had the shock of my life. This is in part why it was difficult to speak with you. Since Melissa has been very put off by intimacy because she directly correlates it to failure, I've tried different ways to encourage her, including counseling, but she is stuck. So please pardon me, but I am somewhat retrogressive, like when I was a much younger man, filled with an energy that requires a certain type of release. I'll leave you to guess what I've been up to lately.

What might we have done, where might we have gone, had we been a couple? Practically-speaking, younger me had fewer means so a restaurant meal and a movie would have been it. Just looking into your eyes across a Formica table, or feeling your fingertips graze mine in a carton of popcorn would have been thrilling. I imagine I would have struggled to concentrate on the lit screen before us, but would have focused on the woman beside me, feeding herself salted snacks in the flickering light, absentmindedly licking her buttered fingers, unknowingly sending me through the roof tiles of the cinema. But the past is relegated to the past and nothing further can truly come from it. Let us indulge in possibilities of the future. I'm not saying that these are probabilities, but the mind enjoys an unchecked freedom. Pick any or none of them, my thoughts globetrot from the spotless to the unchaste.

A. Drop off Teddy at the sitter's, forget your shoes, and meet me at the Sock Hop on Lincoln highway. I twirl you around, your skirt and petticoats rising just enough to reveal your dimpled knees and your ruffled shorts underneath. Your swinging ponytail sweeps my face and I inhale the scent of your shampoo. Afterwards, when we're breathless, we leave the dance floor and order the famous PA Farm Fair milkshake, using two straws out of the same cup. We laugh when we bump noses. Later you tell me I'm your Sweetheart.

B. Bring Teddy to a daycare that stimulates him, then drive for a day trip to the New York Public Library. We discover a little used nook among the stacks, reading passages from famous romantic novels to each other as our bodies squish together on the overstuffed loveseat. I pretend not to notice every time you move a wisp of hair from your face, you gently stroke my hand in unnecessary attempts to get my attention. Between paragraphs of Austen and Michener, we catch each other's eye, draw in as if by some magical force, and share a tender kiss. Your eyelashes brush my cheek when you look up again and I melt into your gaze.

C. Take Teddy to a beloved maiden aunt who holds out her fleshy arms to him as soon as she sees him and fly with me to Killington, Vermont for a weekend of powder-packed snow and a buried Swiss chalet. We ski until our faces flush with fatigue and then we trudge to our abode where a hot meal and mulled cider await us on the hob of a crackling fire. We kiss deeply in the foyer, overcome by our passion for one another. Our body heat escapes our polyester snowsuits when we unzip and our sweat cools us too quickly. We excuse ourselves and change modestly into fluffy robes whose terry cloth comforts us immediately. We eat our meals and play a special wooden edition of Trivial Pursuit, marveling at the intricacy of it, in brave attempts to thwart our mounting desires. Finally, the intense activity of the day catches up with us. Too drowsy from the exercise, victuals, and heat of the fire, you fall asleep asking the question, "How high is a regulation basketball hoo..." and your robe slightly parts accidentally revealing your left breast burgeoning with milk because you forgot to pump. I fall asleep shortly after, dreaming of you, releasing all of my tension in my reverie.

D. Bring Teddy with us on a month-long stay in Dordogne, France. We rent a small Airbnb villa outside of Périgueux and trek "Le Pays de la Soif et la Terreur" while slathered in sunscreen and packed with plenty of water. You delight in comparing and contrasting the plants of this arid climate to those of the Grand Canyon, sometimes rubbing the fuzzier ones on Teddy's cheek. You warn me not to make rock cairns and I blush sheepishly, which you mistake for heat stress. We decide to forgo the next day's hike in the blazing sun and opt for a cool foray into the Caves of Abri Castanet. Teddy charms the personnel there so much we are permitted into the sections only scholars enter for preservation purposes. He falls asleep, completely relaxed in your baby wrap, but we are equally silent in awe of the ancient graffiti. Later, we dine in a two-star Michelin restaurant where we savor foie de gras and artisanal cheeses, which we wash down with perfectly matched wine. Back in the villa, Teddy who had woken and behaved exemplary for a baby at dinner, goes back down for bedtime, and we pursue the earthly delights that rustic images on limestone walls inspired.

I have to go soon, but if any of these scenarios reflect your feelings, or if you have different visions about what we would have done, write back.

Cordially,

Gil

Email 19

Amanda Vero to Gilbert DeRoquedu

(October 2019)

Dearest Gil,

Yes, oh yes, your scenarios delight me! From chaste to titillating, you ran the gamut of all my feelings about us. Thinking of what "might have been" is bittersweet but reveling in the by and by is downright marvelous. I don't know which scenario I liked best, honestly. Everything sounds wonderful, exploring possibilities and commonalities between us. (Note to self: Buy buttered popcorn and sit next to Gil in a movie theater.) My analyses correspond to your same lettering system.

A. You don't know it, but I took swing-dancing lessons a few years after Mom died as a diversion of sorts. In other words, I'm surprisingly good at sock-hopping. Oh, and malted milkshakes are my favorite. (This scenario reminds me of Ludus love.)

B. I've never been to the New York Public Library. In fact, I've not experienced much fun in New York City. Early on in our dating, Peter and I boarded a bus tour, but it was 2002, so we visited the site of the World Trade Center and the church nearby where firefighters rested while working to find lost comrades in the 9/11 destruction. It was very sobering. We did manage to find a deli and order pastrami-on-rye sandwiches as well as hot coffee in those famous blue paper cups with the white urns on them before they were retired. The sandwich was tasty, but the coffee wasn't. Your trip with me sounds much more enjoyable. (This scenario's love is Ludus crossed with Eros.)

C. We don't have a maiden aunt, or even a grandmotherly type since Peter also lost his parents but packing Teddy off with Peter somehow would work. My mind(?) is drooling over this one. (Goodness gracious, this is Eros all the way.)

D. I haven't been to that region of France, but I have been to Paris for two weeks. I'm glad I went, I really liked the artwork in the Louvre, and riding the elevator to the top of the Eiffel Tower was cool, but I feel like we (it was Peter's and my honeymoon) missed the heart and soul of France, like its culture, or the people or something. The closest I felt to anyone else was at a fountain in the Jardins de Tuileries where we watched children use sticks to push wooden boats. Your vision seems much more personable, even the artwork is more intimate. (The ending could be Eros, but your thoughtfulness regarding my interest in flora and fauna is total Philia. Beautiful.)

You didn't add a fifth scenario, but I'll gladly try.

E. Take Teddy with us, but this time in a stroller which we push along a creaky boardwalk, not at the ocean's edge, but on the Eastern shore of the Chesapeake Bay. The scents of tar and estuary water create a bouquet that is at once new and familiar. Teddy is enchanted by seagulls that pitch and dive for garbage in the water. We comment on the intertwining of charm and trash. For lunch, we dine on crabcakes, crab fluff, and imperial crab. For dessert, we share a slice of Lady Baltimore cake, research the recipe, then wonder if the owner used raw egg whites in the heavenly frosting. We decide it's an adventure and don't complain. After lunch near a marina, we find a shady spot under an American chestnut tree in a public park. You wait patiently while I nurse Teddy, but after I lay him down in the stroller to nap, you hold me close in your strong arms, and we kiss while the tidewater softly laps the docks.

Gil, exploring these ideas has been a remarkable journey and flexing my own creativity feels fabulous. Thank you.

This isn't nearly on the level of the pleasure that your scenarios provided, but I hope it can paint some pictures in your mind. The nurse-in was a bust. (Haha, aren't I punny? Sorry, I couldn't resist.) The restaurant was closed, so we stood outside instead of eating inside, which would have made more of an impact. Also, only five of us showed up, which is equally less effective.

According to the pix on their website, WRUMIRS has much bigger crowds for Chinese Food Days, so I don't know what happened here. It seems to me that a nurse-in is more important than whether a Chinese restaurant turns a profit. Of interest, I did feel a ferocity that I hadn't felt as a mother when I exposed my breast to the open air while standing on a sidewalk. Eliza was right to phrase this action as "guns out." All I could think was the more anyone would try to shame us, the more I planned to expose myself. "Come and get them" I thought, and then I remembered that's a quote from Leonides from The Gates of Thermopylae. Weaponized motherhood indeed.

I should go because in a few minutes, I will trick-or-treat for the first time as a parent. So excited!

So many loves fill my heart,

Mandy

P.S. I have no problem with what you indicate you've been up to lately. It is healthy and normal considering the difficulty you're experiencing at home. And obviously, I am going through something similar. However, I have just benefited tremendously from your brilliant mind, as well as from your photo, so I hope to return the favor. If it helps you, I took a picture of myself earlier today

(#selfiesarethenewnorm) in the outfit I was wearing when I saw you, though the pose is frontal, not posterior. I have now embedded it in the body of this email below my postscript. If you would prefer not to receive photos in the future, please let me know.

P.P.S. I too relieved tension, though not in any dream, but in my bathroom, behind a locked door, surrounded by fuzzy blue floor mats and bath towels. I suppose that's not nearly as romantic as anything that you think of (you have such a powerful imagination!), but a woman can only sustain her self-control for so long, especially after having drunk her morning coffee. Your profile picture is equally inspiring, with your eyes that seem to smile knowingly just at me and the roundness of it, (imposed by the app, I guess) reminds me of the Sun. Three times I warmed to your radiance today.

P.P.S. the love referenced above is Philautia. Okay, I'm done now :)

[link to photo]

Email 20

Gilbert DeRoquedu to Amanda Vero

(November 2019)

My Dear Mandy,

Thoughts of you consume me when I should be working on my research, but what is the point of life if I spend it only poring through old books? Why should I spend any time on the black scratchings of decrepit men, long dead before today, when I can be dazzled by your vibrance instead? Your bright smile lightens my heart, your intellect reawakens my mind, your maternal heart stirs my own paternal feelings, and your beautiful shape rejuvenates my unseen middle. While I was glad to know you as a young woman, today's bliss is greater because I know you even better. I never want to lose you again to Father Time and I will fight for our love in all of its iterations, armed with the knowledge that you love me too.

I am reminded of the famous Greek Seikilos Epitaph, "While you live, shine, never at all should you suffer. Only for a little while is there life. Time demands fulfillment."

I may best express it here:

White arms, bare charms, she cast her face

Toward the ships at sea

The fleet did sail upon that day

Recorded history

Her countenance carved a firm place

In our mythology

Yet who was she who launched the ships -

Simply a pale body?

Beauty does merit lore for sure

But character is key

For what are eyes and painted lips

Without the soul set free?

Our poet sang she wove a cloak

To name the ones who battled

Since she was thankful to the men

Her honor fixed, unrattled

Some find Helena of Troy woke

But   Homer   rhymed   her   chatteled.

Today, Love launched a thousand drops

Into a vessel dear,

Her alabaster skin has built

A figure de Plaisir

Yet by her words my pulsing tops

As   my   heart   does   draw   near

Far greater than Yore's gorgeous deed,

This statuesque Mommy

Does write her life and lessons learned

But I long to more than see

Feminine wisdom embodied

In Sud Pennsylvanie

    Love,

    Gil

Email 21

Amanda Vero to Gilbert DeRoquedu

(November 2019)

My Darling Gil,

You astound me. Just when I thought I couldn't be carried further away by your affection, you have transported me on lines of verse. I don't even know this kind of poetry, I had to look it up, but now I think I could identify Common Meter if someone put a quill to my head. I can respond with the only type of poetry I know how to compose - a Haiku.

In Lippincott West,

Two lovers hotelled, undressed,

Their Eros confessed

Love,

Mandy

Email 22

Gilbert DeRoquedu to Amanda Vero

(November 2019)

My Dear Mandy,

It gives me intense pleasure to make arrangements to see you in the near future. My weekends are booked solid through November, but I will be able to arrange a weekend for us in December, before Christmas.

Today, I nearly skipped down the stairs at the University of Pennsylvania, where I am attending a conference on a proposal to exhibit a necropolis found in 2016. A rainy morning and eighty shackled "desmotes" cannot deter this silly man. And it doesn't really matter what we do together, the time between us is what has importance. Just because we may meet at a hotel does not force us into any particular activity, though I can't deny confessing my Eros to you plays on a loop in my head. But I can think of other pleasures too.

A round of trivia? I will forfeit all my points to you. A race with you on inflatable hopper balls? You will bound ahead, my heart with yours, my fleshly desires with your bouncing bottom. We can read passages of favorite works to one another, lying in each other's arms. You have given this middle-aged heart flight in ways that I have not been able to express for some time.

This reminds me of addressing something I had not before, and now I have even more reason to because I want to embrace you, all of you, in one piece, not pieces. Perhaps it is selfishness on my part, but would you please not experiment further with your flight costume? I am deeply concerned you could break bones...or worse. Don't just think of me though, consider Teddy. How well would he be with a mother who was recovering in the hospital, or one who could never hold him again?

But I digress, there is much joy to be had in speculating our future together. I must go and lunch with some "old heads" and discuss how to raise money for the proposed exhibit. Bleh, boring, but You...alluring. I can't even compose a proper poem today; I am so happy for us.

Much love,

Gil

P.S. I hadn't thought to categorize my fantasies, but your descriptors are very appropriate. We are on a "remarkable journey" and the path we have taken seems to be leading us to Pragma.

Email 23

Amanda Vero to Gilbert DeRoquedu

(November 2019)

My Darling Gil,

You say that this pleasure to plan your visit is yours, but I am writing to tell you that it is also mine, yet I don't think either of us has less of it, but more upon its allocation. That this newborn Love defies the Laws of Earthly Physics speaks to its Divine nature. I cradle it in my heart and pray for our continued blessings.

If you can refrain from skipping down a flight of stairs and not risk breaking your neck, then I can be equally pragmatic and not build prehensile wings. You asked with such affection and consideration, how could I not put it aside? But I can reason beyond that, and I hope to be equally humble. I have no need to gamble on a science I haven't really studied, and the Laws of Earthly Physics definitely apply to it. You are right to be concerned on several levels and I am mollified that I hadn't considered Teddy's need for me to remain healthy. Thank you, Darling, for having brought this to my attention. In place of my arms, my heart will continue to soar.

As for our actual meeting, it will need to be from a Saturday morning through Sunday afternoon. I have a standing invitation to scrapbooking weekends at a Bed and Breakfast in Gettysburg which runs in that timeframe. Peter has treated me to this monthly break from our household for years, so I will just say I am there. If he needs to contact me, he can always reach me by cell phone. As to where we will stay, I don't want anyone to recognize me, so I suggest picking a hotel far enough away that we can be discreet, but local enough that I can drive back quickly, if I need to. Would a hotel in Hagerstown work for you?

You mentioned reading our favorite works. What is your favorite book or poem? I feel like there is still much about you I don't know. Here is a funny meme I just saw on social media - If you could be a casserole, which one would you be? I'll give you mine - I'm a Hot Fruit Compote, which is classy at the outset - does anyone use the word "compote" anymore? - whose fragile glass dish has nerdy corners and presents transparently, and whose steaming ripened fruits are bursting with sweet juices, but woe betide the unsuspecting consumer who underestimates the hot buttered prunes therein for overindulgence betrays the gourmand and the indignation is public.

Love,

Mandy

P.S. I feel a little silly asking you about keeping our weekend discreet, but I would be mortified if either Peter or Melissa found out. How can you be sure about protecting this clandestine lovefest? Is your phone private? On my end, I control the dashboards to our phones and WIFI since paying bills on time is my superpower and bill-paying is Peter's Kryptonite.

Email 24

Gilbert DeRoquedu to Amanda Vero

(November 2019)

Dear Hot Buttered Prunes,

You don't frighten me in the least. I will devour your sweetness with gusto, but with a napkin tucked under my chin to catch your dripping juices and I will partake of you near the necessary facilities. If there are any negative consequences, I hope they won't last too long.

If I am to be reduced to a casserole, then I am your Moussaka - dressed as Greek or Turkish, but really a European revision. Filled with French béchamel and Italian tomato sauce, I present many layers to consume and every serving of me is as square as the dish in which I was baked. Unsuspecting consumers may receive a squirt of my hot sauce if they handle me vigorously.

A hotel in Hagerstown will work just fine. I will book one as soon as possible. As for discretion, Melissa does have access to my primary cell phone, but not to my other phone, which I use only for work purposes. You are the delightful exception.

Speaking of housekeeping, I will need to travel to Russia in a couple of days and stay there for a few weeks, but I would like to remain in touch with you. However, I'm not sure I will have access to my usual email. Would you be willing to download the Gobbledygook app? Its encryption will allow for long messages like our emails, but also shorter texts with photos, videos (if you would like to see my travels) links to other things, and if I'm incredibly lucky, connection to you in real time. You indicated that you have control over your phone, so I'm hoping this is something you can do. If you can't, then I'll just reread your emails during the day and dream of you at night.

My favorite book? That's easy. It is The Secret Garden (TSG) by Frances Hodgson Burnett. There is something very moving about parents realizing the worth of children, the repair of human relationships, the afflicted seeking God, and people finding one another, as well as God, in nature, even if the gardens were very contrived. I struggled to finish L'Engle's A Wrinkle in Time, (AWIT) an equally excellent book, which was a required reading for school, after I had discovered such a beautiful book, such is TSG, but I did finish both, though AWiT lends a harsh and cold quality. I tend to remember them together because I was so taken with TSG, but forced to read AWiT, so the intensity of the experience lingers to this day. I suppose that's not a book most cis-het men cite, but it is mine and I will duel you if you deride it in some way. Okay, not fight, but I will wrestle you, pinning you flat under me, then kiss you until you beg for mercy.

I must now spend some time preparing for the conferences in Russia. These boring machinations may take me away from writing to you, but they won't conquer my heart because I will always fight for our love. From the depths of my dusty cabinets to the heights of my next flight, you have my undying affection.

Ever thine,

Gil

Gobbledygook

Shared file of Amanda Vero and Gilbert DeRoquedu

(November 2019)

Mandy: Dearest Gil,

I have downloaded the app as you requested and am reaching out to you here. The idea that we might communicate in real time makes my heart beat faster. I don't know what I'll say. I hope I can be witty. You are so precise in your language. I will still write in email form though when we are asynchronous, opening and closing with "Dear Gil" and "Love, Mandy" because it will be easier for me to find your words in between.

Photos and videos? Squeee! I would LOVE to see where you travel to, what foods you eat, what the libraries and markets look like? But my burning question is: Why are you going in the first place?

I don't have exotic travels to plan for here, just the life of a stay-at-home mom. I'd like to write that it's always charming, but I am unpleasantly surprised more often than not. Take trick-or-treating, for example.

From my childhood in Philadelphia, I remember trick-or-treating as a fun activity, especially in a populated neighborhood full of rowhomes where we lived. After school, Mom would give me an early dinner, then help me into my homemade costume. Then, she would turn me loose to work both sides of our street. It was fun to visit every home, receive compliments on my costumes, hear the thunk of whatever treats the hostess delivered into my pumpkin, then saunter over to the next house. There were often steps to climb to the porch, but sometimes there weren't. I would fill my large pumpkin, race home, dump the candy whatever vessel Mom decided would hold it all, then head out again for more of the same. At the end of the evening, Mom would help me out of my costume, and I would sit at the dining room table fishing out my favorite treats to eat that night, in addition to the popcorn balls and apple slices with homemade caramel sauce Mom made. Completely sugared up, I would crash about an hour later and my parents would help me to bed. I guess what I remember most is my quasi-independence and my parents in the background.

This year was my first attempt at being a parent to a trick-or-treater. Teddy was still adorable in his bread loaf costume, and I was experienced enough with it to know I could change a diaper on the fly, but it seems like everything else was outside of my control.

Since we planned to eat dinner then trick-or-treat in someone else's neighborhood, Peter had to scramble away from work early. But traffic was slow, so he was delayed. That was the first problem. We drove twenty minutes away to join our church group at Bev and Bill's house. My potluck dish of "Yoda heads" which were stuffed green peppers with olive eyes were soggy by the time we arrived. For a Star Wars themed meal, they had made sense to me initially, but then the idea of eating the innards of a character's skull put other parents off. Peter and I hurriedly ate ours because I wanted to show everyone how safe they were, but no one else dared. And then I was stuck with a grumbling digestive system because I ate too fast. I also stained my Princess Leia costume with tomato sauce which looked monumentally stupid. Then it was time to go trick-or-treating. No, it was time to take pictures in the front yard. Guess which baby didn't cooperate, but bawled his eyes out instead? I think Teddy could sense my tension. After several tries, another mother loudly suggested, "Maybe he'll be ready for pictures next year." I whisked him away and worked ridiculously hard not to cry over something that really isn't that important. Pictures taken; it was time to leave. At that moment, I turned my attention to the neighborhood. This wasn't the concentration of city dwellings, but wide suburban homes, with acres for backyards, and no sidewalk connecting any of it. I had thought that Peter and I might take turns holding Teddy for a few houses, then returning to Bev and Bill's, but one hard look at the frontier before us meant that we would be out for the entire two hours, so we had to extract the gangly stroller out of the car and load it up with whatever we thought we might need. For two excruciating hours, Peter and I pushed the stroller along the street, waving our phone lights and yelling along with the other parents at approaching cars that were driving too fast. Only for the first few houses did we park the stroller in the front yard, carry the baby to the front door, receive treats and compliments, then walk back to the stroller and try to convince Teddy he needed to go back in it. The whole ordeal was incredibly disruptive for the poor child, so we stopped trick-or-treating after the tenth house but that meant we received no more treats because I do have some sense of adulthood. Meanwhile, the older kids went back and forth to the tarmac, asking their parents to carry their pumpkins in between houses. For all of their running and hard work, they barely filled their pumpkins. Finally, the two hours ended, but did we return to Bev and Bill's home? No! Her parents wanted to see the grandchildren and since they lived in the same neighborhood, we landed there. Okay, the mulled cider was a nice touch, and I could use the bathroom, where I changed a sleepy Teddy. Then I nursed him privately in a guest bedroom while I munched on candy corn and cookies. Later, Peter and the other fathers walked back to Bev and Bill's house to retrieve their cars and pick us up at her parents' house so we wouldn't have to walk back also. In all, I was very exhausted. I really don't know if I'll do it again while Teddy is a baby. Since he won't remember, it shouldn't matter, but that's just one example of my expectations rooted in my childhood memories that did not meet the reality of my life. Is Halloween like that for you too?

I hope you have a safe flight. Please let me know when you arrive if you can.

Love,

Mandy

Gil: Dear Mandy,

Thank you for your well wishes, I will let you know when I have arrived safely. In the meantime, I'm packing, but I will gladly make time to write to you.

Your description of Halloween in the 'burbs is quite the eye-opener. I suppose it's not much different here outside of Pittsburgh, but trick-or-treating is not something Melissa and I do. Since we were childless for most of our marriage, we didn't have any reason to participate in the holiday, except to dress up for some costume contests at a local bar.

Melissa and I like to explore fresh craft beers and our local tavern has a selection of forty-one taps, so every weekend that I'm home we try something new there and if a contest falls on a Saturday night, we wear our fancy dress. Last time she was pregnant with Alastor, so she wore her Pilgrim costume to which I added a scarlet A over her big belly. I went as a newspaperman, i.e., dressed in a shirt and hat made from old newspapers. We didn't win. On occasion, we have joined Harmonia's parents to trick-or-treat with her in Pittsburgh proper, but it has been a casual affair and we usually wrap up early because she doesn't like sugar as much as most children do. Trick-or-treating with a baby sounds grueling. Considering our special circumstances, we may hold off for several more years.

To answer your question, I am traveling to Russia to delicately discuss the remote possibility of returning some pieces of Greek antiquity to Greece. These topics must be broached with the utmost care and consideration because European countries have plundered Antiquity for its treasures for millennia and only now, through modern sensibilities, do the heads of such countries begin to perceive this as wrongdoing. For the historical pieces that landed in France, Italy, etc., centuries ago, there is little hope of retrieval, but the pieces I will address were looted in the nineties, so there is more of a possibility of their return to North Macedonia, from which they originally came. These discussions must be had in ways that save face, or through which there is something else to be gained. I have been entrusted by the curator of a museum in Bitola to offer some pottery in exchange for the Macedonian tomb and the warrior outfit encased within it. Should negotiations succeed, the museum in Bitola will receive the items in question by the end of my stay.

For my food and drink, I will partake of the offerings at a local restaurant. The food is plain - think cucumber and cabbage-based dishes, but wholesome and cheap. There are fancier venues with tempting menus, but the prices are for oligarchs and I'm already a persona non grata here, so it's best if I patronize places where those who would see me as their enemy aren't as likely to be. For this reason, I will not freely roam the markets either, but in the past, I have visited the Izmaylovski market in Moscow. However, if you've seen one matryoshka doll, you've seen twelve (okay, couldn't resist the joke here) so I don't need to do it again. At some point I would like to explore the Danilovsky food market, but this is not the trip for that. We can make time for it together in the future.

You asked me about my favorite book and turnabout is fair play, but what I really want to know is: What is your favorite movie?

Love,

Gil

Mandy: Dear Gil,

Your trip sounds stressful. I hope the hotel has a gym or a pool for you to build up endorphins or something. I don't know if I could survive on dishes routinely based on cabbages and cucumbers, but I think if I was with you, I wouldn't even notice how plain it was. Matryoshka dolls aren't my thing, so I would skip that market, but the food one sounds intriguing. I've just researched it and the description makes it sound like something one would find on the ancient Silk Road. Maybe we wouldn't have to visit Moscow, where you have some legitimate concerns, but rediscovering points along remnants of the original Silk Road might be interesting, no?

My favorite movie? That's easy - "The Godfather, Part I." I've seen it twenty-five times now and each time, I take away something new. Part II is a close second with Michael masterfully running the show, even willing to kill his own family, but in Part I there is a depth of familial connections that feels absent in Part II. Please never speak to me about Part III, I couldn't bear even a conversation about that awful film. That is all I have to say about that.

I'm surprised you didn't ask me about my favorite book, but it is and has always been...Charlotte's Web by E.B. White. I had a puppy around Fern's age in the book and I did exactly what she did - carted him around in my doll carriage, loaded up baby bottles full of milk and filled his tummy. The only thing different was that he was allowed to sleep on my bed. Well, I grew up with him too, giving him walkies and kibbles later on for years, so that was a major difference. I still cry when I read the ending. Maybe I'm supposed to pick a more grown-up tale, but Charlotte's friendship and loyalty make me think of Ralph's (that was his name) purpose in my life. As an only child, I can't tell you how meaningful Ralph was to me, so Charlotte's Web resonates the most. Isn't it funny that we both like books with young headstrong female characters of about the same age?

Sometimes, I get bored when Peter is away at work and I have to nurse Teddy, or he's already sleeping. Because it is all so interruptive, I've recently turned to common romance novels that won't matter when I pick them up, put them down, nor finish reading them. They may not equate to the drama of your reality television, but I promise you, they're just as trashy. I've taken the liberty of lifting an excerpt from <u>The Scorch of His Torch</u> by Lavender Fields

"Jessica pressed her weary forehead against the outside wall of the conference room. The presenter, deeply engrossed in the thirteenth slide of his detailed sales presentation, didn't see her leave. From the first slide through the twelfth, Jessica furrowed her brows, trying to make out the tiny numbers this fool in front of her failed to enlarge in consideration of his audience. At the thirteenth, she could take this excruciation no longer and sought behind her the glowing red dot over the door she knew to be an exit to a darkened hallway. In one smooth motion, she seized her bag and swiveled around to face the door, pushed it quietly open, and walked through. It shut behind her just as quietly as it had opened.

The cool plaster of the wall soothed her aching muscles and gave her time to think. She need not return to the presentation; the slideshow had already been emailed to her. From the comfort of her hotel room, she could enlarge the numbers and process the data. She could wet a washcloth and hold it to her forehead for even more relief. She laughed at herself for how disengaged she was from the social scene of her office. Anyone else would have availed themselves of the hotel bar at the mere possibility of an excuse and would have joined the vibrant nightlife of the Town hours later, but not Jessica. No one would ever mistake her for a party animal. Her mind turned to her next challenge - moving surreptitiously around the corner into the next hallway, past the presentation in the other conference room, where the door was open, and she knew he sat in attendance. Now was not the time for him to see her again.

Their love story was decidedly *not* the stuff of legends. She had simply interviewed him, the CEO and founder of his flashlight brand, "Scorch's Torches," as an inspirational piece for her sales company. He was indeed a light, so-to-speak, in the darkness of his youth. He had beaten the odds of an upbringing through foster care and founded his company with just a little seed money from one of his foster mothers when he was still quite young. It wasn't much really, most kids that age would have spent it on brand name sneakers, but young Wyndham Scorch had the foresight and a few leftover materials from a hardware store to make a mold and melt a particular composite plastic whose properties he recognized as ideal for casing flashlights. Lightweight, yet strong, these plastic, waterproof flashlights could be dropped from anywhere, down a steep cliffside, even into the hottest campfire, yet still work. Prized by climbers to the top of Nepali, they caught on in a proverbial flash with every amateur hiker who coveted such hipness. Wyndham didn't know the chemical make-up at the time, though he would learn it, but intuitively composed exactly the right plastic for the perfect product. Well, near perfect.

Invariably, customers from Great Britain became easily confused and insulting. Phoning headquarters to enquire about this new flashlight, inattentive callers who only heard the phone number mentioned on the radio, responded to the admins' greeting of "Thank you for calling Scorch's Torches. How may I be of service to you?" with an irritated "What?"

Just as invariably, they would sputter, "What kind of company name is "Torch's Torches?" An exchange of corrections would occur until the caller understood, but then, in the relief of clarity, the caller, feeling a more personal connection to the company, would order multiple flashlights. Sales in Great Britain were up, not down, and so the confusion and its ensuing exchanges remained. Wyndham's meteoric rise was noted by several organizations, Jessica's included. After the interview, he suggested they take coffee. One date led to another until they almost, but did not, reveal themselves fully to one another. Oh, but she wanted him. They had hugged, traded a shy kiss or two, and once, he had referenced his "candle" burning for her, but she was unsatisfied. Her desires caught her unawares in the oddest of places - bending over the hamper to reach down for clothes, she could imagine him taking her hips and thrusting her from behind. Kneeling on the floor to water some plants on the lowest level of her étagère, she looked up for a moment, and imagined him, looking at her, as she delivered raw pleasure to his greatest sensitivity, the strong scent of her fertile potted plants mimicking the perfume of his essence. But then, it all came crashing down.

On the merest pretense of a misunderstanding, created by his own ridiculous internal dramas (What did go through this extraordinary man's head? She wondered as she ruminated over their breakup for the zillionth time) he had outright dumped her, by text. He ended it with a flimsy suggestion that they remain pen pals and a closure of "Peace Be with You" as if she could peacefully let their relationship go. In her stern breakup response letter, she framed it in more contemporary terms. He had "undertaken a major decision, affecting them jointly, without consulting her first," but they both knew she was stung by his sudden discard of her. Was the misunderstanding really the reason? Did he have a sidepiece? She didn't know, but she did have pride. Except for a brief exchange of where he could find the dried, dead husks of flowers he had once given to her, there had been no more communication for nine months. She did not text and she definitely did not call him. She even blocked him on all social media. She most certainly did not beg for him to give her a second chance or try to work it out. Aghast at his stupid, but decisive actions, he did not reach out to her either. Why, oh why did he break up with her? He could hardly name the reason; it was all so silly and dumb.

He should have known better. She was one of those literal types who took him at his word and did not guess his other meanings. She never did see how deeply he had fallen for her so that the slightest miscommunication brought all of his insecurities to the fore. He desperately wanted to measure up to her standards in life and if he didn't meet them, well, he couldn't bear her breaking up with him. He did the only thing he could think of at the moment, he broke up with her.

So, they remained, two souls once united by modern technology, now divided by it. And she was not to be trifled with. She may not have grown up in the foster care system like he had, but she had street smarts and an iron core of will and righteousness. She had seen right through his attempts to draw her into pseudo communication through his fake profiles on social media. After liking each other's posts, then following each other, he had slyly encouraged her whip smart trolling of fools on the Internet, which she did with ease, but then she dropped the bomb in a private message to him. "I was tolerating this as a gentle connection between us, but I think better of it now as this charade is disrespectful to both of us. Please stop following me as Plain Wayne. Peace Be with You." Re-using his closure was the crowning touch. He pretended he didn't know her but did agree to stop following her. In shame and embarrassment, he eventually deleted the account, flummoxed as to how to reach her in a way that didn't require him to grovel to her.

Jessica knew none of his inner turmoil, but she did know he was here, at this hotel, this very day. She had seen his hungry look from across the lobby earlier that morning and correctly interpreted his yearning to speak to her, to give him a second chance. She knew she had to avoid him at all costs or risk being dumped by him again for some other silly reason he invented.

She tiptoed down the hall and gingerly made her way around the corner. The door stood open, and she sensed people inside, but she realized that the attendees were facing away from the door and focused on their narrator. Quickly she walked by, but she did not escape his notice. He had been waiting for a moment like this. While she had been a pillar of stealth escaping her conference, he was not. He stood up, then tripped over a chair leg, flew into the air, and landed across the laps of four coworkers, the youngest of whom in whose crotch his face had smacked. "Owww " his coworker groaned in pain. Wyndham scrambled off the laps as quickly as he had alighted them. The presenter halted her presentation. "Is there a disturbance back there?" she peered through her glasses. "Yes, I am terribly sorry," said Wyndham. To his co-worker he apologized profusely. "I'm alright," declared Dave, a little shaken, but otherwise recovered.

Gathering the shreds of his dignity, Wyndham dusted off his designer suit, picked up his briefcase, and under the gaze of forty pairs of eyeballs, walked to the door leading to the hallway. In an instant, he forgot his spectacle, all he could do was look at her. She was here, from her straight brown hair gathered in a plastic brown clip (oh how his heart fluttered at the familiarity of it!) to her bright blue eyes, her baby doll mouth (oh how he wanted to kiss it again, and again, and again) to her rounded breasts that he wanted to fully discover, to her...oh, she was looking at him awfully hard, one eyebrow cocked.

"What do you want?" she asked, each word punching the air. He had no convenient answer.

"I...," he began weakly.

"You!" she began her attack. "You! You do not know yourself as well as you think you do. You relegated us to pen pals if I recall, yet you have written nothing. How dare you try to speak to me! Are you not a man of your word?" she asked.

He looked at her, deep into her eyes and drew closer, her reddening cheeks egging him on. Now he wanted very much to hold her. She kept looking at him but did not put any distance between them. He reached her and embraced her firmly. And in that moment, that relief to have her in his arms again, he knew exactly who he was. His piercing eyes penetrated her. "I am a man, at times a tempestuous, passionate, and ridiculous man, a man, no less, but I am not a man of my word. I am a man of my wick." and he finished his soliloquy, pressing his throbbing member against her. Liquifying under his intent gaze, replaying his speech in her mind, she knew she should reject him at once, but he was so strong, so familiar, so...male. She couldn't judge him for identifying with his genitals, because she was about to forgo all reason, on account of her own pulsing button and the warm welcome she would give to him began to run down her thighs."

So, you see, Gil, this is what I can pick up and put down as needed. If it were any shallower, I'd use it as a candy dish, lol.

Today, I read as far as

Gil:Oh my God.

Mandy:OMG, Gil are you here?

Gil:I am. What happens next?

Mandy:What?

Gil:In your trashy romance novel. It's bloody terrible, but I want to know - what happens next?

Mandy:Oh, haha. Well, you know, more throbbing members, some quivering thighs, and explosions of some sort.

Gil:I may have to download it and read it on the plane tomorrow.

Mandy:Oh wow, that's hilarious.

Gil:What's hilarious?

Mandy: You are someone so staid and serious yet here you are reading a trashy romance novel. You have a wonderfully open mind. You did establish what an ardent feminist you are capable of being with your Helena of Troy/me of South Pennsylvania poem, come to think of it.

Gil: Well, there is that. I like to think that I'm more evolved than my hairy brothers, but only time will tell. What remains is that I have a deep desire to overpower you physically, when we get together. You may find yourself at my mercy, should we play Twister, for example.

Mandy:I'm not afraid. In fact, I welcome you to test your agility against me. I hope I prove a worthy opponent, though honestly, I can't see myself opposing you in any way, but more likely submitting to your every whim.

Gil:I am Twisted up in you.

Mandy:I certainly hope you will be.

Gil:It's getting warm in here.

Mandy:Oh yes, I'm on fire.

Gil:Then would you like to read a fantasy of mine?

Mandy:Yes, oh yes, please Gil!

Gil:Very Well. We are camping in the Grand Canyon in late September. After a long day of kayaking on the Colorado River, we pull up at Football Beach where no one else is because it's out of season. We prepare our camp, you set up the fire, I pitch the tent. I don't tell you, but I place a bouquet of flowers in a vase for you and light a candle that I secreted inside my pack. You cook a nourishing meal over the fire, then we split some gooey s'mores. We wash it down with a cabernet sauvignon. After a day of strenuous exercise, I strip you, rub my hands with a scented oil, and massage your aching muscles. You are so relaxed, so peaceful, I become aroused. You see my arousal and release me from my constricting clothes. You invite me into your mouth, looking right into my eyes, gauging my pleasure with every movement of your lips and tongue. I sense that I might climax at once, so I pull out, wanting to savor everything. You have me so excited, I gently push you onto the sleeping bag and go down on your drooling mound, fingering you in all the right places, until you reach your ecstasy with soft moans and reddened cheeks. But I can take no more, and I mount you, thrusting my hardened affection into your warmth until I completely lose control. We fall asleep, a tangled heap of oils, fluids, warm breaths, and soft skin. In the morning's first light, we wake up and do it all over again, drifting off afterward for another sleep cycle. When we wake up again, you prepare the coffee.

Mandy:Gil, this is extremely exciting. You make me want to quench my fire.

    Gil:By all means please do.

Mandy:Quenched. Thank you for waiting patiently.

    Gil:My absolute pleasure. I will have my own to quench later.

Mandy:Wowie.

Gil:But you mean more to me than any prurient interest. I mean that.

Gil:Dear Mandy,

You inspire me so. Please indulge me by listening to me sing to you. I made it in my car before I entered the airport, so you are my sole audience.

[video link to Gil's cover of "Longer" by Dan Fogelburg]

Love,

Gil

Mandy:Oh my God, Gil, I LOVE it. What a beautiful voice you have. I'm not just your sole audience, I am your SOUL audience. Thank you, thank you.

I could not love you more. Please accept this modest rendering of Annie's Song by John Denver as a token of my deep and abiding affection.

[video link to Mandy's cover of Annie's Song by John Denver]

Gil:Dear Mandy,

I have arrived safely, having been spurred by your well wishes, I'm sure. Thank you for your soft singing. I have listened to it several times now. It is my hope that I can fill up even more of your senses when we finally see each other again, as God intended. That you picked the song my mother used to sing to my father's accompaniment on his wooden flute can be no accident, but a Divine occurrence.

Currently, I am situated in a would-you-believe-it-? Hilton hotel. You would be surprised how relatively cheap a decent hotel room is in the heart of Moscow. I will upload pictures in a few days. Just imagine an American hotel room with all of the usual amenities, but floor-to-ceiling windows and the tall curtains to cover them. Today, I will just stay in the room, preparing my notes to speak to the curator of the museum where the warrior outfit and tomb are located. There is a very formal procedure, and one must be very prepared. My breakfast of pancake, caviar, salmon and sides of exotic fruit and cold cuts was very satisfactory though. A little too satisfactory. I may need to make some time for the hotel gym. In fact, I just spent more time than I would like to admit watching Russian television, not so much for the shows, but their commercials that address certain societal needs in ways American Puritanical standards don't allow, like the images of real breasts in breast pump ads.

Tomorrow, a colleague will pick me up and take me out to lunch, but it will be a quiet affair. I would much rather explore the touristy areas with you. I can't imagine anything more transcendent than snuggling with you in the nooks and crannies of Saint Basil's Cathedral. The weather is already chilly, though not cold enough to warrant a fur hat, so my wool knit cap will suffice. If you were here, I would kiss your bubushka'd face and we would marvel at the ancient stonework.

Afterwards, I would take you back to the hotel room, draw a bath in the wonderfully deep tub they have provided, then undress you and lead you into the steaming waters. After you relaxed a bit, I would give you a deep muscle massage, kissing you at many intervals. You would relax so completely, so utterly, that your breasts would let down and you would find yourself in a milk bath of your own making. Eventually, our passions would overtake us, and I would draw you out of the warm basin, to the queen-sized bed where I would wrap you, still dripping wet, in me. For now, I will just imagine you under the golden duvet, instead of these extra pillows.

I am feeling some jet lag, so I will wrap up here, but I hope to see you in my dreams.

Love,

Gil

Email 25

Blaise Ayers to Amanda Vero

(November 2019)

Dear Mandy,

I couldn't help but notice your issue and I'm so sorry that happened to you. I thought you did a really nice job trying to comfort Maximus. He's already forgotten it according to Marisol. And thank you so much for hanging back during the rest of the hike so the other kids wouldn't be so concerned.

In the future, you might consider preparing for such a situation by having the necessary items stashed in your car. I don't get mine anymore, so I had nothing to offer. Eliza's sweatshirt almost did the trick though. She's really a peach.

Also, when you agree to a meetup, can you come closer to the time it starts? That way, the other moms aren't left in limbo awaiting your arrival. Thanks again. Hope you feel better soon.

Warmest regards,

Blaise Ayers,

President of WRUMIRS

Email 26

Amanda Vero to Blaise Ayers

(November 2019)

Dear Blaise,

I am so sorry that I arrived late and that this happened. I had no idea it was coming because Teddy's breastfeeding has been stopping it, or so says all the research, so I didn't have anything. Per your suggestion, I've just finished packing my car with necessaries. Thank you for updating me on Maximus' state of concern. I'm really glad he's had no lasting effects.

Also, per your suggestion, I will be timelier. The way I can change this is to figure out how long it will take to drive to a playdate the night before, then stick to the time I need to leave when I leave my house. Thank you all so much for having waited for me and if you would please thank the others for me, I would appreciate it. Again, I apologize to everyone.

Sincerely,

Mandy

Email 27

Blaise Ayers to Amanda Vero

(November 2019)

Mandy,

Sounds great! No worries. We look forward to seeing you at the next playdate (on time! lol) :)

Blaise Ayers,

President of WRUMIRS

Gobbledygook (cont'd)

Shared file of Amanda Vero and Gilbert DeRoquedu

(November 2019)

Mandy: Dear Gil,

You are truly amazing. I'm so filled with emotion; I just want to string together a bunch of emojis, but I don't want to be that inarticulate either. I cannot, cannot wait to truly be with you after all these years. The coffee shop meeting was nothing compared to this. You will need to prepare yourself because I will pounce on you like a declawed cat who hasn't hunted a mouse in years, but into whose vision, one innocent little murine just happened to wander. In fact, I may pounce on you several times. I may nibble a bit, but I promise I won't bite. Okay, that's probably not as romantic as I think it is, but that's where my mind has wandered to at this moment.

It probably has to do with the immense embarrassment I had today.

Certainly, the morning started out well enough. Our Little Tourists group took a planned hike to Strawberry Hill Nature Preserve. It's a bit of a drive from Lippincott, but it really is beautiful. Along route 116 West, the forested hills recede from the road and the land flattens superbly so that the vast fields and farmlands blend into a patchwork of greens, blues, and golds, as if one is driving through a Van Gogh painting. Then, out of nowhere, Strawberry Hill rises on the right side. Turning right onto Bullfrog Road means driving straight into the forested foothills of the Blue Ridge Mountains but the road rises smoothly, and parking is easy to find.

Teddy fell asleep early on the hour's drive, so I didn't feel too bad waking him upon taking him out of his car seat. I had to baby wrap him because the trail we were taking wasn't paved. It was a very good thing I had used the bathroom before we left because the bathrooms here were locked for the season, but I might not have used them anyway because some of the moms were standing stiffly as if they had waited a long time for me to get there. Certainly, their children were milling about in a very uncontrolled way. One check of my phone and I realized I was twenty minutes late. So, I tucked Teddy into his pouch sling quickly and smiled, hoping that I hadn't made them too mad. Finally, Teddy was snugly wrapped against me, and the group started off. There were a few sticks on the ground, so between looking out for them, avoiding gross mud puddles, and trying to direct Teddy's attention to squirrels, birds, other children, I completely missed that I was getting my period, that is, until I felt something warm and very runny start to gush out of my underpants.

There we were, in the middle of the woods, with the nearest bathroom locked, and blood was staining the thighs of my mom jeans in big splotches. I couldn't take Teddy out of his wrap because it was just a pouch sling, the type that has a little premade hammock and buckles, etc., so it can't be used like a sweatshirt to cover my stains, plus I would have had to carry him for the next forty-five minutes. I tried to think what I could do and hung back a little from the group, but eventually a toddler noticed the blood on my clothes and said, "Mommy, Mommy, hurt, hurt!" so then everyone turned around. There was no hiding it and I was really embarrassed. All the other moms just froze, looking at me, like I was some fourth grader who didn't know how to handle her period. The best I could muster was to tell the little boy who alerted everyone to my period that it was okay, that I was not hurt, and sometimes mommies bleed. Apparently, that wasn't the right thing to do either because the other moms just curled their lips and remained in their same positions. I didn't know what to say, but I kept repeating, "it's okay, I'm okay." Eventually, Eliza broke the game of statues and offered me her sweatshirt to tie around my waist. It worked perfectly and we completed the hike, with Eliza, Danielle, and Lawrence, who was in Eliza's more sensible strip-of-cloth baby wrap, (Gosh, how I envied her for having that one!) keeping us company the whole time. I thanked her for what she did and promised to wash and return her sweatshirt immediately. She was just so breezy and said, "Oh don't worry, just get it back to me when you can." We ended the hike at the planned time, and I drove home vowing never to go on a hike in the woods again without wearing a pad. And more supportive shoes. Wearing a baby while hiking does not make for happy feet. I'm also going to use the strip-of-cloth baby wrap more because it would make a better cover in case of any disaster. After everything, I cried in the shower, I was so incredibly embarrassed at my own lack of preparation, my lateness, and I was grateful for Eliza's friendship. I feel better now because I'm clean, dressed, and back in control, but my cheeks still burn while I write this.

In unrelated news, I've finally discovered something Greek about me! After we came home from the hike, and I had attended to my necessaries, lol, I rubbed my aching feet. Upon close inspection, I realized that my second toe on each foot is longer than each big toe. I wondered if this was a genetic thing because it seemed frightfully weird, and I am always on the hunt of understanding conditions that may arise in Teddy. And you've probably already guessed - I have Greek toed feet! I don't know why, but I cried a little at that too, knowing this connection between us. It's silly, isn't it? Why should I feel so happy that my toes are Greek? Ugh, is it my period again? (I hope this feminine function doesn't bother you. Clearly it affects me, lol.) But I love that the form of feet was considered so "aesthetically-pleasing" you can find them on ancient statuary.

I've got to go and prepare dinner. I think I'll make Spanakopita, lol. No, really, I need to use up some bagged spinach and I have eggs galore. Bye for now!

Love,

Mandy

Gil: Dear Mandy,

That sounds like quite the unpleasant ordeal for you. No, I am not put off by menstruation. Periods are part of the normal human female experience and not shameful, dirty, or disgusting. I don't think I would have handled that mess any better than you did. Melissa still gets her period, but we never discuss it, and it is rare that I see her evidence, though shortly after she had Alastor, she left a large amount of used material in the trash can for too long and our dog, Aristophanes, had gotten into it. The memory of it still makes me queasy, but it is not knowledge of menses itself. Certainly, I am not attuned to her cycle as we are rarely intimate, but those times I have seen her stained panties, she has agreed to wash them before adding them to the laundry.

I do need to let you know that typing this is difficult right now as my arthritis in my hand has started to act up again. Usually, this requires pain meds for a few days, then settles down, but it means that I won't be able to form responses to your emails. However, I delight in reading your words, so please keep writing if you can find the time.

As for your Hellenic feet, I anticipate caressing this version of The Golden Ratio even more, though your furry pediment will have most of my attention.

Write soon!

Love,

Gil

Mandy:Dear Gil,

I'm so sorry your arthritis is acting up! I understand that you can't type as much, but I will miss your words. I think you mentioned this app takes photos? So, if you have any photos of something interesting, I would be glad to see it. If you can't take photos because, I don't know, Russia gets secretive about stuff? I'd be glad to look at any other photos you have to share, including those of your family. I hope they are well. I bet they miss you as much as I do now, if not more. I'd miss you a whole lot if I were married to you, for sure!

I'll try to fill in the void here since you can't participate as much, but I'm afraid it's not very highbrow. Eliza tells me there's always something going on, especially during the holidays, or as she likes to call them, the Holidaze. I don't know, I've never been part of a mom's group before, so I do not know what's in store for us.

Sometimes, I wish Teddy would be older. He's adorable, whether he's babbling or watching the elephant over his baby activity mat. He likes to hold my hair, though at times he's a little too intense and winds up pulling it instead. He burbles and coos but has no real words. I'm hoping he says "Mama" soon. According to all of the literature, he should be doing that, but he hasn't yet. It's yet another way I feel a little outside the group. I know what I do is mostly normal, but like, I can't participate as much in crafts, for example. Teddy can't even sit up, much less glue macaroni to a paper plate. And he can't eat candy, so I try not to eat any because it's usually for the kids, not the adults. I never quite know where I fit in.

Yesterday, I took him to the Playground Pals, but he can't go down the slide, or climb on the jungle gym, or ride the seesaw. I did manage to put him in the baby swing, but the equipment dwarfed him so I stuffed a blanket in the seat with him, but I worried the whole time that he would fall out, so I pushed him gently in it. After some initial adjustment including questioning babbles and wide-eyed stares, he rewarded my efforts with his beautiful smile. Still, what we could do was very limited compared to all of the kids running, swinging, sliding, etc. And their moms are different too. While they reminisce and empathize with my "baby days" as we call them, and they took turns holding him, which really warms my heart, they have sooo much else to talk about than being short on sleep. They have all of these interesting problems like teachers they try to avoid. They all know who the bad ones are and who are the great ones, but we're like five years behind any of this information. Their figures are better, I don't know how they do it and they all, I swear all, wear bronzer. I would just look fake if I wore it, but these ladies know what they're doing.

I'm sorry, I'm just feeling very off tonight. You are like my diary. I hope that's okay. I wish I had something more serious to tell you. I feel the pressure of wanting to convey adult topics, but I don't seem to have that. Do you have any ideas? I hope you're well.

Love,

Down in the Dumps

Gil:Dear Mandy,

Here are the photos as promised. I hope they raise your spirits. I don't have many of Melissa and Alastor because she's a bit camera-shy and she doesn't like the pictures in which he looks slack-eyed (which is most of the time), but I'm partial to these.

Love,

Gil

[link to Gil's photographs]

Mandy Dear Gil,

Thank you soo much for the photos! This is exactly what I needed to see; they raise my spirits so! Your family is just beautiful. Thank you again for sharing them.

I apologize for my earlier insensitivity. I let my emotions get the best of me the day before yesterday and because of it, I couldn't see how insulting I might sound, considering all that you're going through with Alastor. You bring much joy at a difficult time.

I was thinking that one of the reasons I got a bit down was as I mentioned, I don't seem to have a lot of intellectual topics to discuss. I know this isn't my fault, I'm reveling in All Things Domestic, but one of the happiest times of my life was when I attended high school. Trivia with you was great, but what I really thrived in was English class, especially when we analyzed books. I used to pour great energy into my essays and always awaited the teacher's grade with breathless anticipation. Do you think that we could read some books and take turns analyzing them? Maybe we pick for each other books we've read that the other person hasn't. If you would be agreeable to that idea, you could pick the first book for us.

I saw your photos first thing when I got up this morning, but we had chores and activities, so I am just setting down to write now. Some days I do absolutely nothing and other days, I'm a whirlwind of activity. I don't quite understand the ebb and flow of my energy, but I make the most of it when I have it.

This morning started off with the housework. I don't know about Melissa, but I don't feel I've finished everything until I've dry-swept the floors. I'm economical though. After one side of the dry sweep cloth is covered in dust, I flip it over and use the clean side. We're comfortable enough that a few wasted dry sweeper cloths won't put us in the "poor house," but I economize where I can. Teddy napped while I cleaned, though I had to delay unloading and reloading the dishwasher because the clanking of mugs, plates, and pots might have disturbed him. Once he woke up, I took time to nurse him, then laid him on his activity mat on the floor of the kitchen

156

while I baked a tart and worked on the dishes until I ordered the dishwasher to run while we went grocery-shopping.

Another way our family saves money is to shop at the generic grocery store. Most of the items are manufactured by the brand name companies so there is no loss of quality, but the labels are different. When I was a girl, the generic labels were only black and white, but now they have color printing and pictures so one doesn't feel stigmatized. Do you shop at such a store, or do you buy brand name? I kept Teddy in his car seat, put it in the shopping cart and took a picture, which I'll include below. Isn't he adorable?

Because most WRUMIRS members spend time with family, our monthly potluck for November was bumped up to today. We met at Blaise's house, and I brought onion tart which was a total hit. So many moms are tired of kid food so adult cuisine is eaten with gusto. (Note: I did not serve the gusto, they provided it, lol) The tart is so easy to make too. All one must do is sauté six onions in butter, add some salt and pepper, then dump them into a pie shell and bake for a half hour. Because the onions are already cooked, they're not swimming in their juices, but what they do release helps them to solidify (congeal? But that seems like the wrong word) on the pie shell. By the time it cools, this savory, buttery tart cuts easily into neat wedges. (Confession: I may have just written out this recipe on the off chance that you could suggest it to Melissa, considering her lack of variety. If you can't suggest it to her, I will understand, but be a little sad you can't have a taste of my cooking for variety's sake.)

Eliza brought Swedish meatballs which are always a crowd-pleaser. I've never quite gotten the knack of mixing the grape jelly and ketchup to perfect the sauce, but hers were unbelievably delicious. She's one of those moms who worries that her kids don't get enough protein, so she's always looking for recipes that will make meat more palatable for them. I saw them eat it, but they didn't return for seconds like I did. Eliza is so generous. She saw that I really liked them and sent me home with a plastic container full of her extras. I think I should do something nice for her in return, but I haven't yet landed on what that could be. I'll have to mull that over.

For the craft part of the potluck, the kids did the classic hand turkey. The most adept drew around their hands, then cut them out, painted them, and added embellishments. I hadn't thought to bring some of mine from scrapbooking, but next time I can bring the ones I no longer have a use for. Does Melissa scrapbook too? I was able to draw around Teddy's hand and added a couple of feathers. It's sweet memento of our time with the group. Watching other moms interact with their children was revelatory. I don't think I'm one of those "Not MY kids," but I saw behaviors which I hope my family can overcome.

Marisol, who is one of the most unflappable people I've ever met, is mom to Maximus who's a holy terror. I hadn't understood how a mom like her wound up with a kid like him, but today I saw something that clued me in. Since Maximus is two, he was able to hold the crayon and began to draw around his hand, but after he finished his second finger, he just put the crayon down and walked away to play with the toys in Blaise's family room. Marisol didn't make him finish it at all. One of the best things we can teach our children is to complete projects that are assigned. It's not how pretty or well they are done, it's that one finishes them. This is something I think is important and I will work hard to instill it in Teddy. He didn't like having his hand trapped for the drawing part, but now is the time for him to begin to understand that we complete projects. Plus, his tiny hand-tracing is super cute. I can't wait to show it to my in-laws.

After the potluck ended, we went home and parked in the driveway. Since Teddy had fallen asleep in his car seat and I didn't want to wake him to move him, I just put my seat back and fell asleep too. It's still warm enough that we could stay inside of the car with the windows cracked for fresh air. We slept for an hour and a half. Then I put him in his stroller, and we walked the dogs for an hour. For dinner tonight, we'll have my first attempt at Bibimbap, which is a Korean dish. This reminds me, did you have a nice meal with your colleague? There are many helpful videos across the Internet and Peter is supportive of my different cooking adventures, so off I go, but not before I attach a few photos so you can see what my family looks like.

Love,

Mandy

[link to photos of Mandy's family]

Gil:Dear Mandy,

There is no need to apologize. You are living your life, existing as your authentic self, and doing everything you can to stimulate your child. I will always have Alastor's condition to deal with. Receiving other people's normal everyday responses to situations which have nothing to do with my child's prognosis is a part of that. Please never hide your essence from me. Your genuine nature is one of the things I cherish most about you. And you don't have to be exuberant about life all day every day, that's just not possible for anyone. I want to know everything about you and that includes the mundane as well as the breathtaking.

My arthritic pain has subsided so I can take more time to write to you and try to describe my day-to-day. Right now, I'm taking a break from researching a topic that I was suddenly asked to speak about a few days ago. Having not been prepared, I am in the bowels of Lomonosov University library, piecing together what I hope will be an acceptable speech about the conclusions of the workroom found in Elis to be that of Phidias, a sculptor of antiquity. My colleague at the university is a professor of architecture, but a Phidias enthusiast on the side so he has exclusive access to documents and information I haven't seen yet. His knowledge about Phidias' techniques and accomplishments is invaluable, but he hasn't organized it because it is a pastime of his rather than his life's work. The library has set aside a series of shelves in an effort to catalog his findings on some level and that is what I am plowing through. This endeavor is tedious, isolated, and dreary. Your colorful descriptions about your domestic life give me the mental boost I need to keep going and they correspond more than you know.

While the artwork you describe is thin and temporary, it is nonetheless associated with the holiday. In fact, you wish to share it with others. Phidias' marble statues and pediments, while obviously less ephemeral, celebrated human anatomy, were brightly painted, and equally aimed at holidaymaking, albeit more worship than anything else. But Thanksgiving in America recalls its Protestant origins, so it is not far-removed in purpose, just a vastly different form of it.

Last night, I dined at the home of the colleague who invited me here in the first place. I had forgotten my silk slippers to wear in his home, so he leant me the "home shoes" he reserves for exactly these occasions. Since my socks are worn in places, I accepted them, but I couldn't shake the feeling that I was wearing someone else's foot funk. It didn't help that the babooshes were thickly padded with an odd squaring of the toe space because it just added to the sensation that I was walking on nasty sponges the whole time. His wife served a typical Russian dish known as "herring under a fur coat" and tea cakes for dessert, so I wasn't further put off during the visit. I also drank a good bit of vodka with my meal, forgetting to pace myself, but it also made our next adventure more interesting. Mikhal is a war-reconstruction hobbyist, so he led me to his garage where he has fully reconstructed the Battle of Poltava, largely based on the engraving by Nicolas de Larmessin. I spent a few hours nodding my head and smiling at the minutiae of his construction, like the threads of fiber from wads of cotton that best imitated the smoke of cannon fire in the scene. At the end of the long night, I felt as if my own head was filled with cotton wool. I woke up with a small headache, nothing I can't overcome. Later today, I plan to swim in the hotel's heated indoor pool.

In answer to your first question, I would be delighted to read and analyze a book for you, as well as assign one. Give me a few days to think of something I hope will reflect our mutual interests.

Regarding your third question, no Melissa does not scrapbook. She used to paint pottery but hasn't since Alastor was born. Her collection of painted ceramics was so overwhelming at one point that our bookcases were overflowing with cat mugs, bearded gnomes, and impractical unicorn plates whose cornices always stuck up in the middle. Now that she's focused on Alastor, I've taken to removing a knick-knack here and there to a special box in the attic I have for such a purpose, making sure to leave other very similarly finished pieces in plain view. So far, she hasn't noticed. If she still doesn't notice in six months, I'll donate the box to charity. This way, she has what is meaningful to her, but doesn't clutter our home with items that other people might use or derive equal pleasure from.

Lastly, Melissa handles all of the grocery-shopping. Mostly, she patronizes the popular chains, but occasionally, she makes bulk purchases from warehouse-type venues, which saves us money. Your onion tart sounds delicious, and I am not surprised that it was devoured by the other moms. I am beyond suggesting meals for Melissa to make, but I hope you cook for me one day. In the meantime, I will savor your words and photos.

Love,

Gil

Mandy:Dear Gil,

I would dearly LOVE to cook for you! I will make you the onion tart when you visit. You can either eat it or take it with you, I'll just put it in a plastic container. It's safe enough to keep at room temperature for a while, no problem.

I can't stop thinking about you. When you wrote that you would kiss my babushka'd face, I thought I could try to make that happen, as I can't be there, but I am with you in Spirit. Attached below is a picture of me in a kerchief I bought just for the occasion. The pattern is Matryoshka dolls in case you can't make it out.

Even though you are far away, I feel you hovering behind me, just over my shoulder. If I look back and up, your eyes will meet mine with a warmth that sends chills right through me. You are light and darkness, heat and coolth (that's a word you know), vibration and stillness. Bending over the washing machine moves me in a rhythm that I want to engage in with you. I linger over thoughts of kissing you. I imagine our tenderness day in and day out.

I will wait for your suggestion of a book for us. Honestly, I haven't read any real books for decades. I surf the Internet and read various articles, but that's about it. My bookshelves are fair to bursting with unread volumes I've collected over the years. I wonder if you'll pick something I already have. Peter's great collection is of movies, so I never want for a feature film. He does read my books from time to time, especially the science fiction ones I inherited from my dad, but I don't think novels are his genre, so if you pick one of those, I'll be in less conflict with him. If our analysis goes well, I might join the WRUMIRS subgroup of Wines and Lines. I'm not sure how wine helps literary analysis, but maybe it loosens tongues enough to voice opinions. I do remember the shy kids in my class when it came to "Dissertation Day" as my teacher called it.

I looked up the sculptor Phidias since you kindly clued me in on your recent topic. He was obviously exceptionally talented, but what stood out to me was the parallel between his Elgin marbles considered stolen by Greek scholars, as well as many British people, and the profoundly serious business about the Macedonian warrior. I wonder if you were asked to mention Phidias as sort of a recall of the distasteful business of looting antiquity and therefore, something that might push the delicate bargain into your favor. I also researched the Battle of Poltava and discovered that Peter the Great wasn't always so great. Anyway, I was pleased to learn something new in Adult World and I thank you for leading me there.

Thank you also for comparing a toddler's craft so favorably to ancient works. I hadn't thought of it that way, but your perspective is refreshing. Today, I cleaned a stubborn stain from the toilet bowl. Does that have classical parallels too? (I'm trying to be funny, not snarky, if you can't tell.)

You are wise to try to remove extraneous items from your home, especially if other people can put them to better use, rather than clogging bookcases. I would be elated if Peter ever took such initiative to clean clutter from our home. Of course, if he gave away the wrong knickknack, I'd be livid as I'm not sure he knows entirely what I treasure, but I imagine you know Melissa better than Peter knows me, considering you've been married longer.

Speaking of homelife, I have something in common with your colleague. No, I don't create models of famous battles, though that is popular in Lippincott and Gettysburg. Many toy shops cater, not to children, but to battle enthusiasts who have retired to the area and delight in recreating combat in three dimensions. Anyway, I digress. The point is, we take off our shoes in our home. We don't demand guests to do it, nor do we provide anyone with slippers if they do, but there is something to keeping street shoes off of our floors, especially now as we have a little one who spends time there. I guess the argument could be made that the dogs bring in street germs, but would you believe I actually wipe their feet before they enter? Their paws would track in the worst germs I think because they trek through the grass where other animals have eliminated. Of course, that's not nearly on the level of eating cat poop when they find it and trying to lick Teddy sometime afterward, but mercifully, that is not an everyday occurrence. This is probably not the romantic topic you envisioned. Moving on.

I don't know about you, but I am looking a little forward to Thanksgiving. This will be our first with the little one. I bought a Thanksgiving bib, but not a silly Pilgrim sleeper because I think those take away from the somber part of the holiday and I am Thankful, read: deeply grateful. This twenty-pound gift came straight from Heaven, as far as I'm concerned. It doesn't take the holiday to make me feel this though, this sentiment courses through me every day. He inherited my past, promises the future, and is my Present. His very existence will make the pumpkin pie sweeter, though I don't think he'll be able to make football interesting to me. Peter can't shut up about the Ravens, who are playing that night. He will be wearing his favorite purple jersey. He wanted Teddy to wear one too, but I put my foot down. I compromised and will dress him in a lavender sleeper when he needs to be changed for night-night though. For the game, I will make Peter's favorite appetizer jalapeno poppers. What are your family's plans for Thanksgiving?

Love,

Mandy

[attached photo of Mandy]

Gil:Dear Mandy,

I've just returned to the hotel at midnight to find your sweet message and beautiful photo. We've had some kind of breakthrough, I'm not sure entirely, but things may move faster than I anticipated, which means I'll return sooner than expected, which means I'll see you sooner. I'll leave you to think of the ramifications of these developments.

Thanksgivings are quiet affairs for us. The most excitement we have is waiting for the popcorn to start popping in our special popcorn maker. It's one of the foods Melissa doesn't screw up, so I try to save it for special occasions. Sometimes Harmonia joins us for dinner, then she and Melissa spend all hours of the night camping out at Black Friday events. I don't know why they do it because they complain every year, without fail how numb their toes were, how obnoxious the people waiting next to them were, how much they waited for the bathrooms once the stores were open, and more often than they would admit, how no Black Friday products were left on the shelves. I guess it's a bonding thing, but I don't understand it. If the game is on, I'll watch it, but I don't feel compelled to. Lately, I've taken to nuzzling Alastor and relaxing in front of old tv "specials". Do you remember those still-frame types of productions? The animation seems to hold his attention and I like sharing a piece of my childhood with him.

As for your conclusion about the dog whistling of the Elgin marble looting distaste, I can't say you're wrong, but I can't say you're right either. Negotiations like these are persnickety, and saving face is paramount, but this speech may not fall on the ears intended for my original travel reason, so I can't say it will have any bearing on it. I will say that your intelligence matches your beauty. You are stunning inside and out. I hope to know more of your inside, however, and I don't mean in just the concrete sense, though there is that as well.

In looking for a book for you, I've landed on <u>Fanny Hill: Memoirs of a Woman of Pleasure Illustrated</u> by John Cleland. I read it years ago and was shocked by it, but that was the time before the Internet. I wonder if we're all a little desensitized now. What do you think of this proposal? You won't hurt my feelings if you decline it. I can think of another.

Love,

Gil

Gil:Dear Mandy,

     I can't sleep. What are you up to this

Mandy:Hi Gil! I had just jumped on. Are you still here?

     Gil:Hi

Mandy:Hi! Okay, I wrote that already. What time is it there?

     Gil:It's 5am.

Mandy:Ohmygoodness, shouldn't you be asleep? Who else is going to fight for the tomb of the Macedonian?

     Gil:My mind is far away from here, nestled in the hills of South-Central Pennsylvania.

Mandy:Are we speaking of the hills dotted with two cows who are returning to the barns, in need of milking?

     Gil:Actually, I'm more interested in the valleys there. Does a little farmer need to do some milking?

Mandy:Yes, but then I may return and listen to you ponder the valleys here.

     Gil:Deal.

Mandy:See you in twenty.

Mandy:Okay, I'm back. The farmer has turned in for the night, the ranch hand is playing games in the drawing room, and I'm relaxed in my bed.

     Gil:Has it rained recently?

Mandy: No, I'm afraid the weather just hasn't made time for that. Sometimes clouds gathered, but the timing for rain was poor.

Gil:I think when I visit, I shall come to a particular valley and quench my thirst.

Mandy: Oh? Do tell!

Gil:I believe there is a very special valley, one that is welcoming and warm whose moisture rises and falls over and around a little boulder and coats the opening of a dark crevasse with a water that delivers a sweetness, but also a bit of a tang. I should like to come to this particular valley, and part the banks of this most secret riverbed with a gentle touch, taste that rare liquid, and run my tongue over the small boulder, while burying my nose in the mossy overgrowth. Does this sound pleasurable to you?

Mandy: Yes, Gil, I want to cry. No one has ever said such a beautiful thing to me. Is it your will to run your tongue over that structure? because I wouldn't want you to feel compelled. Also, it is more like a pebble, I'm afraid.

Gil: It would be my extreme pleasure to run my tongue round and round this special structure, no matter the size, slowly at first, then quickly for a very long time, as long as it would be needed. I would also probe the crevice simultaneously until it rained and rained.

Mandy: Gil, I think there will be a thunderstorm in a minute.

Gil: If I were there, I would put on a raincoat and enter the crevice. I would also spend time exploring an uppermost cavern as I conveyed just how deeply I love this landowner.

Mandy:KABOOM!

Gil:Mandy, you are so very special.

Mandy:KABOOM #2!

Gil:I think it will rain very hard in my room tonight too.

Mandy:KABOOM #3!

Mandy:Gil, thank you. Thank you for expressing your desire for South-Central Pennsylvania. I'm not sure I've ever celebrated living in this valley so well.

Gil:Anytime. Do you feel sleepy yet?

Mandy:Yes, I do.

Gil:Good. Then you should probably get some sleep.

Mandy:Okay, thank you again. I love you.

Gil:I love you too.

Mandy:Goodnight.

Mandy:Dearest Gil,

I woke up early, thinking of you, of us, and composed my thoughts below.

Shelter me in the morning

When Day's first rays try to separate us

You bend low, shielding me with your kisses

While below covers

We are fully united

The Light finds our eyes

And dances between them

Yet the sun shall not rend asunder

This joy

Serve me in the afternoon,

When I sizzle with peak desire

And these delights, drenched in sunshine

Flare for you again and again

My fire is for you alone

Do not err young man or you risk

being cast upon the dark heap

Of others who tried and failed.

Possess me in the night,

When darkness bears witness to your masterful strokes

There is no refuge from your unchecked strength,

You bend me to your will, rushing me to you,

Flexing your muscles with every rock-hard fiber

You penetrate my enthusiastic core

You satisfy your desire with vigor,

My merest independent words and deeds overridden

As your drive dictates

Gil, I need you.

Gil: Please see my response below:

Jet

Plane

Sky Train

Aural Melee

Aerial Ballet

Engines Thrust

Mechanic's Trust

Reclined, he rides the Wind that whips the Dust, his mind

Buoyed by steel, soars to her, to embrace

The Love he always knew

That was right before him

Right to the side of him

In the whimsy of trivia

In the depths of a canyon

In the parallel contrails of,

Marriage, Parenthood, and

Religious Contemplations,

They will copilot Life's Journey

This Day Forward

Evermore

Amen

Gil: I   am   coming   to   you   My   Dear

Mandy:Gil, does this mean that you are coming
sooner?

Gil:Yes, my Love, it does. The Russians decided to hold more discussions on the subject and therefore resolved the issue earlier, so my flight has been rebooked and I am coming straight to you. I understand that our plans may not be exactly as we anticipated.

Mandy:Oh my beautiful Gilbert! I am practically breathless. I will not worry about the details. The important thing is that we get to be together wherever we are. You have my heart.

Gil:As you have mine.

Mandy:I've prepared something for us, in keeping with your Greek traditions.

Gil:By all means, My Dear, go ahead.

Mandy:I've had our names and an image of stefana etched on glasses for us to break. And I have embroidered bags for the glass shards for us to keep always.

Gil:That is very beautiful Mandy.

Mandy:We are beautiful Gil.

Gil:Yes, we are.

Mandy:Goodnight my love

Gil:Goodnight my heart.

Email 28

Amanda Vero to Eliza Dupont

(November 2019)

Dear Eliza,

Thank you so much for being so generous when I needed your help. I have washed and dried your sweatshirt several times now. I know I could drop it off on your porch, but I was wondering, would you like to have a playdate? I'm guessing Danielle is in school, but if you and Lawrence are available, we'd love to have you. And I'll have plenty of coffee.

Sincerely,

Mandy

Email 29

Eliza Dupont to Amanda Vero

(November 2019)

Dear Mandy,

I would freakin' love to have a playdate with you and Teddy! Thank you so much for thinking of us. Would tomorrow morning be okay? Like 10am? Yes, Danielle will be in school, but I don't get my act together most mornings until at least 9am. And yes, I'll chug all the coffee you have to give. I can bring Morning Glory muffins if you like.

See you soon,

Eliza

Email 30

Amanda Vero to Eliza Dupont

(November 2019)

Dear Eliza,

Morning Glory muffins sound perfect. 10am it is!

Sincerely,

Mandy

Email 31

Amanda Vero to Eliza Dupont

(November 2019)

Dear Eliza

Thank you so much for coming over. The gift basket of tampons and sanitary pads is hilarious, but also useful! Your muffins were absolutely scrumptious, and Lawrence was so very gentle and sweet with Teddy. You should be really proud of how your kids are turning out. They've clearly learned so much from you. Would you like to come over next Thursday morning as well?

Sincerely,

Mandy

Email 32

Eliza Dupont to Amanda Vero

(November 2019)

Dear Mandy,

Thank YOU so much for having us over. It was exactly what we needed too. We will definitely come again next Thursday morning. And you're welcome for the basket!

See you soon,

Eliza

Gobbledygook (cont'd)

Shared file of Amanda Vero and Gilbert DeRoquedu

(December 2019)

Mandy:Dearest Gil,

You will be my favorite early Christmas present to unwrap. Ever since I can remember as a little girl, a relative has always given to me a Saint Nicolas Day present, like a precursor to Christmas. It's as if you unconsciously echo the traditions of my family, almost like you have already joined it. But I don't need the trimmings and trappings, I only want you. The gift of Christmas was one of Divinity made flesh. I feel that your early arrival recalls that sentiment. By no means am I supplanting God with you, but your presence is a testament to the Divine connection between us. I haven't yet figured out where we will meet, but I ask that you text me when you feel you are getting close.

Yesterday, I had Eliza and Lawrence over for a playdate and it was Heavenly! Lawrence is the sweetest toddler. He kept offering Teddy different toys which Teddy reached for. Lawrence also kissed

Teddy from time to time, melting both mine and Eliza's hearts. She brought these fabulous Morning Glory muffins that she made and left the extras for us. Peter chowed down on three this morning, which I wish he wouldn't have done, but I didn't catch him in time. Hopefully, Eliza will bring something else yummy when she comes. I think I told you I already like her cooking, yes?

Eliza spent time telling me other stuff that had happened in the group long before I came. She's been in it since Danielle was a baby, so she's seen a lot and she's held different Board positions. One of the ones she told me about was this subgroup called "Plan Aheads." It was a scheduled playdate once per month of moms swapping freezer meals so that everyone could have something different to eat instead of their usual menu and as frozen meals, one only had to cook them, not spend time preparing them. The concept was great, she said, and the first Plan Ahead playdate went off without a hitch. All the moms brought these awesome dishes, well really, they were portioned out in plastic freezer bags or containers. Eliza said it was the first time she had zucchini boats, for example. Zucchini boats aren't exotic or anything, but different from the usual fare she served her family. However, at the next swap, some moms couldn't make it, so they sent their food in, but she could tell that there were fewer vegetables, and less meat, plus the portions seemed smaller. By the next swap, of those who bothered to show up, everyone only brought in large, flavored portions of rice or pasta. It was as if they had all run out of ideas. By the fourth swap, well, it wasn't a swap, the group finally disbanded, lol. I consider myself lucky to receive her baking because she knows Quality.

Speaking of baking, I've decided to participate in the Christmas Cookie Swap. I know I don't need these treats, but my family never held this tradition, so this is a way I can be a part of something like that. All I have to bring are cookies and I'm pretty sure my family's Molasses Tea Cakes will be a hit.

I've got to go, or I'll be late to a Playground Pals playdate.

Love,

Mandy

P.S. I've started to read <u>Fanny Hill</u>

Email 33

Blaise Ayers to WRUMIRS members

(December 2019)

Dear Fellow WRUMIRS Moms,

I am excited to announce our annual WRUMIRS celebration is scheduled for December 7, 2019. Don't forget, this is a Climbing the Walls event (no kids, no husbands). As always, it is a potluck, assignments for dishes are as follows based on the first letter of your last name: A-D cutlery/cups/paper plates, E-J desserts, K-P proteins, Q-T vegetables, and U-Z appetizers. (I decided to mix it up a bit, so the same people aren't stuck with the same assignments year after year.) We will serve the usual iced tea, lemonade, and water.

Before the awards ceremony for Board members, both incoming and outgoing, we've added something new. This year, get ready to flex your mom skills because we plan to host the Mom Olympics. These feats of motherhood have been overlooked, but here they won't be.

Are you Mom enough? See you then!

Blaise Ayers,

President

Gobbledygook (cont'd)

Shared file of Amanda Vero and Gilbert DeRoquedu

(December 2019)

Gil:Dearest Mandy,

I am scheduled to board my flight tomorrow morning at 8:00. It will take ten and a half hours to fly to you, but since Moscow time is nine hours ahead, I will arrive in Washington DC close to ten in the morning, barring unforeseen interruptions. It will take me an hour or so to rent a car and drive north from the airport. At that point, I will need to crash, not only from the jet lag of tomorrow, but also, the residual jet lag from the first trip. Therefore, I will be ready for you in the evening. The rest is up to you.

Love,

Gil

Mandy:Dear Gil,

That is perfect! I walk the dogs every night near the woods of the National Military Park of Lippincott. While the park is closes at dusk, it's not well-monitored and on moonlit nights like that of tomorrow, I take them along the Bridenthal Trail after I put Teddy to sleep. Peter spends his time with his Guild while I can take hours with the dogs who are always thrilled to go Long Walkies. I'll bring them special treats so they will be calm and happy. The signs to the Bridenthal Trail are well-marked. You can park in the parking lot of Chopsticks Restaurant so as not to attract any attention, then walk over. I should be able to join you at 8:30 p.m. I cannot wait to see you. I've barely eaten this morning. I have managed to bake two onion tarts, however, one of which I'll bring for you. I am so excited and happy.

In other news, the annual WRUMIRS meeting will be held the night after tomorrow night. We're hosting the Mom Olympics. I can't wait to participate. Even if I can't do anything right, I think I'll have a lot of fun trying. For my appetizer assignment, I've decided to make my dates stuffed with blue cheese spread and topped with pecan halves. They are sweet, savory, crunchy, soft, and creamy, plus the dates remind me of you :)

Much love,

Mandy

Mandy: My Adonis,

I can't even bring myself to write poetry about our lovemaking, I am so overcome. Our connection is so beautiful, so exquisite. My only regret is that we did not love each other sooner. I wish I had stayed connected with you back then, that we might have married, for if every night would have been like tonight, I would want for nothing. That we encountered that outdoor chapel I had forgotten existed feels like another touch of Divinity. Our union, our glass that cannot be unbroken, feels blessed by Our Creator. Nothing, not one thing can break this covenant. We are truly, truly meant for one another.

I cannot have you in this moment, but we are locked together in my heart, and for that I am grateful. As I go through my days, I will relive every hour, every minute, every second of our consummation. And if my memory ever falters, I know I can replay the videos you sweetly asked to take. You are dearer to me than I ever thought possible. My eyes are opened, my flush is constant, my heart beats faster, my thoughts are far, far away from the day to day. I will forever search and wait for that other moment, when we can share what we have with the rest of the people we love. Until then, I will learn to be at peace with the communication we do have before us.

I hope you have a safe drive to Pittsburgh. I love you dearly.

Mandy

Gil:Right back at you, Kid. <3

Love, Gil

Gil:Dear Mandy,

I am safely back in Pittsburgh, and I feel the same about us. I will try to plan another rendezvous with you soon, but we cannot be too careful. No good can come from the pain of our Others. We must care for them too, knowing someday, the moment will be right to break such news to them, gently, firmly. For now, though, we will relive each moment of "our union" as you rightfully call it, and none shall rend it asunder.

Semper Fidelis,

Gil

Email 34

Gilbert DeRoquedu to Family and Friends

(December 2019)

Dearest Family and Friends,

As 2019 draws to its inevitable close, we take this time to review and refocus on those who are nearest and dearest to us while the world pauses its infinite busyness.

Alastor continues to make wonderful progress in speech-language and physical therapies with his doting caretakers. Just last week, he crawled toward Aristophanes, who never fails to deliver the comedy (see photo below). However, Alastor capped that just yesterday when he said, "Mama" and looked straight at Melissa. It was a thrilling moment for all of us. She and I celebrated with a Peach Melissa, but substituted honey for the simple syrup, which we felt was most appropriate for the occasion. The baby enjoyed the non-alcoholic and non-sugared peach puree version of course, then slept soundly.

Melissa manages to astound me every day with her incredible care of our little boy. He would not be where he is today without her. Not only does she deftly arrange his therapies, his socialization, his nutrition, and his amusements (check out that big smile of his on the swings), she heads the outreach committee of the Trisomy 21 parent group to find those parents in similar situations and lift them to the same sweetness of this unique parenthood. She sustains the cheer of our household with her newest ceramic figurines and homey casseroles. Rare is the day when she hasn't served her family a piping-hot dish of the familiar and nutritious. Next week, however, she will take a much-deserved break from the kitchen, as we celebrate our twenty-third anniversary with a dinner at Chez Unique, a two Michelin starred restaurant in Aliquippa.

Recently, I was privileged to travel to Russia to assist in the repatriation of some Macedonian antiquities. I encourage you to virtually visit the Museum of Macedonian Antiquity, whose link can be found here: xyz.mma.org, where you can see the restored treasures. For the upcoming year, I am scheduled to speak at engagements in Greece, France, and Turkey. If you plan to travel in any of those countries, I'd be glad to meet up with you at our mutual convenience. Having visited many significant sites in the past, I can give you a few pointers and recommend some restaurants in the area.

At the risk of sounding overly sentimental, I see travel to the far-off places as greater than just visiting touristy sites. On my return trip from Russia, I became reacquainted with a former colleague. Having just traveled from the Hubei province of China, whose capital city of Wuhan had recently adopted Chalcis, Greece as a sister city, he detailed the extensive plans he had developed there for cultural exchanges. Art exhibitions, student swaps, community events, academic presentations, and musical productions, including virtual ones, will bring Greek and Chinese people together in ways that the Silk Road never delivered, and yet, the desire to know new things, to understand different peoples is eternal. I encourage you in your travel because the ways by which folks seek to reunite, to recognize our commonalities, is nothing short of Divine. It seems to me that when we see the humanity in others, it's as if we've reassembled ourselves to reflect the image of Our Heavenly Father back to Him.

Last month, Melissa and I had the honor to serve as ushers in our local church. Not only do we praise Our Creator with prayers from our lips, but with the service of our hands. We could not be more grateful for the many blessings He has bestowed upon us. We continue to live by His laws and uphold the Gospel as told to us by His Only Son, Our Lord.

May You Have a Very Merry Christmas.

Much love,

Gil, Melissa, Alastor, and Aristophanes

[photo of DeRoquedu family]

Gobbledygook (cont'd)

Shared file of Amanda Vero and Gilbert DeRoquedu

Mandy:Dear Gil,

I just realized that I didn't thank you for the exquisite Matroyshka dolls you gave to me. While I treasure our physical connection, these "babushka'd" faces remind me of us. I put them on my kitchen windowsill above the sink, so I lose myself in fantasies of us while I wash the dishes. I hope that my scrapbook gives you similar flights of fancy.

Now I am starting to get into the Christmas Spirit, looking forward to chocolate goodies in my stocking though you will make the holiday much sweeter! I will need exactly that boost too because things might get quiet in the mom's group during the last days of December. Most people associated with academia talk about leaving here to visit their families of origin, not that I envy them by any means, (plane travel with kids must SUCK), but I will miss the camaraderie of moms. Today, I shopped with Teddy for Peter for our private holiday before the insanity begins. What's that, you ask? Insanity? Why, yes. On Christmas Day, we will leave the comfort of our home, then head to Baltimore for another of Peter's family's wacky holidays. Every year, we end the day, wondering why we ever started out in the first place.

Perhaps it's gauche to speak of Peter's family, but their dynamics cannot be quietly put aside. Yes, some day, we plan to tell our Others, but I am perfectly fine with not upsetting our apple carts anytime soon because what divorce does to families is frankly, horrendous. Peter can't help it, he's just a pawn in their stupid head games, but to stop attending holiday get-togethers wouldn't feel right either. Basically, Peter's parents split when he was a kid, back in the eighties. From what I understand, these people went loggerheads at each other, badmouthing whatever parent was picking up or dropping off, blaming the other one if his diabetes was poorly managed, and gossiping about each other to their respective families, so that, Peter and his brother always had to choose sides wherever they went, which made every day some kind of hell and holidays absolute infernos.

Since both parents have died, there is not so much drama feeding the fires, but our Christmases require us to visit every branch of the family that split in some way. Oh, and did I mention that not everyone on any side gets along? That's right, we visit FIVE places every Christmas. With Teddy in tow for the first time, we will brunch with Peter's stepmother and her new husband, then lunch with Peter's Aunt Deb, have tea and cookies with Peter's Aunt Deb on his other side, yes, it's that confusing, then dine with Peter's only living grandmother who doesn't speak with one of the Aunt Debs and isn't related to the other. Since Peter's brother's family will come here from Hawaii, we will all caravan together. After I nurse Teddy for night-night, we plan to return to the hotel where Peter's brother is staying. His brother will put his kids to bed, and we will DRINK at the hotel bar with everyone else also commiserating about their family celebrations.

I swear, if we don't have drinks planned for the evening, I don't think I will make it. And the bar is extra comfy cozy with couches around a stone fireplace. Maybe it's déclassé, but last year, we did this exact thing and then took off our shoes, put on those crazy Christmas fleece-lined socks, and put our

187

feet up on the coffee tables, while the fire glowed before us. The four of us laughed and laughed about how ridiculous it is that we pile into our cars like Keystone Cops and drive away every year, but we keep doing it. It's a little fuzzy, but I think we also played some games then too. Peter will rent a room at the hotel again this year, so after we say goodnight, we'll only have to retire upstairs, which is way better than driving home after hours of drinking. It was and hopes to be an awesome way to end such an insane holiday.

What are your Christmases like?

Love,

Mandy

Gil:Darling Mandy,

Today, I am compiling notes from my trip, preparing a report to the Hellenic Society, but I would much rather be living my future. As I caress the lock of hair that I freed from your scrapbook, I breathe in your essence and remember our time together. You are at once near, yet far, distant, yet intimate. Alas, I cannot fabricate any more of you in my presence, but my heart beats as fiercely as if we were consummating our love again. I look very forward to our next time together.

I did read <u>Fanny Hill</u> on the plane back to the States, but I have not written an analysis. I had forgotten the amount of erotica in this book. Initially, this book was to be a distraction from my thoughts of you but combined with my anticipation of our meeting and the graphic descriptions, I struggled to keep from announcing my keen interest in the subject matter to my fellow passengers. I plan to write something when I can summon a calmer state of mind.

Your Christmas sounds as difficult as your Halloween. Are all of your holidays like this, or just those two? How shall I fortify myself for your description of Easter?

Just like our Halloween, our December Christmas is exceptionally low key. My family never did much, just exchanged a few gifts on Christmas Eve, so Melissa and I trade a couple of token gifts that evening and have a ham, one of the few dishes she prepares without cheese, for Christmas Day. We don't say much about it because her side of the family celebrates in January, and we don't want to seem like we've succumbed to American influences. I suppose our January Christmas is quite the opposite of our other holidays though. With family and friends, we participate in many processionals to the various church services, neighborhoods for caroling, the Monongahela River (to bless it), and family homes where we feast on all the delicious "roast beast" we can cram into our mouths. (I do take antacids along with me for this purpose). While there is much activity, it is well-planned, and to the best of my knowledge, everyone gets along, even the divorced families.

I must return to my work now, but I hold dear not only the parts of you that you have gifted me, but the ones I cannot touch.

Love,

Gil

Blaise Ayers to WRUMIRS Members

(December 2019)

Dear Moms,

What an exciting whirlwind of an adventure we had on Saturday night and the perfect way to wrap up our fantastic year! Many thanks to everyone from current Board members to past Board members to future Board members (looking at you, Bela! lol, just kidding, no pressure). The speeches were great, the mom gifts from the thrift store were funny, and our mutual appreciation of our services to each other throughout the year warmed my heart.

But seriously, did anyone outshine the fabulous Eliza? Eliza, you were simply AMAZING. No other mom juggled more sippy cups, matched your reading speed of The Very Hungry Caterpillar by Eric Carle, or finished more kid puzzles in the timed minute. Hands down, Eliza Dupont is the MOMMEST of ALL TIME.

In other news, we are working to install a new app for our group that will allow us to group chat and share more media in ways that we didn't before. Stay tuned!

Warmest regards,

Blaise Ayers,

President of WRUMIRS

Email 36

Bela Rekker to Blaise Ayers

(December 2019)

Dear Blaise,

I had a wonderful time at the banquet, thank you so much. I just wanted to tell you that I'm still using a hand-me-down monitor and console and an old flip phone, so I won't be able to download the new app. Can you please email me any pertinent information, by any chance? I don't want to be disconnected from the group in any way. I hope that's okay.

Respectfully,

Bela

Email 37

Blaise Ayers to Bela Rekker

(December 2019)

Dear Bela,

That's absolutely no problem. I'll just forward you the emails I write. However, you won't have access to the comment fora or the shared files of photos. Don't worry, we moms stick together!

Warmest regards,

Blaise Ayers,

President of WRUMIRS

Email 38

Bela Rekker to Blaise Ayers

(December 2019)

Dear Blaise,

Thank you so much for understanding and forwarding me the important stuff. I really appreciate being able to stay connected to the group. I've never felt so accepted for who I am and what I believe in like I am in WRUMIRS. All of you mean more to me than you will ever understand. And if I inherit any newer equipment and can download the app, I'll let you know!

Respectfully,

Bela

Eliza Dupont to Blaise Ayers

(December 2019)

Dear Blaise,

Thank you so much for your kind words. Obviously, I had a lot of fun at the Mom Olympics. I hope we do it again next year.

I was wondering, since Mandy and new moms like her have joined WRUMIRS, do you think they would benefit from an anonymous advice column? I'd be glad to run it weekly, asking on Mondays one question a week that other moms emailed to me, but I wouldn't give away their names. I could collect the advice other moms send to me, then publish their answers anonymously on Fridays. That way, we could see the advice that we give to each other, and we could file it under our Resources tab on our website so if new moms needed it, there would be a place they could find what people in the group think. What do you think?

See you soon,

Eliza

P.S. If you or any Board Member already have a question, I could use that as the first one.

Email 39

Blaise Ayers to Eliza Dupont

(December 2019)

Eliza,

I've run it by the Board, and they think it's a super cute idea. I look forward to reading your column! It just so happens that one of the Board members did have a question if you would like to use it. Here it is: What can I do to motivate my second-grade son to settle down to do his homework after school?

Let me know if you have any issues,

Warmest regards,

Blaise Ayers,

President of WRUMIRS

Email 40

Eliza Dupont to WRUMIRS Members

(December 2019)

Dear WRUMIRS Moms,

I hope this email finds you well and ready for…the HOLIDAZE. Just in time for this crazy season, WRUMIRS is now offering a Weekly Advice Column! That's right, if you have a burning question that you would like to ask anonymously, I'm here to publish it for you. I'll take all the questions and put out one per week.

Conversely, if you would like to offer advice anonymously, please email me your advice and I'll publish it once a week so everyone can read it on the same page as any other answers I receive.

As it turns out, we already have our first question:

What can I do to motivate my second-grade son to settle down to do his homework after school?

Please email me your answer and I'll publish it anonymously for you on Friday. I look forward to reading all of your advice and fostering that camaraderie we moms are known for!

See you soon,

Eliza

Gobbledygook (cont'd)

Shared file of Amanda Vero and Gilbert DeRoquedu

(December 2019)

Gil: Hi, are you there?

Gil: Sweetums?

Gil:Sugar Plums?

Gil:Maybe now isn't a goo

Mandy:Hi

Gil:HI!! I thought maybe Teddy goes down for naps about now, but then I thought I missed you.

Mandy:No, you didn't miss me.

Gil:How are you?

Mandy:Fine. How are you?

Gil:Just fine? Not spectacular? Not effervescent?

Mandy:No, just fine.

Gil:You don't seem like your usual bubbly self. Are you sure you're, okay?

Mandy:I've been better, thank you.

Gil:What's wrong?

Mandy:Nothing. Mom problems. Nothing important. How are you?

Gil:Tell me.

Mandy:It's stupid and I feel very crossed up and confused. I'm not sure. Maybe you would prefer to tell me about your workday?

Gil:There's not much to tell about my workday, just typing up some notes on my recent trip.

Mandy:Well, that's a pleasant thought. Did you type up anything about us?

Gil:Those notes are filed in my heart.

Mandy:Swoon.

Gil: So what's happening in South Central Pennsylvania that has you full of angst? Did another mom spill her wine on you? Or (gasp!) on Teddy?

Mandy: No, nothing like that. I kind of wish it was as simple as that. I did spill some coffee on the rug, come to think of it, but I cleaned it up right away. No, we had our cookie swap playdate.

Gil: That hardly sounds like a dramatic event.

Mandy: Well, it wasn't per se, but it was sort of what was said. And I'm not sure I handled it well,

neither. It started out fine, don't get me wrong.

Gil: I'm here for you Mandy.

Mandy: Yes, but no. I wish you were here, I'd be wonderfully distracted.

Gil: Please tell me. Maybe we can work through it together.

Mandy: Yes, okay. I do appreciate being able to tell you what is heavy on my heart. As you can

with me.

Gil: I know. Please go on.

Mandy: Okay, fine.

You should have seen the cookies on Marisol's table. They were all so festive, I was momentarily transported to my childhood when my mom used to make distinct kinds of holiday treats. I remember not being very keen on the oatmeal lace cookies, or those melt-in-your-mouth meringues, and I turned up my nose at those old fruit cake slices with the heavily dyed "fruits."

Gil:I know exactly the ones you're talking about. I can practically reject their taste from here.

Mandy:But you wouldn't believe it Gil. Seeing that assortment of old-timey cookies made me tear up a little, maybe because it was such a surprise. Those images recreated from the seventies weren't supposed to be there. Come to think of it, I added to the nostalgic collection because I brought my Molasses Tea Cakes which are archaic for today's palate of crisped rice and marshmallow fluff, or cookies squeezed from a prepackaged tube. Anyway, I printed the name on a little sign which I placed next to the plate. Then, I put Teddy on the floor with a soft ball and just wallowed a little in the emotion of it all, where the past (the cookies) and the present (my darling Teddy Bear) were caught in one sweet moment together. Then one of the moms came over, picked up one of my cookies, tasted it and complimented me. She asked for the recipe, but I told her that my family forbade me to reveal it to anyone. Once upon a time, my ancestors had a cookie shop in Philadelphia that made and sold these cookies for the Christmas season. Everyone loved them so much that the business profited enormously. It was bragging a little, but I'm always trying to offer tidbits of what I think is interesting to get a conversation going further, so I told her that one year, the family's earnings were so great, they gave my great grandmother a pony.

"Can you imagine such a gift?" I asked her, and then she, all agog, was like, "No, I can't."

"And they must have had extra, extra money to care for him. His name, unsurprisingly, was Molasses, lol," I piled on.

So, I was telling the mom this rich family history when a different mom came over and tasted one of the cookies and that's when things turned "South," literally. Or north maybe.

Gil:Were your cookies made from real mole asses?

Mandy:What?

Gil:Sorry, I couldn't resist.

Mandy:Oh, no, ha ha. But Georgia, who is African American, took one bite and said, "Oh, you made some Joe Froggers". And I was like, "What? What are you talking about?"

And she was like, "I'm talking about Joe Frogger's cookies".

Gil:Who's Joe Frogger?

Mandy:Exactly! So, I explained to her, "No, these are my family's cookies. They've been in my family for generations. I don't know any Joe Frogger."

I swear, Georgia looked me up and down and said, "Look, I know Joe Frogger's cookies when I eat them. These are them. Your family lied to you."

And I was like, "My family did NOT lie to me. This is super weird."

"Are you calling me a liar?" she asked, and I told her, while I was starting to shake, "No, I'm not calling you a liar, but you are calling my family liars and that's wrong...and rude."

"I'm no liar," she said.

"Well, this isn't, doesn't feel right. Like you don't have proof." I was stumbling over my words at that point.

"The proof is in the cookies." she said.

"This conversation makes no sense." I told her. By then, all of the other moms had filed into Marisol's dining room. Teddy crawled over, wanting me to pick him up, which I did - that's when I knocked the coffee over, but I had a towel handy - but I didn't feel a lot better. Everything was off and I didn't know how to solve it.

Then she asked, "Does your family have any connection to Massachusetts, by any chance?"

And I was like, "Uh, yes? What does that have to do with anything?"

And she asked, "Marblehead, Massachusetts?"

I slowly nodded my head because that's exactly where my great grandmother's mother grew up.

And she was like, "Every Black person there knows these cookies by heart. Like my own family who's from nearby there does. Why? Because a Black man invented the recipe, but a bunch of white families are always claiming it as theirs!" Then she literally started rattling off the exact ingredients, including the super-secret rum, and all of their correct measurements. This recipe was given to me by my paternal aunt, who got it from Grandmama, who got it from her mother, who got it, I thought from her family, etc. They acted like these cookies were sooo special when we had them when I was little, like they were leaving open the opportunity to sell them again or something if we all kept it secret and my aunt gave me the recipe with a promise that I wouldn't give it to anyone but family. Yet, here was this person just completely revealing everything like it was common knowledge. Plus, she had added extra facts about white families stealing it as theirs.

Then Maxine, she's another mom who oversees the Activists subgroup and has an eight-week-old named Hepzibah (I really love that name) said she had heard about white families pilfering the recipe as their own because she's very well read and progressive like that. She even pulled up an article on her phone to email to me since I didn't know about it. I just stood there feeling stupid, my cheeks burning off my face. Finally, Eliza suggested we just take the sign and change it to "Joe Froggers" instead of "Molasses Tea Cakes." I did that, but I felt weird. I didn't know if I was too slow to change, or if my family was just racist, or what. I didn't know how to feel. I still don't. Mostly, I feel embarrassed and confused. Like, was my family the kind of white family that stole from Black people? If so, did they steal anything else from the Black community? Does Georgia know even more about this stuff? Does Maxine? Does Blaise? I want to ask and then I don't want to ask.

Gil:Hmm. It sounds like it had a rough beginning, but then things smoothed over.

Mandy: Yes, sort of. I fixed the sign, then we all collected the different cookies to assemble batches for our families, but I could barely look at Georgia. I didn't talk much more. I just shuffled Teddy from one hip to the other while I filled my plate, made some awkward excuse about him needing to stick to his nap schedule, and practically ran out of the door. I wouldn't have felt quite so overwhelmed if I hadn't been feeling so nostalgic up to that point. Still, I feel like I learned something, but then didn't handle it well.

Gil:You might have handled it better.

Mandy:Yes, but then I didn't know how to reapproach the topic. Like what does one say? "Hi Georgia, do you have any more information about how my family may have profited off of Black people? We didn't have slaves. Does that count?" I couldn't confidently summon any approach, so I dipped. What would you have done?

Gil:My family immigrated only a couple of generations back, so we don't have anything like that.

Mandy:Oh. No history of your family profiting off of Black people, I guess.

Gil:Not overtly, no. In a general sense, I suppose with unequal wages, voting, etc., but the Civil Rights movement solved a lot of that.

Mandy:I guess. Still, I feel like I'm not quite getting it. Do I give her some cherished heirloom from that side of the family to make up for their wrongdoing? Do I give it to Joe Frogger's family? How does that work? What if she thinks the heirloom is ugly? How do I fix this?

Gil:I think you're getting ahead of yourself. Why don't you take a nap?

Mandy:Yes, I should do that. I'm sorry. I'm very out of sorts. Maybe I'll feel better later. Should I reach out to you then, on my walkies?

Gil:Actually, I won't be available. Melissa and I are dropping Alastor off at the sitter's and heading to a colleague's house to play Bridge.

Mandy:Wow, I didn't know you played Bridge. That's old school!

Gil:It's something we've learned that we enjoy together, so we make time to do it once a month.

Mandy:That's lovely! I'm really happy for you! Sometimes, Peter and I team up to fight Minotaurs virtually, but I think sitting at a card table with another well-educated couple, sipping Mint Juleps or the like, trading quips about recent voyages or antique finds would be more enjoyable. And teaming up with you would be tops, like when we killed in Trivia.

Gil:It's nothing like Trivia, it takes strategy, not blunt knowledge. And we drink Whist cocktails.

Mandy:Oh, I get that, but the thrill would be similar for me. I've never heard of a Whist cocktail. It sounds equally upper-crusty. I feel I've missed something.

Gil:You haven't missed anything. Look, I've got to go. I hope you feel better.

Mandy:Thank you.

Gil:Kisses.

Mandy:Goodnight

Mandy:Dear Gil,

I hope this missive finds you well. I'm happy to report that I'm doing better. Just when I thought that I was going to be stuck in a low place, I miraculously turned around, and all in the space of less than twenty-four hours. I have so much news, I hardly know where to begin, but I think I will start with us. Yesterday, as I was scrolling through my social media, I discovered a Bible retreat sponsored by the Protestant Women's group in Maryland, planned for next weekend. Normally, I do my scrapbooking retreat then, but I could register for a "Bible retreat" instead, and spend the weekend with you, if you become available. The retreat is relatively cheap, so I don't mind losing the money and we could book in a room nearby and park my car at the retreat parking lot so our geolocations would be correct if anyone looked at our phone activity for any reason, (not that I think anyone would). Would you be available? Does this appeal to you, by any chance?

The other news is that I think I can do some things to raise awareness about an important local issue, and this ties with Black Lives Matter demonstrations, so maybe in a roundabout way, I'd be giving back to the Black community somehow. So, this morning, since I was wallowing in guilt and feeling misplaced on a lot of levels, I took Teddy for a walk around the Lippincott Battlefield. The wooden hatch-crossed field barriers, rolling hills, stone farmhouses, and stately monuments quilt a pastoral scene that's very restful to the eyes. Yet, the knowledge that cannons thundered here, bayonets plunged deep into the guts of enemies, and smoke plumed among men's screams prevents a truly peaceful contemplation. I took Teddy out of his car seat, bundled him warmly since it's drizzly out and walked among the Confederate monuments on Dixie Row. I don't know if the witness trees that border the edges of the Battlefield there judged the men, then, or frown against the casual tourists now, but I felt them watching me, so I was careful and respectful of my movements. But then, I started thinking - why should I be so respectful of the Confederate soldiers? Why am I being practically reverent to men who shot at valiant defenders of the United States of America? I mean, these Southerners chose not to be Americans, didn't they? And what were they fighting for? It wasn't anything noble! Why are there statues here? What are they doing? So then, I looked at those statues, I mean, I really LOOKED. And guess what I read? This, after already reading how "noble" they were, dedicated to the "Boys of Virginia" -

"We, the Descendents, will never forget their valor, their ardent defense, their Heaven-Sent purpose."

What? Their purpose to kill those who would prevent them from enslaving others was "Heaven Sent"?? Whose Heaven? And these descendants! This statue was erected in 1913, fifty years after the Battle of Lippincott when Virginians were lynching Black people left and right! Lynchers! That's who erected this statue! And others. It's disgusting! I visited other monuments that were equally appalling, most of which were erected in the 1960's. It's funny. When I first looked at these statues, I saw them as historical because they depict soldiers of the battle, but most of these monuments went up during the Civil Rights Movement. I ask you, which people would pick that time especially, when Black people were being hosed down for peacefully demonstrating for voting rights, would white people want to commemorate ancestors who saw Black people as "property"? Racists, that's who. I can't think of any person with internalized equality who would erect effigies of defenders of slavery. It just doesn't make any sense. These statues shouldn't be here. My eyes are wonderfully opened. I am considering writing a Letter to the Editor of the Battlefield Times. It is my hope that locals will recognize how incongruous these monuments are to the ideals of American Equality. Have you ever known statuary to exist for such a perverted purpose?

Love,

Mandy

Gil:Dear Mandy,

It is not infrequently the "purpose" of statuary comes up among my colleagues, though the need usually it arises from an archeological request. When the purpose of the statuary such as religious reverence, military victories, or historical events, is determined, any fierce debates that had arisen, die down. "Perverted" is too charged a term for these relics, though it is not unheard of those certain depictions of pedophilia are characterized as "perverted." In antiquity, there was always "a bad guy", but agreeing absolutely with any one group is only the ranting of a novice to the discipline. Our (my) research has always uncovered some prior insult that has, if not fully justified, then rendered the ensuing attack more understandable. This is an area where I would tread very carefully if I were you. From your words alone, many Battle enthusiasts who are steeped in history retire to the area, so I wouldn't be surprised if you received very pointed feedback from your Letter to the Editor. Can you share it with me before you send it, please?

Love,

Gil

Mandy:Dear Gil,

Thank you for sharing your professional perspective. While I truly value your input, I feel differently than you do on this one. I can understand statuary for strictly religious purposes. In antiquity, the statuary was needed to give worshippers something concrete to fix upon since most were illiterate. Additionally, larger statues might have inspired awe. In fact, I don't think that has really changed since we use statuary in our religion today. As a side note, I find it funny that the people who claim to follow God directly defy His commandment to not make anything in His image, but that's beside the point. Religious statuary had purpose then, as it does now.

Historic events and military victories rendered three-dimensionally probably served the same purpose to the illiterate. I can't deny that there are mythologizing elements to some of those too, and it makes me appreciate what you do even more.

But while the Civil War was over one hundred fifty years ago, I can't relegate it to antiquity. Not only are there a ton of contemporary writings like legal documents, personal letters, speeches, military descriptions, etc. preserved, so there are uniforms, paintings, military-issued and personal effects, and photographs. I mean, I know that there was a Civil War photographer who posed dead soldiers for his photos, but the bodies of the soldiers and the rocks at Devil's Den in them were real. Even the bushes in the photos are as they existed at the time of the Battle of Gettysburg, etc. But let me revisit the writings because I've really been digging into this.

We have the Constitution of Confederate States of America that explicitly endorses slavery.

We have Alexander Stephens' speech in which he defined slavery as the "cornerstone" of the Confederacy.

We have the Letters of Secession from the states that split from the USA.

And anything newly found corroborates what's already here.

These statues, however, defy the existing reality. Yes, some of them describe real events, but others are intertwining religious purpose like that Mississippi statue. My original point still stands - only racists would consider Confederate purpose to be Divine. The rest of us understand that all people were made in God's image and that includes...Black people.

But the most damning of all is that the enslaved people weren't a grand Enemy. There's no society which all of these African Americans had prior to being tortured together - they came from multiple countries, backgrounds, languages, etc. They didn't organize themselves into "enslaved," others forced them into it. The enslaved were an Oppressed People. And it wasn't their own army that mounted a response to the attack on Fort Sumter, but a military body of United States of America, who eventually engaged in a full out war, fighting the stupid secession with abolition as a side issue. That's a totally different understanding than what you usually encounter, no?

Meanwhile, I've been offering this information, these truths, if you will, on social media, as an attempt to head off any arguments that I might encounter after I publish the letter. This way, I am learning in real time how to sharpen my points, so that people can't come back at them. It doesn't really stop those dedicated to ignorance, but I'm hoping people on the sidelines re-evaluate their understanding of the Confederacy.

Anyway, when I've written the letter, I would be interested in your feedback.

Love,

Mandy

Gil:Dear Mandy,

I understand your desire to write a letter to the editor, but I say this with sincere concern - don't send one. While you make some interesting points, your rhetoric is far too inflammatory to engage the public, let alone any academics who might support your assertions. If you must write something, you might consider consulting a Civil War historian from the area, from the University, first. Do you ever socialize with any of those professors? Or their wives? And don't forget, the Confederate soldiers were just doing their duty, engaged in warfare because wealthy plantation owners put them there. Most of those soldiers didn't come from families who enslaved people, they were just "boys" bravely fighting for what they were told to.

Love,

Gil

Mandy:Dear Gil,

I've reread your words several times, but you don't seem to say I'm wrong, just that I might say it wrong. I don't quite understand why I need to tiptoe around this subject. You say that the Confederate soldiers were brave and while I guess that's true, doesn't their ignoble purpose kind of undercut that? Like, weren't there brave Nazis, diving in to sacrifice themselves in some way so that other Nazis wouldn't be killed? But we don't really acknowledge that stuff, right? Because their purpose wasn't noble. What the Nazis did was contrary to basic humanity. So…we don't erect statues to them. In summary, statues to the Confederacy are wrong. Yes, I agree with myself, LOL.

Love,

Mandy

Gil:Mandy,

The Nazis were completely different than Cofederate soldiers. They were Nazis. There is no comparison to the Holocaust they perpetuated. The Confederates needed their enslaved people to stay alive. This is a poor tangent. Some of the enslavers even treated their enslaved very well. I am not comfortable continuing this conversation, so I'll stop here.

Gil

Mandy:Dear Gil,

I know it's not apples to apples, but it's the bigger picture - there's literally nothing honorable about the Confederacy. I'm not saying their atrocities are the same, but also, just so you know, the Nazis first needed the Jews to stay alive in forced labor camps. The Final Solution didn't come about until the end of the war. And there are tons of examples of enslavers killing the people they enslaved, especially run-aways who were caught, as examples to others not to do things the enslavers didn't like. Plus, babies died from malnutrition and people died from disease because enslavers didn't give them sanitary situations. Over the course of four hundred years, infrequent murders on private plantations added up. Also, how many experiments were done on African Americans who had no agency, all in the name of "science"? Isn't that a Nazi parallel? And don't get me started on the number of Africans who died during The Middle Passage before they even reached America. That was a very treacherous journey. (Sorry, I know this isn't organized, but I want to get all my thoughts down before I forget them.)

Obviously, I agree, the manifestations of the Nazis and Confederates were different, but their ideologies were both abhorrent.

Anyway, I'll try to put my thoughts down in some cohesive way. I'm not sure how I'll tone down any rhetoric, but I'll try. Thank you again for your input. Since you aren't keen about this subject, I won't bring it up again in the near future with you, but I think I will run it by my mom's group. Maybe if our activist subgroup foments enthusiasm for the topic, my letter to the editor will be better received by the rest of the community.

Much love,

Mandy

Email 41

Amanda Vero to Blaise Ayers

(December 2019)

Dear Blaise,

Thanks again for a great night at the annual banquet. I thought the Mom Olympics was hilarious and Eliza is very deserving of the title.

I was thinking, since the Activists are Us often concern themselves with injustices, might that group consider protesting the Confederate monuments on the Battlefields of Lippincott or Gettysburg? I've been reading the inscriptions at Lippincott and they're atrocious in rhetoric, waxing reverent for those defenders of enslaving people. We could even tie it to the Black Lives Matter demonstrations from the past years because current racist police brutality is tied to the habits of slave catchers who targeted Black Americans.

What do you think? Or should I just run this by Maxine instead?

Sincerely,

Mandy

Email 42

Blaise Ayers to Amanda Vero

(December 2019)

Dear Mandy,

I too had a great time at the banquet, thanks so much for coming! And thank you for bringing your scrumptious appetizers. I must have eaten six of them.

With respect to demonstrations, Activists Are Us considers fights over Confederate imagery too controversial to confront. The Battles of Lippincott and Gettysburg are inherent to our tourism industry and the statues are touchstones for those whose ancestors fought there. We Activists don't want to raise too much fuss. We just try to be a gentle and persistent presence, like moms are known for, but thanks for reaching out! I hope someday you can find some peace in this matter because there is so much more to life than fretting over bronze and granite sculptures. Kiss that beautiful baby boy of yours for me :)

Warmest regards,

Blaise Ayers,

President of WRUMIRS

Gobbledygook (cont'd)

Shared file of Amanda Vero and Gilbert DeRoquedu

(December 2019)

Mandy:My Dear Gil,

Since my phone needs to recharge and most parties are otherwise occupied, I can take a little time to write. I daydream constantly of our togetherness, of more tender moments shared, of everyday smiles returned, of coffee drawn from the same pot, of spoken words breathed together. I continue to be incredibly happy with what we have given to each other so far.

I so appreciate your willingness to assign a book to me and I look forward to your critique of Fanny Hill. After I finished it yesterday, I rated and reviewed it on xyz.readmybook.com. The review contains a mild spoiler for other readers. I did use the word consent, and I still stand behind my review, but after having used that word, I decided to look up other critiques of the book, as well as the history of its publishing. Mr. Cleland was arrested for having written this salacious tale, but since he had written it from a debtor's prison, his newest stint in jail wasn't that unfamiliar. He withdrew the book, but it persisted in society, even to the point of accompanying the text with illustrations in 1827! But I digress.

I've read several articles about themes of consent in this book. Basically, many of these scholars come down hard on the consent that seems to be given, that it is disingenuous because it is often done to appease either the other parties involved, or the readers of the time. Part of the reasoning is due to the amount of pain often described in most of the passages about sexual activity, and I certainly agree there is much of it, but I am of a different opinion.

The fact is, I have very rarely, if ever, felt pain with sex. I happen to really, really enjoy it, but this, this is the thing that has withstood the centuries since Mr. Cleland wrote his book - society dictates that women are not supposed to delight in sex for the sheer pleasure of it - sex must always be accompanied by some reason, mostly gratification for the other partner or procreation. It, more than now, is still described as a "duty." And yet, I cannot generalize beyond my own experience and state that women in general like sex as much as I do because they don't tell me. Surely, no other mothers/wives I know ever share a coffee with me and then announce to me how much they like sex with their partners, how good it feels in the moment, how it brightens their lives. This never, never happens in my world, nor can you politely check in among your colleagues. It is interesting to note, however, that the purpose of the clitoris is strictly for pleasure, but even in this modern world, I, along with most people, didn't know the full structure of it until a year or two ago. And, I can't say I've done a good job in pursuing all of the ways to satisfy it, but I have every belief that we will luxuriate in exploring this together :) That the world would be so longtime ignorant of an organ dedicated to the zenith of sex speaks to how taboo it still is for women to like sex very much strictly for its bliss. As I'm sure you know, the opposite is true for men.

Men are so freely allowed to express their joy for sex, that my ninth grade Biology teacher, when imparting all of the whys and wherefores of procreation stopped his lecture at one point, threw his arms wide, and loudly proclaimed, "I LIKE SEX!". I was a bit shocked by the statement, but he suffered no consequences for having said it. Men are not expected to provide some other reason for engaging in the act but have it for how wonderful it feels. Certainly, there is an easily identifiable apex of ecstasy for men, but it is my belief that women might also have such a detectable point, especially if more attention is given to the anatomy specifically intended for this purpose. Additionally, women in the throes of passion sometimes cry and moan in ways that might mimic those of pain, so I do wonder if, at least for the more voyeuristic passages in the book, if Mr. Cleland was truly trying to describe exultation, but then backed away from that to describe it as cries of pain, for the readership, in order to abide by the standards of society. And so, it is my belief that the disingenuity surrounding consent in this book is not the various ways that non-consent is masked, but that so much pain was written in. Of course, I can't speak for all women, and I wouldn't diminish the pain some women often suffer, nor would most women have experienced pain at some point in their sexual histories, but this level of pain so often might be very infrequent, as I believe sex for women is supposed to be as pleasurable as it is for men. And men not being a monolith, may have experienced pain at some point in the process as well, so Mr. Cleland too readily left that out.

Another thought I have about the book is that so much of the debauchery seems remarkably consequence-free - no social diseases, no uncontrolled violence, no unwanted pregnancies, not so much as a period, and no permanent anatomical damage despite much wounding, especially as the male member is often described as weapon. The lack of protection that surely would have resulted in some of the above-named consequences, but we know that at those times it barely existed.

I'd like to note that for prostitution, these accommodations written in the book bordered on delight, as they were couched in trust and safety under the watchful eye of Mrs. Cole, and therefore, a good bit of fiction. Having read The Happy Hooker by Xaviera Hollander (have you read this too?), I have a fair point of comparison, and while Ms. Hollander equally escaped permanent damage and wrote about her activities in the best light, there was a seamy side to the quality of her engagements - some partners had questionable motives or needed to be subdued, she suffered crabs at least once, she was jailed in "The Tombs," some clients had gross proclivities, and pimps or other madams betrayed their "girls." In Miss Hill's world, there is stability, financial independence, camaraderie with women of the same age, rich and handsome clients, absolute discretion, and cleanliness (for the time), excepting the one young man. I only read one passage about wild deception, and that was the willing part of Miss Hill. I am certainly horrified by the passage about the poor young man.

In this day, it's easily seen as a lack of consent from a vulnerable person, but I don't fully trust Mr. Cleland's description either. In those times, deaf-mutes were often confused for people who were developmentally delayed, so I'm not entirely sure this was not the case for him. And if he were deaf, he might not have heard the cries of pain from his partner. Still, her facial expressions should have registered that for him, and Fanny tried to pry him off, which also should have alerted him to the pain he was causing, but if he were developmentally delayed, then the lack of consent was more on his side than hers. Because Fanny acted like she was happy with the act, our consciences are relieved in some way in her direction, but continually disturbed for him.

As for the sadism/masochism, I was a bit surprised that the man wanted to indulge in both to such an extreme, but that was probably a plot device, and again, I'm encountering this with modern understanding - that one is either of one tendency of one or the other, but not both equally. Side question: If the man was so experienced in this way, why did it take him and Fanny a while to find a comfortable position for both?

Mr. Cleland has incredible talent for turn of phrase, but my favorite was his description of John's parts as "a wren peeping its head out of the grass". That's just adorable.

Lastly, the ending was abrupt and unbelievable, so ham-fisted, but I assume Cleland was asserting he had morals of some kind in order to avoid being arrested. Obviously, it did not work.

In the end, I'm glad I read the book, but I am sorry it wasn't better literature. I thank you again for assigning it to me. I look forward to your response. Oh, and the book I picked for you is: The Killer

Angels by Michael Shaara (if you haven't read it, of course). I just read it right after Teddy was born because I needed something substantial to look at while I had to nurse him so much as a newborn. And now, this subject has relevance for me.

Did your onion tart make it home? If you ate it, did you like it? I'm not fishing for compliments, but I would really like to know if you enjoyed this homemade meal. (Hint, hint: I would love to cook more for you if you like it and will do so on our weekend getaway.)

Much love,

Mandy

Gil: Dear Mandy,

Thank you for your fascinating write-up. It had been years since I last read it, but you brought much back to me. Yes, I agree the ending was awkward and didn't fit the pacing of the rest of the narrative. I don't quite understand that, but Cleland was better at describing sex than he was delivering plot. I hadn't read The Happy Hooker, but I've certainly heard of it. You make some good comparisons.

I will read The Killer Angels with a fresh perspective, but I don't relish reading your analysis. Please try to refrain from commentary on the misplaced sentimentality over Confederate forces. I know exactly where you stand and while you might not mean it, I couldn't bear more patronizing from you nor arguing with you.

Lately, in addition to my arthritis flaring up, I've been feeling a bit under the weather, so I'll sign off here, but I'll make tentative space in my calendar to meet with you the weekend before Christmas for our "retreat."

Love,

Gil

P.S. I did eat some of the tart after I pulled over halfway through driving home that night. Maybe my palate is defective in some way, but I couldn't taste or smell it, so I honestly couldn't give much of an opinion. Since bringing it home to Melissa might raise some questions, I had to throw the rest away, but I thank you for your sweet (read: savory) gesture.

Mandy:Dear Gil,

I'm so sorry I come off as patronizing or argumentative. Please know that I don't mean to sound like those things. I thought we were having an intellectual debate, but I can understand how you might feel, so I won't do more. I do hope you enjoy reading our next book despite everything.

You mentioned you feel under the weather, and I have been suffering something similar. (No worries on the onion tart. It's such a strong buttery and onion-y flavor, I've smelled like sweaty armpits for days after, so maybe it's good you didn't have more. And I do understand why you couldn't take the rest home. I assume you have an easier way to deal with the scrapbook, or you would have mentioned it too.)

Actually, I've had a runny nose and can't smell or taste anything either, plus, I'm super exhausted lately, which has made nursing Teddy even more challenging than usual. However, I do feel some good because I know I'm giving him my antibodies if I'm fighting something off. He seems okay, he just has a runny nose too. There must be something going around. Peter is sick, coughing a lot, and he has a fever. I don't know how we got this, but we've obviously been around people lately. Come to think of it, Peter finished giving his final exams last week and has spent his time at home on the computer, so I'm not sure who he's been around. Maybe Teddy and I brought something to him. Usually, these kinds of flu clear up after a week or two, but I keep a close eye on Peter because his diabetes predisposes him to serious complications like pneumonia, etc. Back in 2004, when Peter had SARS, we had to go to the hospital, but they fixed him up right quick with steroids, nebulizers, etc. and told us how to manage it early on so he wouldn't get to that point. He's not doing well. I guess this is on my heart because it's coming out in my letter to you, and I feel like I want to cry. I'm sorry for everything wrong. I'm going now.

Love,

Mandy

Email 43

Eliza Dupont to Blaise Ayers

Dear Blaise,

I know I proposed this Weekly Advice Column (WAC), but I don't think it's going to work out for me to continue it. Today is Thursday and I've collected all of the "advice" for the question someone asked, but the responses make no sense to me. It's as if these moms never researched information from real child behavior experts. Absolutely nowhere did anyone suggest things like "Give him unstructured play before he does it" or "Schedule twenty-minute breaks for him every hour" or "Take a walk so he can use up some energy and get his endorphins running."

A question about helping a kid to settle down to do his homework is a simple behavioral question, not a health one, but these moms don't seem to know the difference, nor where to find true answers. I will gladly hand it over to anyone else who wants it.

See you soon,

Eliza

Email 44

Blaise Ayers to Eliza Dupont

(December 2019)

Eliza,

You took on this project and no one asked you to. If you don't want to do it, just publish the first responses that people gave to you in good faith and wrap it up. I think you're being very judgmental about people's reactions to the question. We don't judge each other at WRUMIRS, so I'll not judge you for wrapping it up, but the next time you come to us with an idea like this, we're going to give it a lot more thought before we okay it.

Blaise Ayers,

President of WRUMIRS

Email 45

Eliza Dupont to WRUMIRS Members

(December 2019)

Dear WRUMIRS Moms,

I am terribly sorry, but due to unforeseen circumstances, I will not be able to continue the WAC Attack column as planned. I am publishing the responses from the first question below because they were sent, but I will not publish any more questions or responses. If anyone else is interested in taking it over, please talk to Blaise.

As promised, here are the responses I received, in no particular order. Please do not respond to the responses. Many thanks in advance.

Question: **What can I do to motivate my second-grade son to settle down to do his homework after school?**

1. I've had this same problem with my elementary school-aged child and what worked for us was lavender oil. Just a dab behind each ear ought to do it because lavender is so calming. If that doesn't work, try verbena instead. Good luck!

2. Sometimes homework is a real challenge, especially after a long bus ride. The best thing you can do is get your child into the habit of doing homework every day after school at the same time. If the school doesn't assign homework, you assign the homeworks of your choice. I recommend this educational website [link to educational website].
3. I highly recommend Dr. Heathcliff at Mason-Dixon Chiropractic in Littlestown. He's been a chiropractor for twenty years. He always fixes whatever ails our family. For a while, my little one wouldn't potty train right, but once he gave her a few adjustments, she used the toilet like a pro. He's very good with kids.
4. This sounds like a situation for amber jewelry. Amber is known for its healing properties like soothing anxiety and the thyroid. It doesn't matter if you choose a bracelet or a necklace, it still works great.
5. Attention Deficit Hyperactivity Disorder (ADHD) is prevalent among children of this age, especially boys. The school counselors should be able to evaluate your child and determine if there is an issue. Once your child officially shows signs of ADHD, then they can recommend a psychiatrist who can prescribe an effective medication to calm your child down. My child has had great success with Ritalin. Lack of appetite is a side effect, but the focus and concentration are totally worth it.
6. Just do the homework for your child. You can probably imitate your child's handwriting pretty well. The teacher won't be able to tell. Just go over the answers with your child to make sure they know what they are.

See you soon,

Eliza

Gobbledygook (cont'd)

Shared file of Amanda Vero and Gilbert DeRoquedu

(December 2019)

Gil:My Dear Mandy,

You are quite forgiven for everything and are rendered as blameless as a newborn lamb. I can only imagine the sheer stress you suffer as you juggle the care between your loved ones, barely affording time for yourself. If I were there, I would take you in my arms and give you all the comfort I could. Is there any arrangement I can make for you? A parcel I could send to you to make this time easier? I won't write much because my hand still aches, and I know you don't have time to spare.

Affectionately,

Gil

Mandy:Dear Gil,

Thank you for forgiving me and for understanding. No, I don't need anything, just for Peter to get better. Thank you for your offers though.

Sometimes I have no time and sometimes I have too much. I'm lost right now while I keep trying to take care of them. Teddy is fine, but Peter doesn't seem to be improving. I ask him if he wants to go to the hospital, but he says "no," so I try not to keep asking, but I'm scared.

What is good is that yesterday, when both were sleeping, I decided to dye my hair brown. I wanted to tell you, even though I'm middle-aged, you make me feel young again. I look at those dolls and sometimes smile through my tears. Hopefully, when you see me next, you'll see the younger version of me again and remember some of the ways we both decimated our intellectual opponents once upon a time.

Peter just took medicine which will knock him out for a few hours. I'm going to Nips and Blips now, which may help me to feel a little normal.

Love,

Mandy

Email 46

Eliza Dupont to WRUMIRS Members

(December 2019)

Dear Fellow Moms,

Recently, I was saddened to learn of a local family espousing the pseudo-scientific rhetoric of discredited former physician Andrew Wakefield and the anti-vaccine movement. If you've never encountered the anti-vaccine movement, you're in luck, for their conspiracy theories — about pediatricians and other health care providers, pharmaceutical companies, and government health agencies- are deeply founded in misinformation, if not outright lies.

When I raised my concerns regarding the presence of anti-vaxxers with other members of WRUMIRS, where the proportion of potentially vulnerable babies, toddlers, and pregnant mothers runs high, I met with a bizarre and ardent defense of neutrality toward all "parenting philosophies," as if rejecting the guidance of evidence-based medicine constitutes a mere difference of opinion. I wondered why other parents in the group, particularly those associated with a respected academic institution like Battlefield University, failed to speak up in support of vaccination when many long-time residents of this tourist town retain vivid memories of the horrors of polio, measles, pertussis, and other deadly, communicable vaccine-preventable, childhood diseases.

Researching policies in the community, I have since discovered that the Battlefield University on-site daycare honors waivers of immunization, signed by parents who choose not to vaccinate merely for "personal reasons". Some children genuinely can't be vaccinated for valid medical reasons (such as the immunocompromised). In those cases, the parents often keep these medically fragile children away from kids who might infect them with everyday germs. However, these waivers for simply "personal reasons" allow for easy, unfounded exemptions. While I believe the daycare staff caring for babies to be fully vaccinated, they will simultaneously permit unvaccinated children throughout their facility. Concerned parents can't even learn who is and isn't up to date on vaccinations, for communicating those records would violate the daycare's policy.

Due to my concerns, I am asking anti-vaccine parents in this group to please identify yourselves. When we can identify those who choose not to vaccinate due to your misguided beliefs, we can make informed decisions as to how much we will expose our children to yours. I, for example, only welcome into my home children who are up to date on their shots.

To those members associated with the University, I ask you to please consult your most learned faculty steeped in the knowledge of life sciences and public policy on this issue, which should lead you to require immunization on the American Academy of Pediatrics (AAP) recommended schedule at the on-campus daycare. You may prevent unnecessary illness, or even save a life.

See you soon,

Eliza Dupont

Email 47

Blaise Ayers to WRUMIRS Members

(December 2019)

Dear Fellow Moms,

If there is one thing WRUMIRS prides itself in, it is raising up other moms, no matter our parental philosophies. Where else can we be moms without other people judging us for what we do or don't do? We need this basic humane acceptance of each other, to know that our differences don't truly divide us. Even our own children will judge us for our parenting choices at some point, but for this moment in time, you may find other like-minded adults. If you don't agree with another mom's choices, please keep that negativity to yourself. Think about how you would like other moms to react if you adopt a particular practice. Every mom, like you, is doing the best she can, and all have researched a lot to get to this point. If you can, please try to point the mom in question to other moms who share her same philosophy so that she doesn't feel so alone. This is how we support one another.

Yesterday, a community member had a negative reaction to another mom's parenting philosophy. Her outburst affected many other members in a subgroup. I will not name the person, nor comment on the philosophy, but I will remind you this uncontrolled behavior is not tolerated in WRUMIRS. Many moms are short on sleep, for example, and even what might seem like an offhand comment can cut deeply, so actual yelling and cursing is prohibited. Our updated guidelines now reflect this prohibition. Again, if you have a problem with another mom's parenting practices, please keep it to yourself and just focus on those who think like you do.

The community member in question has been eliminated from the group, as has her most recent email since she continued to find reasons to divide people. You may notice a change in our roster, but please do not comment on it. And please do not gossip about them, just keep raising each other up because that's what we do.

Warmest regards,

Blaise Ayers

President of We Raise Up Moms in Real Solidarity

Gobbledygook (cont'd)

Shared file of Amanda Vero and Gilbert DeRoquedu

(December 2019)

Mandy:Dear Gil,

I am sorry to read that your arthritis is still acting up, I hope it passes quickly. By any chance, do you see a doctor for it? You contribute so much to the world and to me, I hate to see anything slow you down. I will miss your words again, but for now, you can relax a bit by reading about my mama drama because today, extraordinary things happened, which took my mind off of my heartache.

I don't know if you know, but I deal with a lot of "woo" moms in WRUMIRS. They're not pushy about their philosophies in the least, but if a person asks them about why they co sleep, or use elimination communication, or choose not to vaccinate their children, they explain their research, usually which comes from the internet. They don't seem to cite sources I'm familiar with, but they are very polite, so I don't say anything.

Perhaps I am a little smug, but I don't worry about Teddy catching anything related to not vaccinating because he is perfectly up to date with his shots. In fact, he had his boosters at his six months' visit and his next round will happen next week when he turns nine months of age. I continue to nurse him, so he ingests some of my antibodies too, though the doctor said the antibodies in breastmilk aren't as effective for babies after two or three months of age. Still, the nutrition and hydration of breastmilk is specifically targeted to the baby's needs as the breasts are triggered by changes in the baby's behavior. For example, my breasts respond with a greater volume of milk to Teddy's frequent nursing from growth spurts, so even if my body can't help Teddy fight a specific illness, it can give him the best nutritional support he needs. Therefore, I don't feel the need to say anything when anyone else brings up the topic, but my friend Eliza didn't act respectful at all.

Our Nips and Blips group had met inside my Lippincott Lutheran's nursery, and we were sitting in a circle on the floor, where I am often happy because not only is it such a bright and sunny room, but I also really appreciate the advice that some of the "old heads" dole out. Additionally, I know that I am accepted to breastfeed my child as he needs it, and I don't have to think about covering up. Seeing other uncovered moms offer their breasts to their children really normalizes that for me because there's nowhere else, I can receive such validation of my own practices. Even when I attend church, I always throw a baby blanket over Teddy's head in the rocking chair in the nursery. I don't think we'd be received well if I didn't. But that's beside the point.

Anyway, I was sitting there happily feeding Teddy on the floor with the others, when Georgia mentioned she just found out that Pennsylvania law allows unvaccinated children in daycares, including the one at Battlefield University. Marisol quickly said it wasn't true because she had to fill out a form with all of Maximus's vaccinations before her daycare would accept their application. Then Georgia corrected her and said, "The only requirements for the parents of unvaccinated children are to skip filling out that form and sign a waiver stating they don't vaccinate." Then Bela spoke up and said that's precisely what she did when she enrolled Portia. And that, My Dear, is exactly when the feces hit the whirling blades.

You should have seen the expression on Eliza's face. She flushed purple and then said in a very deep voice, "What?." Bela must be used to this kind of reaction because she was just so breezy. It was like it was her time to shine. She smiled and explained that Portia needed care and since so many moms from WRUMIRS recommended the daycare at the University, that's where she had enrolled her, so she had signed the waiver. Almost immediately after Bela finished her explanation, Eliza shouted, and I quote, "You stupid cunt! You can't bring your unvaccinated kids into daycares, mommy groups, and church nurseries! Babies who aren't fully vaccinated are grouped there! My God! What in fuck's name do you want to happen?"

Gil, I was so shocked, my jaw dropped, then froze there. I've never heard a mom be so disrespectful to another mom and I didn't know what to do for several seconds. When my drool fell on my arm, I remembered then to close my mouth, but my eyes couldn't shut, they were glued to Eliza who was scrambling to pack her diaper bag and sling-wrap Baby Lawrence. Marisol was the first of us to recover her speech.

"Eliza, that was incredibly rude," she said. Then she reasoned, "Not only are you acting inappropriately and making us all very uncomfortable, but your point is also moot. Most of the children in our group are up to date with their shots, so even if an unvaccinated child does bring in a preventable" [Bela interrupted here and said, "Not necessarily preventable. Most vaccines aren't that effective and so many cause shedding of the disease in the first place that natural immunity is really to thank"] "...childhood disease," Marisol resumed, "then the vaccinated children aren't likely to get it."

"But you don't get it!" Eliza hissed back, "While vaccines are far more effective than Bela gives them credit for, they aren't effective for the children who haven't them yet. Some first vaccinations don't happen until after the first year! And" Eliza added her tone having risen again, "Babies and children aren't considered fully vaccinated until they've received all of their booster shots, which," her voice rising higher yet again, "doesn't happen until just before they start kindergarten!"

Georgia then reminded Eliza that we are all respectful of each other's parenting philosophies, even if we disagree with them, that WRUMIRS is very upfront about this in our welcome letter, and that Eliza owed Bela an apology. Eliza responded by saying, "I'm not sorry in the least" and swept out of the room with Lawrence.

I could feel my cheeks burning over the confrontation and I was confused as to which position, I should take. On one hand, Eliza is right that not all the shots happen in that first year and there must be reasons the pediatricians have. But on the other hand, no way could I support being so vulgar to a fellow mom like she was. And Bela has been genuinely great about breastfeeding advice. I really admire that she tandem-nurses Baby Lilith and Portia, who is three years old. If Teddy nurses until the same age, I will hold the title of "extended breast feeder" as one of my mom prizes. I know you don't have such things in Research World, but it would be meaningful to me. I would much rather a cranky threenager seek his mom for comfort than a stuffed animal, or a pacifier, like I had. Of course, I say this now, but preschooler mom Mandy might feel differently in the future, lol.

So, we wrapped up Nips and Blips exchanging a lot of stunned looks and went home. I double-checked the kinds of shots Teddy would have and Eliza was right, but that doesn't make up for her abuse of Bela. She even sent out an email that night, not naming names, but noticeably clear that children who were not up to date in their shots wouldn't be welcome in her home. I found her email to be decent and informative, but it didn't compensate for her earlier outburst.

Certainly, it was no surprise later that this morning, WRUMIRS put out an email doubling down on not discriminating against other moms for their parenting philosophies. Not only that, WRUMIRS announced that Eliza had been voted out of the group, which meant she and her children would not participate in any activities with us. This seems a little unfair because they're punishing Danielle, who's only six years old, as well as Baby Lawrence, but I chose not to say anything because I don't want to be seen as rude or discriminating either. I even baked an apple pie for Bela to give to her at our potluck tomorrow in order to assuage any hurt feelings that might linger from Eliza's attack. Also, I don't want to give anyone any reason to associate me with Eliza's sentiments because I couldn't bear it if they were to kick me out too. I need this group so badly. There is no support like it anywhere in our community and these early connections lay the foundation for other types of relationships Teddy and I may have in the community. Eventually, I hope to return to the working world, so I will need to network with other women who have successfully transitioned from stay-at-home-moms to working moms. It's all just too precious to lose.

I imagine you'll be asleep by the time you receive this, so I bid you sweet kisses and look forward to your response, whenever you feel well enough to send it.

Love,

Mandy

Gil:Dear Mandy,

I read your email after I woke up in the middle of the night. My medication helped so I will compose a short response.

That was quite an outburst you described. Sometimes, researchers get a little heated in their exchanges, but it usually involves excruciatingly detailed arguments that only the most dedicated among us are willing to follow. We researchers must consider our academic reputations at every point. A failure of reason, a missed insight, or a perceived vulgarity can result in disastrous and life changing repercussions. Such rudeness gains nothing and convinces no one, even if the loudmouth is correct. You are right to uphold the decorum, and not gossip, nor confront anyone with whom you disagree. Just keep caring for Teddy as the fantastic mother you are.

I am feeling a little better otherwise and am currently reading The Killer Angels which I hope to finish by tomorrow. If I dream of guns, drums, and canons, I hope they won't wake me.

Love,

Gil

Mandy:Dear Gil,

I know I said I wouldn't bring up the subject of Confederate monuments again, but since I recommended The Killer Angels to you, I felt the need to take Teddy to the Battlefield of Gettysburg and revisit the site of Pickett's Charge. I was struck by a great many things which I hadn't considered before. It's all tumbling in my mind right now, so I'll try to get it out in some kind of order.

The first thing I think is when I drove by The High-Water Mark, I found myself muttering, "Thank God, thank God Almighty the Confederates lost here." I sweated when I considered how close the Confederates came to winning that Battle too. Remember, Gettysburg was on the heels of Lippincott, where the Confederates had won, so if they had won Gettysburg too, they might have won the entire Civil War, and where would we be today? Moreover, would we still enslave African American citizens? The thought is ghastly. When I drove down Confederate Avenue, I thought those monuments are as artistic as the Lippincott ones.

Each Confederate state monument was one inscribed atrocity after another, decrying their "heroes" who acted "nobly." I could vomit, I was so mad. The more I looked at those altars to white supremacy, the madder I got. Teddy was very patient with me as I repeatedly took him out of his car seat, walked around alternately carrying him or setting him down on the grass for a few minutes, while muttering to myself, then rebuckled him back into his car seat. I've never felt so frustrated, embarrassed at my own inability to perceive the injustice of it all.

So, I am full of piss and vinegar. I'm sorry. I'm out of sorts again. This walk today really threw me for a loop. I am very curious as to what you will say about the book now. I don't think I ruined it for you, the writing is still worth its Pulitzer Prize, but the way this country, well, white people - Black people already knew the Confederacy was shit - treat the Confederacy is a crime in and of itself. If I oversaw statuary, I'd dedicate them to breastfeeding mothers, or something equally noble.

I've got to make dinner. Peter can't eat much, but this has renewed my energy and lifted me a little. I feel something from the abolitionist states. Boston-baked beans and weenies, I think. Write soon.

Love,

Mandy

Gil:Dear Mandy,

I have just finished reading The Killer Angels. With regards to the writing, yes, we agree. It was worth the Pulitzer. I knew the plot, of course, as anyone who has ever studied the Battle of Gettysburg has, but to draw out my emotions took talent. Shaara presents the "characters" very, very well and does the bucolia and the time period great justice. Thank you again for recommending it to me.

That said, even though it lifted your spirits and distracted you a bit from difficulty on the home front, I don't appreciate your reopening the topic of the monuments because you know we are not on the same page. There is no point in responding to you about them, so I will move on.

There are no breastfeeding prizes in antiquities research, but there is a lot of statuary depicting the intimate act between mother and child, so in a sense, it is lauded for eternity, or as long as the statues last. I don't claim a prurient interest, but I have noticed the prevalence of breastfeeding in most countries I've visited. It's just the norm. In fact, I had never heard of a "nurse-in" until you described it last month. Such an overt demonstration speaks volumes to the stigma of breastfeeding in the United States. Again, kudos to you and your group for advocating such a normal activity.

On another front, when exactly would you like to meet in Hagerstown? The weekend before Christmas is coming up and I need to finalize the arrangements if we are to have any success getting together.

Love,

Gil

Mandy:Dear Gil,

I don't think I'll be able to join you in Hagerstown, I'm sorry. Peter is so terribly ill, I had to take him to the hospital emergency room department last night. His lips were turning blue, so I didn't feel like he was making the best decision when he said he would just sleep. The ER doctor diagnosed him with "severe pneumonia" and said they would keep him overnight. Also, if he doesn't improve, he'll have to go on a ventilator. They'll know more in the morning. Even if he's well enough to be sent back home, he'll need therapy and "watching over" (doctor's words) for the next couple of weeks because his body is suffering so. I'm just a crying mess and I don't have a lot to offer. I'm sorry we can't be together. I hope you can understand.

Love,

Mandy

Gil:Dear Mandy,

I do understand and I will make other arrangements for that weekend. Thank you for letting me know.

Gil

Letter 21

Mrs. Amanda Vero to Mrs. Amy Hood (deceased)

(December 2019)

Dear Mom,

I know you're not physically here, but I need you. I haven't felt this way in a long time. Peter is always my rock, but he is so extremely ill. Please pray for us, wherever you are. I hope you can see a brighter future for us because right now, things are looking very dim. Peter had to stay overnight and if he doesn't improve soon, the doctor said he'll have to put him on a ventilator. This is not the way of things, not in my life with Peter. He's always there, kind, and not causing drama. I know it's selfish, but I'm really lost and don't know who to turn to. You always made me feel like I made good choices and right now, I could really use your support. If you were here, I think you would help me fight this swarm of bad feelings.

Perhaps it is the mark of a person ungrounded, but sometimes I feel you're nearby, an angel's wingbeat away. I sense you haven't missed anything but have been by my side through every heartbreak and joy. I feel close to you now, as you might know. I wish you were truly here though. You would hold me as I needed. You would have me voice why I married Peter in the first place. Maybe he was the you I was trying to replace. He has always been in my corner, just like you were. That would explain why I've been falling for Gil - because he replaced Dad on some level. I think you would understand this if you were here. And beyond my current love mess, I want to ask you so many things about being a homemaker when you were.

You obviously battled many things for an exceptionally long time - Dad's unspeakable infidelity, Grandmama's classism, the misogyny of your own family, the sexism of society. I am grateful that I live in these times, that I have earned a degree through higher education (even if I no longer use it), that the #metoo movement occurred, that the Internet provides ways to identify and articulate discrimination, but it is my heart's desire to listen to you.

How did you create a separate peace when you were so isolated from warmth and support? Did your mother provide it to you before she died? I can barely remember Geegaw. It's not important though. What is important is that I know I am not alone in these fights, that you fought them for me long before I arrived, and that you would fight them alongside me if you could. I wish I could tell you that you weren't alone too. The syphilis had turned your brain to mush before you died, but I want you to know, you kept your beautiful spirit about you. Your last words to me were "thank you."

If I can be half the mother you were, I will have succeeded. Every lunch you prepared, every costume you constructed, every math concept you broke down, every playdate you arranged, every item of clothing you washed, dried, and put away - you did it for me. Dad sometimes described you as "vanilla," as if your constancy and effort was banal, but I see now what a unique orchid you were among us. I thought my world revolved about Dad, but he had woven an alternate reality around us both instead, sewing lies and deception into relationships. We shred those ways as women empowered, you in death, and I through an enlightened middle age.

I have loved as I think you might have wanted me too, but Gil doesn't feel good for me, especially now. My heart hurts for Peter, my familiar, my family. I am filled with such confusion. Please help me find my way or I will regret much for the rest of my life.

Much love,

Mandy

Email 48

Gilbert DeRoquedu to Peter Vero

(December 2019)

Got something for ya

[video link #1]

[video link #2]

[video link #3]

Gobbledygook (cont'd)

Shared file of Amanda Vero and Gilbert DeRoquedu

(December 2019)

Mandy:Dear Gil,

While I stress because my beloved husband is in an Intensive Care Unit, I have been handling his accounts, including those of social media. Unbeknownst to him, you sent him videos of our "together time." I don't know why you did this. Is it because we have been disagreeing about Confederate monuments? Or is it because I couldn't be with you this weekend? But that makes no sense. Are you truly that childish? Why would you do something like that? While I had agreed to us being filmed, I did

NOT consent to you sending those images to my husband. Mercifully, I was able to delete the email and empty his virtual "trash" so he will not see them.

We discussed that when the time was right, we would gently, but firmly break the news to our loved ones because we still love them and don't want them to be hurt. These videos would have crushed him. Imagine if he had seen them! You wouldn't want Melissa to see such videos of us either now, would you? How would you feel if I sent her some?

Because I have copies too, you know.

My heart cannot take these abrasions. I love you dearly and need you to be more protective of us. Please, please, never do this again.

Love,

Mandy

Gil:Mandy,

I most certainly did not send those videos; I was clearly hacked. That you thought I might have sent them out in anger shows what little regard you have for me. Of course, I wouldn't send such a thing to your husband. I would never want this dalliance to get out. And I hope that you have the self-respect not to retaliate to Melissa in some way. Perhaps I should have better protected my accounts from hackers. That I didn't secure them is my fault and for that I'm sorry. But for you to even think of gaining revenge in some way raises a glaring red flag to me.

Lately, I've been seeing an overly aggressive side of you which is very unbecoming. Lashing out at me is a direct result of this new behavior. Frankly, it's unsettling, if not downright Evil. I honestly don't know what you'll accuse me of next. We have known each other in the Biblical sense, but it is noticeably clear I don't know you well beyond that.

I think the time has come for us to call the end to this affair. We obviously have much less in common than I thought, and I can't genuinely love a person who would contrive such vengeful tactics and thereby pursue ungodly living. I would appreciate that you do not respond in any way. I pray Peter gets well soon.

Adieu,

Gil

Mandy:Dear Gilbert,

I wouldn't have actually sent the videos because I don't want anyone to suffer such fallout. Since I wasn't clear that I wouldn't really do such a thing, I apologize, but your mischaracterization of me is terrible. I am Evil with a Capital E to you? I told you I was a Sinner from the beginning, but I am no more Evil than any other of His creations. And I testify, quite frequently, I might add. Yet, you accuse me of broaching "ungodly living"! Are you not the slightest bit aware that you are cheating on your wife? Double standard much? Ungodly living indeed!

You imply that you can't love me because of it, but the fact is, you would rather control me than love me. I feel this in my soul. The lack of control you are experiencing is my "agency." What you deem as Evil is your own misogyny by another name. And please take note of your outlandish hypocrisy - you asked me early on not to criticize you in any way, which I respected, but here you promote yourself as judge and jury with regards to my character.

I am distraught over my husband's critical illness. The doctors say they haven't seen anything like it since the SARS outbreak in 2004. You have no idea what I am going through, and you are horribly unsupportive, even if you were "hacked" which I am struggling to believe. Somehow these "hackers" just randomly found my husband on the internet and chose to send him videos of us. Despite this "hacking," you are still willing and able to use the exact same accounts as before. Does that make any sense to you?

Because it doesn't to me.

Because I know how to love a Sinner like you, I will always hold you in my heart and remember the good things we once built together. But for now…Goodbye.

Love,

Mandy

Email 49

Eliza Dupont to Amanda Vero

(December 2019)

Dear Mandy,

It's been a while. How are you? How is your Teddy Bear? I miss our conversations and playdates. Lawrence has even been asking "Bay Bay?" I think that's his way of saying he misses Teddy too. I don't bake Morning Glory muffins so much, but I've just learned how to make hummingbird cake and it is DELICIOUS, if I do say so myself.

I know things are a bit different now, but I am glad to be away from such uncaring individuals like Bela and any other anti-vaxxer in the group. Frankly, those bitches are fucking Evil. How dare they? But I'm getting off track. Obviously, my position hasn't changed.

If I remember correctly, Teddy is up to date on his shots? Does that sound right? Lately we've had a lot of free time and I've used that to think. My kids need socialization with other kids. Removing all other children from the picture isn't right and Danielle is intermingling with anti vax kids already at school but is protected by all her shots and boosters. My main concern is really Lawrence though he's now had at least one shot of every kind since his first birthday was last week.

My point is this: Would you like to start a different mommy group with me? It might be just the two of us for a while, but we would advertise as "Pro-Vaccine" and we would require proof of vaccination. If our mommy group advocates vaccination, then anti-vaxxers would be less likely to be drawn to it. Also, for every member who joins, we would request kids' immunization charts to be faxed directly from the doctors' offices so there would be no fakery. This wouldn't protect us from where we mix our kids with other kids, but it might make us think about those places too. Honestly, I don't know where anyone is safe since Pennsylvania allows parents to exempt their kids from vaccination, but still mix them in with other kids. Right now,

I'm hesitant to go to Toddler Time at the library, for example.

So, does this sound like something that would interest you? We could discuss it some more over hummingbird cake and coffee and any morning will work. We are a lot freer now.

See you soon?

Eliza

Email 50

Amanda Vero to Eliza Dupont

(December 2019)

Eliza,

Besides not being interested in your group, I really have my hands full right now as my husband is experiencing severe illness in the hospital. I cannot afford the time and space in my life for people like you who blow up at anyone they disagree with. Please find someone else.

Sincerely,

Mandy

Email 51

Rodney Vero to Amanda Vero

(December 2019)

Dear Mandy,

Thank you so much for calling us last night and updating us about Peter's condition. Though you are making the best decisions regarding my brother's care, Marsha and I are very distressed to hear how poorly he is doing. That said, we will not plan on anything different for Christmas, unless something changes.

Please know we have not told the children since we are trying to keep Christmas joyful and special for them while they are still young. As for the rest of the family, I will tell those whom I see at each interval, just as we leave, so that we don't upset all of the festivities. I hope you understand.

Of course, we don't expect you to join us for anything you're not feeling up to, but I do hope to reconnect with you at some point. You said that Peter isn't conscious while on the ventilator, so I hope you don't mind if I accompany you to the hospital sometime later, when we aren't scheduled to be with anyone else and Marsha finds something to do with the kids.

Love,

Rodney

Email 52

Amanda Vero to Rodney Vero

(December 2019)

Dear Rodney,

I do understand. Any time that you can spare to visit the hospital with Teddy and me would be appreciated. This isn't how I wanted to spend Christmas and I could really use your company and support, thank you. Hopefully, Peter's condition will improve soon, and it will all be a distant memory.

Love,

Mandy

Dear Cousin,

I hope this email finds you and your family well. I was delighted to receive not only your family's annual Year in Review, but to see your patient dog outfitted in matching Christmas pajamas with the rest of you. Your tree was splendid too. There is rarely a dull moment in your household.

I can't say the same for mine. Don't get me wrong, my family is healthy - we have access to a lot of organic foods, and we've found a chiropractor we like - but this move has proven more challenging than I envisioned. Since I no longer work at the office, I've lost touch with "the girls" I used to hang out with. Sometimes, Ron and I go to bourbon pairings at local distilleries, but we have to arrange for a babysitter and the people we meet there seem too traditional for our tastes. I'm looking for a social scene that, if it doesn't completely align with our interests, at least doesn't damn us for them. From your letter, I know sometimes you're in this area of South-Central Pennsylvania. Are you aware of any interesting venues in York County, something we could visit, some people we could know? I don't mean political organizations, we're in them already, but protests and meetings are hardly family-oriented, much less conducive to the activity of a busy nine-month-old. However, if you can't think of anything, that's fine and I completely understand.

Please give my love to Melissa and the baby, and especially to that sweet dog of yours!

Love,

Eloise

P.S. The next time you plan to come this way, please know that we'd love to have you to dinner. Just give us the heads up.

Email 54

Gilbert DeRoquedu to Eloise Voldesing

(December 2019)

Dear Eloise,

It is a pleasure to receive your email. I will gladly plan a visit and catch up with you and your family in the New Year. I'm often involved in the academic scenes of this area, but a former acquaintance of mine did recently tell me about a group that might serve your interests, as well as accept your politics.

The former acquaintance was someone I once knew in high school and Arizona, but stability is not her forte, so I would caution you in your dealings with her. However, before I decided to protect myself from her waywardness, she did manage to tell me quite a bit about this mothers' group, so you might find something there.

My calendar looks clear for the second Monday in January. Would six in the evening on that day work for you? I could bring a bottle of Chablis if that appeals.

Cordially,

Gil

Dear Gil,

The second Monday at six will work well, thank you. We will have just returned from our vacation in the Independent State of Samoa, so I'll have lots to tell you, plus I will still have my tan for you to envy in the middle of winter ;). If it's not too much trouble, would you please bring an Arneis instead? I know you suffer from a lot of cheese, so I'll prepare a salad Niçoise, with a crab fluff appetizer and baked pears for dessert, no cheese course whatsoever. If you would like anything else, please don't hesitate to ask.

Love,

Eloise

Dear Eloise,

Thank you very much for taking into account my current dietary situation. Consider two bottles of Arneis purchased. Tongues are sure to wag. See you then.

Cordially,

Gil

Email 57

Blaise Ayers to WRUMIRS Members

(December 2019)

Dear Fellow Moms,

It is with a heavy heart that I must report the death of Peter Vero, Mandy Vero's husband. Mandy has given permission to explain that he had been on a ventilator for the past few days, but ultimately succumbed to severe pneumonia the day after Christmas. Prior to his sudden passing, Mandy and Peter had been married for fifteen years. Peter was a Biology professor at Battlefield University and will be greatly missed by both students and faculty. The funeral will be held at Lippincott Lutheran at 2 p.m. .on Monday. If you would like to attend, please DM me so I can let Mandy know to expect you. You are also welcomed to attend two public viewings at Lippincott Funeral Home on Sunday afternoon to express your condolences, though Mandy will not attend those.

At this time, Mandy asks to grieve in private with Peter's family who is visiting, however, she is open to receiving frozen meals, etc. Please DM me if you would like to arrange a time to leave something for her and Baby Teddy.

They have no allergies to any foodstuffs or types of containers. Her address is on the roster and can be used for sending cards as well.

Naturally, she will not be participating in group activities right away, but she does expect to return at some point because our group is her "normal." In fact, considering Peter's loss, the Babysitting Club may help Mandy tremendously. She has told me that she doesn't need to work immediately either but may seek employment in the coming year. If you would like to help her network in the future, she would welcome it, but not until a few months from now. She has extensive experience as a manager in the credit card division of a national bank and a degree in Botany. She just asks that you keep her in the back of your mind for any fitting positions, as well as childcare recommendations for when she does return to the workforce.

If you have any questions or concerns, please don't hesitate to reach out to me. I know this is an especially tough time, but if we can come together for Mandy, then we will truly raise up a mom in real solidarity!

Warmest regards,

Blaise Ayers,

President of WRUMIRS

PART THREE: BATTLEFIELDS

Correspondence 1

From the Desk of Beatrice Fowler, Esq. to Amanda Vero

(January 2020)

Dear Amanda Vero,

I am hoping to reconnect with a person who used to be named Mandy Hood and who worked at Grand Canyon Youth Campground about thirty years ago. I found an obituary (I'm sorry) in which your middle name is Hood. Might you be that same person? If not, I apologize for wasting your time.

Sincerely,

Beatrice Fowler, Esq.

Correspondence 2

Amanda Vero to Beatrice Fowler, Esq.

(January 2020)

Dear Bea,

Thank you so much for reaching out to me. I am newly widowed with a ten-month-old, but stable. If I were in a different place mentally, I'd "Gurrrl" you, but I spend many days trying not to weep uncontrollably. Actually, your reconnection may be the distraction I need. I'm so sorry. I can't keep my shit bottled inside. I have a lot of feelings right now. If you can deal with the teary mess I sometimes am, I'll gladly keep writing to you. Hold your loved ones close, Life is short.

Love,

Mandy

Correspondence 3

From the Desk of Beatrice Fowler, Esq. to Amanda Vero

(January 2020)

Dear Mandy,

First, thank you so much for writing back, despite your painful circumstances. I am so sorry for your loss. Please let me know what I can do for you. You wrote that my letters can be a distraction for you, so I am acting upon this and writing to you what I need to discuss, but if at any point, you need to disengage, I completely understand. We have so much to catch up on. I don't quite know where to start, but I'll back up to where we left off because it's relevant.

I think you know; I was dismissed from Grand Canyon Youth Campground on what can be called the absolute WORST day of my life. I was completely humiliated by the public display of a very private act and left very quickly. However, I am a lawyer now, so while I am still horrified on a personal level, I understand that the wrong was on someone else's part, especially since we have terms for stuff like this, and more importantly, these kinds of crimes get prosecuted.

In this digital age, we know that "revenge porn" is a crime, and worse, subjecting minors to it is "corrupting minors". So, the asshole who did this engaged in exactly the kind of behaviors that a lot of Hollywood starlets suffer post break-ups. What a nightmare. At least mine wasn't broadcast across the internet, but still, I lost my job and a whole lot of self-esteem over it. I don't know if you had the same experience, but many young men in my circles back then were under that stupid "Madonna/Whore" complex. They just couldn't handle women who operated in society without being provocateurs but were happily sexual in romantic relationships. These men were always attracted to me until I returned their sexual feelings. It was as if they didn't want any equal relationship, but considered themselves arbiters of sex, only having it if they "conquered" a woman, then throwing the woman away as a punishment for fitting their broad idea of "lustful" as if we were pieces of used chewing gum. Come to think of it, one of my middle school health teachers taught that females are as disposable as used tape in a demonstration.

I'm totally burning up, I'm so angry now that I'm thinking about this. In class one day, this goon gave a fresh piece of tape to every girl in the classroom, then asked us to stick our tape on as many boys as would let us. Peals of laughter rang out for the next several minutes as girls jokingly rejected or practically knocked each other down in deciding which boys could be stuck with tape. By the time we were done and back in our seats, our tape pieces were covered with sweater lint, most having lost their stickiness by the second or third attachment. It was then that the stupid teacher declared, "See? Girls are like these pieces of tape, the more guys they "attach" to, the more they lose their

256

value. Remember that Everyone. Class dismissed!" I swear, this teacher, this paragon of society, responsible for "molding the minds of youth" literally compared girls with multiple sex partners as fucking garbage. Of course, he never implied that boys were just as worthless (hey, no one is worthless for having sex no matter how many partners they had, nor the types of acts in which they engaged, including those forced upon them without their consent), and now that I'm really delving into this, I'm also realizing how ridiculously heteronormative that demonstration was. Female masturbation wasn't mentioned at all in that class, as if any female sexuality was wrong, while male masturbation was blushingly acknowledged as "normal." Having grown up with this awful baggage, I worked ridiculously hard to hide any sexual relationships - not bringing home boyfriends to my family, never expressing my desires about sex to anyone but my sexual partners, sometimes using risky methods of birth control because I was worried about negative (family) consequences if I would have asked for a prescription, and not even masturbating until I was an adult! Ha! I wonder what the STD rate in that area was if I was going through all of that. At least I didn't catch anything. Yeesh, but I digress.

Anyway, my last day at Camp was a spectacularly horrible day, but it clarified a lot of the misogyny around me and ever since I regained my self-confidence, I have been championing comprehensive sex education. If you have any questions about such things, just email me, I obviously have no qualms about answering them, even the most embarrassing ones.

Okay, so after I crawled away from Camp, I decided to return to university and pursue a Master's in something different than my original major of Native American studies because I couldn't be sure that I would ever be hirable again since Ms. N. said she wouldn't give me any reference.

Finally, the injustice over everything propelled me into Law, and here I am today with my own successful practice in copyright law, which is hilarious because I recently became aware that something I had created before I left Camp (and labeled with my own hidden logo, God I was prescient back then!) was recently profited from by...none other than the asshole who released the picture of me blowing him!

So, anyway, I had been recently looking into suing him for copyright infringement, but I really need to clear things with you first because I think I could use you as a witness. I need to know - do you support my proposed lawsuit, or is there anyone who, from that time, you would feel protective of and not be inclined to bring to justice?

I know this is a lot to lay on you, but time is of the essence, and I need to move on this lawsuit. I don't know if you currently have ongoing relationships with anyone from that time period. Please let me know where you stand and what is going on in your life.

Yours truly,

Bea

P.S. FWIW, I still paint as a hobby. If you would like me to paint a portrait of your departed loved one, I will gladly do so at no charge. Your friendship at Camp is one of the brighter memories I have from an otherwise difficult lookback.

NOTICE: This transmission is from the law firm of Fowler & Associates and may contain privileged and confidential information that is for the sole use of the intended recipient. Use, distribution, or copying of any part of this transmission by an unintended recipient is prohibited and may be a violation of law. If you believe you have received this message in error, please delete it, in addition to any attachments, and inform Fowler & Associates that you have done so. Thank you.

Correspondence 4

Amanda Vero to Beatrice Fowler, Esq.

(January 2020)

Dear Bea,

Your email was a lot to unpack, but I really appreciate your writing it instead of trying to say all that at a sit down. My concentration is poor right now and I can't seem to catch any breaks with my baby who is very fussy from teething, so I reread your letter whenever I didn't understand or forgot something.

I'm totally familiar with comprehensive sex ed because I am in a moms' group and not too long ago, a former acquaintance had explained exactly those terrible things being taught in Adams County public schools before she left the group. And I recently read <u>Fanny Hill: Memoirs of a Woman of Pleasure Illustrated</u> by John Cleland and shared similar thoughts, but that's beside the point.

Yes, I am perfectly willing to help you if I can. I had a negative ending to the camp, but for different reasons. I did see the slide you referenced, and I agree - you were very wronged. I would like to help you in any way I can to right that injustice, though I'm not terribly sure how I can do that.

I do vaguely remember you painting though and if I think hard enough, maybe it was flowers or something? Does that sound right?

It is funny that you mention connections to Grand Canyon Youth Campground. I had made one recently, though it is ended now, but I also feel as if nothing was handled in an adult manner. I am not without blame for my own terrible behavior, and I believe I have paid a dear price for it, but I also feel like there was blame to go around. Maybe it would be good to meet for coffee despite a cranky baby. I need a real friend and a break from roaming this house full of memories. If you can stand sniffly, sinful me and my crying child, would you be willing to meet at Lippincott Coffee House on Saturday?

Love,

Mandy

Correspondence 5

From the Desk of Beatrice Fowler, Esq. to Amanda Vero

(January 2020)

Dear Mandy,

Absolutely! I would be delighted to get together with you. What time would work for you?

And yes, it was flowers. I was very smitten by someone, and I painted something that he inspired me to that I hoped would raise his spirits. The paintings seemed to work, we had a great romance, but his extreme need for privacy spurred him to humiliate me.

I'm curious as to the circumstances you left under too. Did they have to do with a romance that soured by any chance? It seems to me there were some real hijinks that led to such things back then. Thank you for suggesting we meet. It might be fun to reminisce a little together.

Yours,

Bea

Correspondence 6

Amanda Vero to Beatrice Fowler, Esq.

(January 2020)

Dear Bea,

4 p.m. would work well because Teddy is most likely to be up from a nap then. Also, would you rather message or leave voicemails? I don't mind. Every time I get an email from you, it looks so official with the "Correspondence from the Desk of Bea Fowler, Esq." at the top and that notice at

the bottom, but I am downright sentimental that such a long-lost friend found me, so it feels more personal.

No, I didn't leave over a lost love, but honestly, I don't feel like getting into it, if you don't mind.

Love,

Mandy

Correspondence 7

From the Desk of Beatrice Fowler, Esq. to Amanda Vero

(January 2020)

Dear Mandy,

4 p.m. it is. It will be great to get together with you. While I remember you fondly and am very willing to have a personal relationship with you, I also have to note your agreement to be a witness in my lawsuit, and anything you remember about the time in writing, so for now, please continue with my professional email. After the court case, we can totally trade personal emails. And it's fine if you don't want to talk about how you left. Just know that you can bend my ear over that place anytime.

Yours,

Bea

and may be a violation of law. If you believe you have received this message in error, please delete it, in addition to any attachments, and inform Fowler & Associates that you have done so. Thank you.

Correspondence 8

Amanda Vero to Beatrice Fowler, Esq.

(January 2020)

Dear Bea,

Thank you again for reaching out to me and making the time to get together. I'm super glad to reignite our friendship. Again, you've brought back so much and reminded me of the great connection we shared back then. I'm really grateful for the socialization that the Internet provides too, and it led me to you. You are helping me to work through my self-imposed isolation. But that's beside the point. Anyway, I really appreciate you confiding in me what happened between you and Gil. Obviously, your situation was different from mine with him, but his sensitivity hasn't changed one iota. Still, he was incredibly wrong to appropriate your paintings for his own profit. I'm truly horrified on your behalf. Again, he and I are no longer in communication, and I expect we never will be. Anything I can do to help you move this suit forward will make me feel like some justice has been served.

By the same token, I am disturbed, wretched even. I profoundly loved a man who didn't even know how to love, and I loved another man at surface level who surrounded me with a steadfast love I didn't appreciate. My world is wracked in all directions. I don't know which way is up or down. I thought I was down with Peter when I was really up because his death has crashed me to the lowest place. I honestly wish you never are embraced by this kind of affection because its loss is unfathomable. Peter was my Sun when I thought Gil was, but that bastard was just polluted water that reflected glittering trash in a dark alley of confusion. If God is vengeful, I am caught in His vengeance. The only relief I am starting to feel is the righteousness that you begin to pursue. I didn't know I needed any of this. I do now.

On another note, thank you for validating what I said about the Confederate monuments. I know I'm not wrong, but around here no one else seems to be embracing what I've been saying, maybe because the town thrives on Confederate tourism. I had tried to raise awareness in my Mommy group, but the other moms are basically ignoring the information. Your support, however, has inspired me to send my Letter to the Editor of the Battlefield Times. This is a distraction I need. I look forward to getting together with you again. Gotta go. Teddy is fussing.

Love,

Mandy

Correspondence 9

From the Desk of Beatrice Fowler, Esq. to Amanda Vero

(January 2020)

Dear Mandy,

You are most welcome for the support. Anyone with half a brain should recognize that only lynch-lovers and other racists erected those monuments to keep Black Americans down and away from the National Parks. I hope the paper prints your letter. Please let me know how it goes.

In the meantime, I will have the firm representing me send a Cease-and-Desist demand letter to Gil, seeking his voluntary removal of his name from the artwork and for monetary compensation from the stamps. While I don't anticipate much of a response, it's a necessary preliminary step to bringing the case in front of a judge. Though Gil has probably spent all of the money that he received from the US Post Office, especially considering the jet-setting he's been doing for years, it's important to remove his name from the artwork and to credit mine. And maybe, if the USPS regrets their role in this fraud, they'll offer me a new chance to submit artwork to them.

Talking about him today really helped me emotionally too. On many levels, I've already healed, but hearing you swoon over his emails and poems confirmed what I experienced - I did love him and his words were a big part of that. Through the things he said and wrote, I glimpsed the sweet man inside and loved him utterly. Then, by degrees and for reasons unknown, he closed that part of himself off to me and the intimacy we once shared, which I tried to recapture so hard. I wanted him to take that photo of me surrounding his member because I was already feeling the effects of him turning away. I remember now that I thought if he had that photograph in his possession, he wouldn't forget what we had together, but I was wrong, and he eventually used it against me. I was only good to him, though I wasn't without thoughtlessness, but my blabbering about his medical issues didn't come from a nefarious place. His inability to see that made him lash out in unfair ways and clearly, he did the same to you, but I honestly think he had already decided he didn't want to be with us before he brought both romances to hurtful ends.

My relationship with Gil was much shorter than yours with him, but they seem to have run similar courses. For me, and I hope as well for you, there's some peace in that. Neither one of us had done terribly wrong, he just can't handle actual partnerships. And yes, I too cringe for his wife. Thank you again for being so open with your story and willing to testify if needed. You are a true friend and I'm happy to be reunited with you.

Love,

Bea

NOTICE: This transmission is from the law firm of Fowler & Associates and may contain privileged and confidential information that is for the sole use of the intended recipient. Use, distribution, or copying of any part of this transmission by an unintended recipient is prohibited and may be a violation of law. If you believe you have received this message in error, please delete it, in addition to any attachments, and inform Fowler & Associates that you have done so. Thank you.

Correspondence 10

Amanda Vero to The Editor of Battlefield Times

(January 2020)

Dear Editor,

Slavery was wrong. The Confederacy was wrong. Most Americans agree that forcing people who were bought and sold as property to work untold hours under the harshest and most abusive conditions, while simultaneously depriving them of dignity, education, and basic needs as African Americans suffered through chattel slavery, was wrong. Most Americans also agree that any group of people who choose to grab American land in an attempt to carve out their own country with their own set of laws are also wrong.

And yet...anytime I raise the idea that the monuments to the Confederacy, a group of southern states that left the United States of America, created their own country called, "The Confederate States of America" to perpetuate slavery, then declared war against the USA, should be removed from the Lippincott Battlefield, it is met with fierce and baseless opposition.

"You can't erase history!" they cry, but disgraced General Lee never stood forty feet high, nor did angels herald the Confederate troops as depicted by mythologizing monuments to the Confederacy. It's as if the opposition has willingly been gaslit by proponents of the false Lost Cause narrative. When we juxtapose the language of the monuments to the text from the letters of secession of individual states, scales fall from our eyes, and the racist history of these cheap emotional appeals crystallizes.

Mississippi, for example, inscribed "On this ground our brave sires fought for their righteous cause; In glory they sleep who give it to their lives; To valor, they gave new dimensions of courage; To duty, its noblest fulfillment; To posterity, the sacred heritage of honor.", but their letter of secession stated, "Our position is thoroughly identified with the institution of slavery-- the greatest material interest of the world. Its labor supplies the product which constitutes by far the largest and most important portions of commerce of the earth. These products are peculiar to the climate verging on the tropical regions, and by an imperious law of nature, none but the black race can bear exposure to the tropical sun. These products have become necessities of the world, and a blow at slavery is a blow at commerce and civilization."

All Confederate monuments echo this same evil purpose thus rendering their inscribed honors quite hollow.

Certainly, the relocation of Confederate monuments seems like a very removed activity from more immediate actions such as supporting Black-owned businesses, requesting local police to wear body cameras, or reading books about racial injustice.

But in Lippincott, where the traitors to the United States occupied American land until they ultimately lost the Civil War, this is exactly the place to speak out because...monuments to states and people who left the USA to perpetuate slavery are WRONG!

Amanda Vero

Lippincott, PA

Email 58

Blaise Ayers to WRUMIRS

(January 2020)

Dear Fellow Moms,

WRUMIRS is delighted to welcome our newest member, Eloise Voldesing, to our fabulous group! Eloise and her husband Ron Stillman, recently moved to our area from Baltimore for Ron's job as a Graduate Professor of Physics at Battlefield University. Eloise is a stay-at-home mom to baby girl Lilith (nine months old), taking a break from her career as a chiropractic technician. In addition to Lilith, Eloise and Ron have two dogs, both Chihuahua-Beagle mixes, named Spot and Red. In her free-time, Eloise likes to practice yoga and experiment with non-GMO sourced and gluten-free recipes. Currently, Eloise is nursing

Lilith (hint, hint Nips and Blips). Eloise and her family are allergic to gluten and GMO-sourced ingredients. They look forward to many events with our group. Please reach out to Eloise if you have an upcoming event to invite her, or just to say hello.

Warmest regards,

Blaise Ayers,

President of WRUMIRS

P.S. Don't forget to download the new Gobbledygook app and find WRUMIRS there!

Email 59

Bela Rekker to Eloise Voldesing

(January 2020)

Dear Eloise,

Welcome to our group! I just read Blaise's letter to us, and it was such a pleasure for me to read all of the things we have in common, including baby girls named Lilith, lol. I remember thinking, "this name is so unusual," yet here we are. Currently, I nurse her, so I do recommend our group Nips and Blips where we trade a lot of good motherly advice. There's also a February potluck, if you would like to meet more of the group, but you can also bring Lilith to my house for a playdate, if you're interested. Just know that my older child, Portia, will also be there, but she's very good with the little ones.

By the way, do you use oils? I happen to sell oils through my home business and all of my oils are non-GMO sourced too.

Respectfully,

Bela

Email 60

Eloise Voldesing to Bela Rekker

(January 2020)

Dear Bela,

Thank you so much for your warm welcome. When Lilith was born through natural birth in our wading pool, she latched on and we never had any problems, but thank you for the invite to the nursing group.

However, I would love to come to your house for a playdate. We just got back from Western Samoa the weekend before last, so I'm just taking things a little slowly. A private get-together would be perfect. Would tomorrow morning at ten work for you?

Also, my Lilith (great minds think alike!) has had a runny nose since we got back, so I don't want her to give her infection to any formula-fed babies because they have no protection like mother's antibodies like your breastfed children do. So yes, I am very interested in your oils for her, as well as for me. Do you take credit cards, by any chance?

Sincerely,

Eloise

Email 61

Bela Rekker to Eloise Voldesing

(January 2020)

Dear Eloise,

A private playdate tomorrow morning at ten would work perfectly. I'll have coffee and non-GMO coconut seaweed snacks. My address is on the roster. I look forward to seeing you.

Respectfully,

Bela

P.S. I accept both cash and credit.

Email 62

Eloise Voldesing to Bela Rekker

(January 2020)

Good morning, Bela,

Lilith seems to have a bit of a rash on her head. Does it bother you if I bring her? Also, if it doesn't, do you recommend a particular oil for it?

Sincerely,

Eloise

Email 63

Bela Rekker to Eloise Voldesing

(January 2020)

Dear Eloise,

It's not a problem. Rashes happen all the time and the best oil I have for that is verbena vanilla - it works like a charm, it will even help with the runny nose, and right now, I have three-ounce bottles on sale for $15.99, plus tax.

Respectfully,

Bela

Email 64

Eloise Voldesing to Bela Rekker

(January 2020)

Dear Bela,

This is great, thank you so much! I'll be there at ten.

Sincerely,

Eloise

Email 65

Amanda Vero to Eloise Voldesing

(January 2020)

Dear Eloise,

I would very much like to meet you. I just read your bio and see how much we have in common. My husband and I moved up here from Baltimore too. You'll find this area has many Maryland transplants like us, so there is an abundance of restaurants serving steamed crabs, crab dips (including on hot pretzels, combining the best that both regions have to offer), and crab-stuffed dishes like Chicken Chesapeake. And everything has Old Bay seasoning on it, like it's supposed to. You can also find a lot of support for the Ravens, if that's your thing too, though you'll see support for the Eagles (pronounced "Iggles" just like in B-more here too) and the Steelers, but we never have to mention these teams again, if you don't want to. Everyone here roots for the Orioles, of course.

I too have a baby, though Teddy Bear is a boy, I bet he has a lot in common with your little Lilith. I am raising our boy to support women's rights though he can only say "mamamama" right now, especially when he wants something. Still, it's a start. I say "I" because I recently lost my husband Peter to respiratory failure. It has been very difficult to face widowhood, but support like that of WRUMIRS has helped.

Your husband teaches in the same facility as my husband taught though Peter was under a different discipline. I wonder if Ron has heard of Peter? It's okay if he hasn't, but it would be nice to be reconnected with the university in some way, and kind of reassuring that he isn't forgotten, but even mentioned to new faculty. Right now, Teddy and I are cared for because Peter invested in a good benefits plan. He was always thoughtful like that. Is your husband like that too? Husbands who plan and care for their loved ones are incredibly special and I feel very blessed to have had Peter as my husband.

Do you go to church too? I just joined Lippincott Lutheran. It's not quite what I grew up with, but close enough for our purposes. They also saw me through my husband's funeral with a lot of care and concern for both Teddy and me. The nursery is also where our Nips and Blips group meets. Would you like to join it? We're always looking for new members and I'd be happy to introduce you to the other moms.

I love to bake too, though I haven't had much luck with gluten-free dishes. I'm not allergic to gluten, but I would prefer to know how to bake some things so that if people like yourselves came over for a playdate, I could serve such dishes with confidence. Oh, and we, I mean "I", it's so hard to get used to) also have a couple of dogs, full-bred chihuahuas, so I'm guessing their behavior wouldn't be unfamiliar to you. Actually, I have to go walk them right now.

I look forward to hearing from you. Write when you can, but no pressure.

Sincerely,

Mandy

Email 66

Eloise Voldesing to Amanda Vero

(January 2020)

Dear Mandy,

This email is to serve as my only communication with you.

I'm sorry for your recent loss, but I don't need to find out how it further destabilizes you personally. You are far too familiar with me for my comfort. I will not be your needy crutch to lean on.

I understand that we may run into each other both in the group and on campus, but I want to make it very clear that I will not be doing much with you socially, and certainly not for any private playdates. My cousin, Gilbert DeRoquedu told me all about how he knew you in Arizona. That you hurt children in your care and got away with it is beyond comprehension, yet here we are. I won't be outing your old business, but I know what you did, and I don't want you anywhere near my child. If I hear of you touching anyone else's child, I will report you to Child Protection Services at once.

Please do not contact me further.

Eloise

Correspondence 11

From the Law Offices of Peerce, Davis, and Davis to Gilbert DeRoquedu, Ph.D.

(January 2020)

CEASE AND DESIST

Pursuant to Titles 17 and 18 of the United States Code

January 15, 2020

Gilbert DeRoquedu, Ph.D.

124 Piedmont Ave,

Pittsburgh, PA 18094

Dear Dr. Gilbert DeRoquedu,

The law firm of Peerce, Peerce, and Peerce represents Beatrice Fowler, Esq. If you have an attorney, please direct this letter to him or her and have your attorney notify us of such representation in this matter.

We are writing to notify you of your unlawful crediting of "The Flowers of the Grand Canyon Stamps of the USPS year 1999" infringes upon our client's exclusive copyrights.

CEASE AND DESIST ALL COPYRIGHT INFRINGEMENT

Beatrice Fowler, Esq. is the sole creator and owner of a copyright in various aspects of the artwork known as "Grand Canyon Flowers" that you misrepresented as your own work to the United States Post Office on your application #AED09102002 for the purpose of display on US stamps. Under United States Copyright Law, Beatrice Fowler, Esq.'s copyrights have been in effect since the date that "Grand Canyon Flowers" was created. All copyrighted aspects of "Grand Canyon Flowers" are copyrighted under United States law.

RESTITUTION FOR PAYMENTS RECEIVED

It has come to our attention that you received monies from the United States Postal Service for the use of "Grand Canyon Flowers." We have copies of your false statements on the application #AED09102002, as well as check stubs #USPS425102002 and #USPS525112002 deposited by you, in the amounts of $5000.00 and $5000.00 respectively to preserve as evidence.

We demand that you immediately cease and desist your unlawful claim to Beatrice Fowler, Esq.'s work of "Grand Canyon Flowers" by writing to the USPS to inform them of Beatrice Fowler, Esq.'s rightful ownership of "Grand Canyon Flowers" and provide restitution of the fraudulent transfer of the total of $10000.00 to Beatrice Fowler, Esq. by check through certified mail to the physical address at the top of this letter within the next ten (10) days.

Failure to comply with these steps in this timeframe will constitute "willful infringement." Should "willful infringement" occur, our client, Beatrice Fowler, Esq. has granted us full pursuit of all legal remedies which could result in considerable liability and exposure for you.

In addition to this letter, the United States Post Office will contact you in pursuit of litigation for providing false statements to, damaging the integrity of, and financially defrauding the above-named federal institution which is punishable by fine and imprisonment of up to twenty years.

Please sign and return the attached form, along with the check, by certified mail, as instructed above, within the allotted ten (10) days.

Sincerely,

Roger Peerce, Esq.

Letter 22

Amanda Vero to Gilbert DeRoquedu

(January 2020)

Dear Gil-a Monster,

I have continued to give our affair much thought, realizing that you were already doing harmful things to it before you cut us off completely. Since you have removed me from our shared file, I am reaching out to you by letter one last time because I can't help but think of your poor niece who may still receive your relationship "advice". This last letter of mine articulates what I think you would like her to know as a budding young woman. God knows how little you think of "the fairer sex".

Adieu,

Mandy

(With respect to C.S. Lewis)

My Dear Harmonia,

The time has come for me to impart some important relationship advice to you since you are dating and I am, besides being your doting uncle, a "Guy."

Considering your youth, it is high time that we discuss the essentials of how a relationship should and shouldn't work. I imagine someday, you will fall deeply in love, and you will drink great draughts of fresh, wholesome milk from this. But eventually, as taste buds become inured to lactose-laden assaults, some of the sweetness will dissipate, and the relationship may arrive at a point where, for whatever reason(s), it will seem to progress no further. At this time, your Guy may develop "lactose intolerance", or just wish to leave the whole liaison, perhaps to conserve the energy needed to maintain it, perhaps because he would rather spend time with someone else. In either case, he does not owe you a real conversation about it, he may merely contrive a dastardly situation, fault you for suspecting him, then leverage your suspicion of him to mischaracterize you and break off the relationship entirely.

Later, when he realizes his grave mistake, he may come to you, asking to receive him again. (He will have forewarned you about this behavior by uttering "I will fight for our love" or some such nonsense so that this doesn't come as a complete surprise but see it for its true purpose.) What is important to remember is that he is redeemable, but you My Dear, are only redeemable at the point you offer his redemption. In no way are you corrigible leading up to that time, which is why he would not offer you any possibility of improving yourself, prior to ending the relationship.

In the olden days, a Guy might offer an ultimatum to a young woman such as "You'd better change this thing about you, or we're through", but the #metoo movement made young women far too keen about the unfairness of that technique and so, more subtlety is needed. The key here is that his feelings must be considered at all times. The fact that you are a person, deserving of the same consideration you would grant him prior to a break-up is of no matter. In fact, he has worked very hard to not see you as the same type of person he is, full of emotions and unpredictable desires that course   through   him.

He will have decided what about you he likes best and work to only bring that part of you, remaining silent or disapproving should you express yourself any other way. He may use phrases like, "You help me to relax" so that you must check yourself should you want to express something that might be considered counter to relaxation because he couldn't possibly handle it. At first, what you mean to him in this way will be genuine, but in time, as the relationship progresses and you exhibit more sides of yourself, it will become more of a plea. Once he has decided on what you will be to him, you must work to only be that thing, and quite predictable as well, not unlike a robot. If you are unpredictable at any turn, this would force him to risk trust of you in future episodes, and that won't do because your only worth should be as a reflection of himself, not as your own person with reason and agency in the world. One thing you must never express is anger, no matter how justified you are in this feeling by his actions. By expressing any anger, you scare him so utterly, he will be too stunned to try again, because he did not expect his robot to have this.

When he does come to you in recognition of how much better he should have done by you, he will still not get it right. No matter how many ways and wherefores you might spell out his errors in a letter, he will simply respond with vagaries about his faulty thought processes, sprinkled in with some general "I'm sorry"s, rather than sincere and heartfelt apologies for his real and hurtful actions. Some Guys know that they don't know quite what they've done, but if they are still doing this while middle-aged, it is because they prefer their obtuseness to their own real self-knowledge.

Should you take him back, this relationship will again offer you milk, and it will be called "buttermilk", which sounds richer, and therefore, better. Certainly, the milk will look just like the wholesome drink you had at the beginning, but it will be different, thicker, filling you up sooner, and have a sour taste. In no case should you question this flavor, the result of not truly vetting what went wrong prior, and so you will consume the buttermilk, hoping to have the sweetness you once knew, but never achieving it and overfilling yourself with its consumption. Should you dare to question this difference of milk, you will again be found at fault, and he will end the relationship abruptly because it was indeed your fault that you accepted the buttermilk in the first place.

In these ways, he may continue to begin and end relationships, never fully realizing how much more potential he would have had with you as a partner, and you, My Dear, will always have him in the heart and brain, wondering what you could have done better. Please also remember to hold the Double Standard of behavior very close to your heart, so that you can understand how fully unworthy you are. I wouldn't tell you these things if I hadn't known them to be true.

Your Affectionate Uncle,

Gilbert

Correspondence 12

Melissa DeRoquedu to Gilbert DeRoquedu

(January 2020)

Dear Shithead,

By the time you read this, blah, blah, blah. You fucking LOSER! All I ever did for you was cook, clean, and bear your spawn, but you, Dr. Fuckhead, run around, sticking your dick into everyone! How do I know? Because for the first time in my life, I've caught an STI!! My gynecologist is going to call you because she has some questions. I know I've been faithful, but that was clearly useless. Twenty-three years of my life I gave to you and what do I have to show for it? Fucking gonorrhea!! This! This is what I get from our yearly-only-on-our-anniversary-sex? Oh, and don't think I haven't been noticing your shitty swipes of my art! You goddamned dickhead! I am so tired of trying to make this marriage work. I've cooked and I've cleaned, and I raise our child, but it's never good enough for your royal asshole! I have nothing, nothing left to give to this marriage. I don't even have anything to give to another man, you've taken everything from my normal life. I've drunk myself into a stupor every night just to dull some of the pain. Now, I'm the fattest I've ever been, and I have smelly discharge! As if I wasn't feeling like absolute shit every single day! You suggest I lose weight one minute, then come to me the next and get mad because I'm somehow not in the mood. Whose fault is that?? I never fucking know if I'm attractive or not. And you already hate me because our kid was ruined! Well, guess what, Shithead? That's from YOUR side of the gene pool! That's right, I've been learning something from my Trisomy 21 group! That fucking takes the cake! You kiss our child when you come home, but never read him a fucking bedtime story. You don't really want to be his father and it shows. Meanwhile, I look like an asshat at all the Tri 21 groups as I stand alone with Alastor for the umpteenth time. You know what? I'm going to live with MOM. Guess what I found out today besides the fact that you don't care about my health?? The lady who has ALWAYS had my back trusted her instincts about you and hired a private investigator who has been tracking your rendezvous ever since. He delivered the report to her just the other day. She had been sitting on it, but totally opened up to me when I called her this morning in tears. Your "colleagues" have been photographed kissing you on the mouth in Greece, Egypt, and most recently, Russia. Additionally, this investigator has been collecting evidence of inconsistencies in your life as compared to information you told to me, like when you said you were still in Russia, but had already flown to Pennsylvania and drove a rented car to…Lippincott?? Where you parked at a Chinese restaurant, then hiked in the woods for hours? Does that make any fucking sense? you goddamned weirdo! Who knows? maybe you were out there sharing diseases! I hope you never kiss our kid again. God only knows what more you'll take away from him by what you give to him! I've taken Alastor away where you can't get to him or me and I'm seeking custody of him and alimony. If you want to contact someone, you can call my lawyer, Bob Jansen at 717-630-9373. Don't even think of coming to my mom's house because your restraining order has already been written.

Fuck right off,

Melissa

Correspondence 13

Christopher Decapente to the Editor of the Battlefield Times

(January 2020)

Dear Editor,

I have never, not once, been so irritated by this paper like I was the other day when I opened it and read Ms. Vero's account of the Civil War. She doesn't know anything, especially about the Confederate soldiers. Has she ever even served? Because I have! My family fought in that war on BOTH sides. Both sides suffered losses and ALL my family served with honor like they always do.

Who is she to say that my great-great-great-great Uncle Jaspar didn't serve faithfully? She doesn't know what she's talking about. Uncle Jaspar was known for his good stories and his whittling. I even in fact have some of the things he whittled for my great-great-great-great Aunt Marie while he was serving for said army. He walked hundreds of miles in his boots, and he was so smart that when there wasn't any more patches to spare, he made some from the sap and the leaves available.

Besides that, his family didn't own any slaves. He didn't know what a slave was until the war, and someone told him because his family was too poor to own slaves. If Ms. Vero could pause and take a breath, she could see that it was just a war fought for by the rich plantation owners. Those poor Confederate boys, like Uncle Jaspar, were just there doing what they were told so they didn't starve and could send some money home. I'd even be glad to give her a tour. Maybe she might learn something.

So, with respect to the monuments, they should stay because those poor boys fought hard for what they were told to do, and they were there for each other. Therefore, they fought honorably. War is h-e-double hockey stick and Ms. Vero shouldn't stick her nose where it doesn't belong.

Chris Decapente

Lippincott

Correspondence 14

Christina Pablum, Ph.D. to the Editor of the Battlefield Times

(January 2020)

Dear Editor,

In reviewing Ms. Amanda Vero's letter regarding Confederate monuments on the battlefields run by the National Park Service, I note that she does make some good points. However, despite her research, these relics of the past should stay on public land because through them Americans can understand how imperfect the journey toward racial equality is.

To wit, Ms. Vero correctly asserted the Army of Northern Virginia was an enemy combatant to The Army of the Potomac. There is absolutely no argument among all historians that the Confederacy started the entire Civil War by its attack on Fort Sumter on April 12, 1861. This military maneuver cost several American lives and the fall of the fort to the people who were forming their own country titled, The Confederate States of America, complete with its own Constitution. There is no equivocating the Confederacy with the United States of America in terms of morality, patriotism, and military might.

However, these Confederate monuments, the majority of which served to counter the Civil Rights Movement in America, are an impressive, if not misguided, example of American Unity in the face of the Cold War. We must remember that at a time of governmental battles, descendants of both the Union troops and the Confederate troops erected these examples of solidarity against a political movement that menaced the progress of Democracy in several countries. By this unified effort, in recognizing the sacrifices of Confederate forces, the democracy of The United States stood strong against a history that often undermined it. In the National Parks of Gettysburg and Lippincott, Civil Rights demonstrations that questioned America's idea of equality took a backseat to this patriotic display, and Americans felt relief.

Today, we understand how loudly these monuments sell The Lost Cause. What we can do to balance their message is to provide an educational panel near the base of each monument, so tourists who leave their vehicles can read the extensive history and receive a greater message. By comparing the words of the panels to the works of art before them, all tourists, both American and International, will travel through the eras of America's complicated journey of racial equality and arrive at a better understanding of humanity and the forces that can affect us. In other words, don't remove the monuments, contextualize them.

Christina Pablum, Ph.D. in American History

Battlefield University

Lippincott

Correspondence 15

Georgia Zuri to the Editor of the Battlefield Times

(January 2020)

Dear Editor,

This letter is in response to Mr. Decapente's letter published this past week.

Sir, the heartache you feel for those "poor Confederate boys" is deeply misplaced.

While you may know that the Confederate soldiers didn't come from plantations, did you know Lee's army forced ten thousand enslaved Black Americans to work their camps? Or, if you knew that already, have you really explored the meaning of this? Ten thousand people, simply for the color of their skin, were forced to chop wood, prepare food, care for military animals, drive wagons, pitch tents, haul supplies, and march along with the soldiers wherever they went.

These Americans labored not for honor, not for wages, but near starvation, constant exhaustion, living moment to moment under the never-ending threat of armed people who considered them "property."

Those "Confederate boys" upheld the system of forced labor, so they didn't have to do as many tasks as they felt beneath them. Those ones who didn't come from fancy plantations? They didn't question institutionalized cruelty, they enforced it!

Perhaps you don't believe me. Okay, then. Find examples of Confederate soldiers who freed the enslaved, then went AWOL rather than shoot at American soldiers for the express purpose of perpetuating the torture of Black Americans.

And then, when you realize none are to be found, read the stories of "contraband".

That's right. Lee wrote that Confederate soldiers were not to capture Black Americans while north of the Mason-Dixon line. But…every Confederate unit at Gettysburg did exactly that! They rounded up and kidnapped Black Americans, *especially women and children who couldn't outrun them.* Then, these units sold off The Oppressed. Make no mistake. Some poor Confederate soldier wasn't getting kickbacks for this, especially ones who didn't know the system. The sales were happening offsite, among the rich plantation owners.

Then…why? Why would "poor Confederate boys" be motivated to capture Black Americans? Why would these rogue soldiers risk behavior tantamount to war crimes deep in Union territory? Why, oh why did they pursue these women and children, when they weren't finagling the sales or receiving the money? What did these sex-starved soldiers take for strong-arming helpless people?

You know what they took.

You know exactly what they did.

Georgia Zuri,

Lippincott

Email 67

Eloise Voldesing to Bela Rekker

(January 2020)

Dear Bela,

Thank you again for last Tuesday's playdate. I'm sorry I haven't been in contact, but Lilith has continued to be under the weather. I applied your oil per your instructions to her since we saw you, but it's not working. Immediately after our playdate, her rash spread all over her body, though that's pretty much gone away. However, now she seems worse off, struggling to latch, and she's developed a fever and slight cough, in addition to her runny nose never going away. If this doesn't clear up in a few more days, I'm taking her to my chiropractor in Littlestown. I'm frustrated that the oil you recommended didn't cure her of illness. Do you give refunds?

Eloise

Email 68

Bela Rekker to Eloise Voldesing

(January 2020)

Dear Eloise,

Thank you for letting me know. I'm sorry your Lilith is suffering so much, though it does sound like the verbena vanilla did the trick since you were also aiming to cure the rash. By this point, you've probably used most of the bottle.

As a fellow mom, I offer you every bit of advice I know. Why? Because it is also what works for my children. So, no I don't give refunds, but I can gift you a bonus bottle of menthol eucalyptus oil which is what I use for coughs.

Since we saw you last, my Lilith has been fine, but Portia's runny nose and watery eyes contributed to her four-hour nap after Nips and Blips yesterday. I'm not saying that your Lilith gave it to us, but I'm willing to bear the burden of care for my children no matter how it comes to us because that's what moms do. My oil sales are a natural extension of the care I give to my family, but they also provide extra financial support we need. So again, all sales are final, but I'll put a free one-ounce bottle of menthol eucalyptus oil in your mailbox. I hope she heals soon.

Respectfully,

Bela

Correspondence 16

Amanda Vero to Beatrice Fowler, Esq.

(February 2020)

Dear Bea,

I hope this email finds you well. We're okay here. Well, not really. Teddy has been kind of listless and feels like he has a fever coming on. I wish Peter were here, but I have to learn to manage without him. The moms group still helps. I especially appreciate the nursing subgroup. That reminds me.

A couple weeks ago, my moms group announced a new member. I was so happy because she and I seem to have a lot in common, but it turns out..she is Gil's COUSIN! I had written to her, hoping to cultivate some kind of mom friendship and she wrote back quite nastily. Apparently, Gil had gossiped to her about me, so she knew who I was, and she said hurtful things. I had invited her to the nursing subgroup, but since she doesn't want to be around me, I don't think she's coming, which is her loss because Nips and Blips has a lot of helpful information, like last week when Bela recommended introducing fresh avocado as a first food instead of shelf stable rice cereal. Well, maybe it's a good thing if Eloise doesn't come. She really debased me in her email, so I don't want to meet her in real life.

Anyway, dealing with her reminded me of Gil again, so I was wondering - have you heard anything since you sent a Cease-and-Desist letter (if you did)? I think it's been more than ten days since you were going to send it "right away." Maybe you weren't thinking about telling me when you received his response because of whatever strategy you're following, but I am curious how he will handle this shameful situation. And again, I'm really glad that you're pursuing your justice. Just his slandering me to his cousin was like a stab in the back. I don't know if he meant it, but the meanness of their words really got to me. Thanks for everything, even if you can't tell me all of the developments.

Love,

Mandy

Correspondence 17

From the Desk of Beatrice Fowler, Esq. to Amanda Vero

(February 2020)

Dear Mandy,

I had been holding on to this information for a few days, trying to figure the best way to convey it to you, but this space is fine.

On Monday, I received a call from my lawyer, Roger Peerce, of the law firm representing me in the intended lawsuit. They called me after having just received a call from Gil's lawyer. According to Gil's lawyer, who made the call after the autopsy was confirmed, Gil suffered a series of strokes and died. I have decided to rescind the lawsuit and not pursue it through his estate because I don't know that his wife, or his widow now, knows anything about what he did nor am I that keen to collect restitution from her. I think she suffered a lot having been married to him.

I know this is a lot to take, but there is a little more. The reason I know that she suffered is because Gil's lawyer told Roger that Gil may have suffered the series of strokes and died shortly after reading our letters - the Cease and Desist one from my lawyer and your letter, which both arrived in the same mail delivery. He had opened those and presumably read them right before a mail courier had arrived with a letter from Melissa, who was leaving him and filing for divorce as well as custody of Alastor because he was abusive in a variety of ways. Right in front of the mail courier, Gil read her letter, then collapsed. The mail courier called 911, but it was too late. He gave the letter to the police who came after the EMT's called the death and they used it to track Melissa whose lawyer eventually called Gil's lawyer, who called Roger.

The thing is a letter from you was in that collection even though you had indicated that you would never be in touch with Gil again. I can't tell you how incredibly violated I feel that you reached out to that abuser after all we shared, how he had wronged both of us! What could you possibly have written that was so important? Actually, I don't know what was in your letter. The point is your action took me right back to Grand Canyon Youth Campground where I was terribly hurt by people whom I thought cared about me. It wasn't just that Gil double-crossed me, you NEVER reached out after the incident! Why didn't you check on me at our bunkhouse, or ever even write to me after I left? It hurt me so badly that you didn't keep in touch. It was like you were of the same mindset as everyone else, as if I had done something very, very wrong, when I hadn't! I was embarrassed, but I shouldn't have been found at fault for something I didn't consent to sharing! Your loss of friendship really hurt me the most. And now? You literally betray me! Thank God Gil died! Because what kind of lawsuit would I be capable of if you were feeding him a bunch of information? Frankly, I should sue you for breach of confidentiality if that's what you did. That's why I have that notice at the bottom of my emails. Just like my prescience in the past, my professionalism today protects me when I mistakenly trust people. But I don't know for sure what was in your letter, and I think you too have been swallowed up by the misogyny that engulfs us, so I'll just drop the idea of suing you, but also, I'll drop you. I don't need your kind of "friendship." Ever.

In summary, this transmission will serve as my last communication with you. If you try to call me, I'll hang up on you. If you send any email, it will go straight to my spam box. Good luck keeping friends. You really suck at it.

Bea

Gobbledygook

Shared file of WRUMIRS

(February 2020)

Blaise:Dear WRUMIRS,

This is just a reminder that our February potluck is coming up! Taking a break from all things Valentines, our theme is "Snow." Maybe if we make foods that resemble the white stuff, something greater than flurries will actually appear in South Central Pennsylvania this winter.

So far, we have on the menu: coconut snowball cakes, sugar cookies, mashed potatoes, cauliflower casserole, spinach dip with melted mozzarella, a chicken dip and bread snowman, crudités with a snowman made of three baked rounds of brie cheese, and marshmallow popcorn. We're still looking for creative drinks to add this eclectic meal. Just message me before 3 p.m. today and what you plan to bring if you plan to come.

Warmest regards,

Blaise Ayers,

President of WRUMIRS

Maxine: Hi Blaise. I'm sorry, but I can't make it. Hephzibah has a fever, so I don't want to bring her.

Blaise: Oh no! Well, I hope she feels better soon. Thank you for letting me know.

Marisol: Yes, also Maximus is feverish with a runny nose, so we won't make it.

Blaise: Okay, thank you for letting me know. Would anyone else like to bring the mashed potatoes or marshmallow popcorn?

Georgia: Something may be going around. Mosi has been sneezing, but he doesn't have a fever. Has anyone heard from Bela? Portia was at Nips and Blips last week with watery eyes and a runny nose.

Blaise: Oh wow, that's a shame. I guess something is going around.

Marisol: Is it Covid?

Blaise: No, no these aren't the signs of Covid.

Blaise: And I think it's a little soon for Covid.

Mandy: Hi, yes, please include us in the cancellations. Teddy is also spiking a fever. Please keep me informed if any of you find out what it is. Sidenote: I don't think it's Covid. What Peter had resembled Covid more than anything that's going on with babies.

Georgia: Do you think Peter died of Covid?

Mandy: No, I don't think so. I mean, how would he have got it?

Maxine: Actually, I read an article about some virologists wondering if it had gotten to the States earlier than they had detected.

Mandy: But how would it have gotten here?

Maxine: Oh, the usual ways pandemics spread - international travel, or being around those who have traveled internationally.

Mandy: Yes, well he wasn't traveling, he was sitting at home.

Maxine: Well, if anyone he had come into contact with had traveled.

Mandy: Could he have contracted it from someone who spent time with someone who traveled internationally?

Maxine: Yes, that could have happened too. That's kind of how disease spreads.

Mandy: I have to go now

Maxine: Okay, well, I hope Teddy feels better soon.

Mandy: Thanks

Email 69

Amanda Vero to Georgia Zuri

(February 2020)

Dear Georgia,

Thank you so much for having written what you did about the Confederate soldiers. I really appreciate your support. If you ever want to get together for coffee and talk about anything we can do to bring them down, I'd be glad to. I hope Mosi feels better soon.

Sincerely,

Mandy

Email 70

Georgia Zuri to Amanda Vero

(February 2020)

Mandy,

This isn't about you - this is about Black People! My ancestors suffered and Black Americans continue to suffer, whether or not we have those statues. Lippincott was a Sundown town not so long ago and so today; I am still followed around in stores. As the only Black mom in our group, I often wonder why Gettysburg itself isn't a beacon of racial equality since the Union won that battle and changed the outcome of the war.

But that brings me to another thing. Did it ever occur to you that Black People have been fighting those statues? Why don't you raise Black Voices instead of your own? Did you ever think to research who said what when? Have you ever even heard of Frederick Douglass? W.E.B Dubois? Dr. Ibrahm X. Kendi? Bree Newsom? Bryan Stevenson? I heard you trying to talk about the statues to the other moms a few weeks ago. Not once did you ever mention them. And the other moms coming to me to get my opinion was unnecessarily painful. It's like you're in your own white bubble and you don't see how your talk affects people. If you actually want to fight for equality in America, join a group that raises Black voices. Otherwise, keep it to yourself, and definitely don't involve me. That said, I hope Teddy gets better soon. Mosi is on the mend, thank you for asking.

Georgia

Correspondence 18

Cordelia Links for Battlefield Times

(February 2020)

Measles Has Arrived in Adams County

LITTLESTOWN - The first case of measles in Adams County since 2003 was confirmed this week, state health officials said. The patient, a nine-month-old baby, had been brought to Mason Dixon Chiropractors at 3 p.m. Thursday afternoon where a practicing chiropractor noticed symptoms of respiratory distress and called 911. The case was confirmed February 4 and public health officials conducted multiple interviews with the patient to confirm there were no public exposures. It is believed that the measles was acquired during a vacation in the Independent State of Samoa where they have suffered an outbreak of measles since October 2019. It is also believed that the baby did not exhibit symptoms until a little over a week after returning.

At this time, public health officials are treating this as an isolated incident. However, the public should be aware of measles, look for symptoms, and get vaccinated if they haven't been. People unsure of their vaccination or immunity status can request a measles titer check from their primary care physicians. If their measles titer is too low, their primary care physician may recommend the measles-mumps-rubella (MMR) vaccine.

Public health officials recommend vaccination not only to protect members of the public, but also their loved ones who are too young or too immune-compromised to receive the vaccines. Other life-threatening diseases vaccines protect against are polio, whooping cough, tetanus, diphtheria, chicken pox, rotavirus, and Hepatitis B as well as others.

According to the Centers for Disease Control (CDC), there were over 1200 reported cases of measles across 31 states in 2019. "The majority of cases were among people who were not vaccinated against measles. This was noted to be the greatest number of cases since 1992, which does not bode well for 2020.

The CDC lists the first symptoms as high fever, cough, runny nose, and watery eyes, which appear seven to fourteen days after the virus is breathed in. The measles rash typically appears three to five days after the first symptoms. Some measles patients can infect others even before they are known to have the disease.

Complications from measles include pneumonia, hospitalization, encephalitis, and death.

Public health officials advise anyone who suspects they or their child have measles to call their primary care physician prior to arrival at any urgent care or doctor's office.

Email 71

Bela Rekker to Eloise Voldesing

(February 2020)

Dear Eloise,

I saw a news article that said there was a case of measles reported from a chiropractic clinic. I was wondering if by any chance your Lilith was the baby mentioned in the article who had measles? Because Portia has a full body rash right now and she's unwell. If I know it's measles, I can work on combining different oils more targeted for that disease.

Also, if you want to get together, maybe we could have a measles party? That way we can just pass it through the community so all of the kids who haven't gotten vaccinated have a chance at natural immunity. If you haven't read the article yet, you'll laugh at the obvious plug for the CDC and Big Pharma. A measles party would be a great way to combat it.

What do you think?

Respectfully,

Bela

Email 72

Eloise Voldesing to Bela Rekker

(February 2020)

Dear Bela,

My baby's health is none of your business. Please respect our medical privacy at this time as we have respected yours. I did not divulge our previous playdate to the public health officials because I believe in your right to privacy. I will let you know when we are available to get together for another playdate.

Sincerely,

Eloise

Gobbledygook

Shared file of WRUMIRS

(February 2020)

Blaise: Dear Moms,

As several people have backed out of the February potluck due to illness, we're postponing it until the end of the month, but please keep your fingers crossed for snow!

Warmest regards,

Blaise Ayers

President of WRUMIRS

Georgia: Hi, have any of you seen the article about measles in Littlestown? Should we be concerned?

Marisol: Oh my God, I hope it's not measles! Maximus has a fever and just started a rash on his forehead. I'll make an appointment with the pediatrician right away.

Blaise: Are you sure it's measles?

Georgia: Well, it's in Littlestown at least. Probably a few other places too.

Mandy: It's measles. I'm with Teddy at the hospital. They have him on oxygen.

Marisol: You were going to tell us when?

Mandy: I just here. Teddy is sick.

Maxine: It's measles. I'm with Hephzibah now at the hospital. Bela brought Portia in too.

Mandy: Where are you? How did they get measles?

Maxine: We're downstairs in a special positive pressure room in the ER.

Georgia: If all our kids have or had it, someone brought it into Nips and Blips.

Mandy: Who brought it in?

Blaise: Well, we don't know who had it first.

Georgia: The article said someone who traveled to Samoa. Do we know anyone who was there?

Maxine: We do now.

Marisol: Wut?

Maxine: I asked Bela if she knew anyone who traveled to Samoa, and she said Eloise.

Marisol: The newbie?

Maxine: Yes. According to Bela they had a playdate a couple weeks ago. And she sold Eloise some oils because baby Lilith was "poorly."

Marisol: Ohmygod

Georgia: Well, Mosi seems better. Maybe it will be okay.

Mandy: My baby has respiratory distress It is NOT okay

Mandy: My child's lips are blue because someone else's kid didn't get vaccinated didn't CARE

Blaise: Hi Ladies, we do need to keep it respectful here.

Maxine: My newborn is sick Blaise. The anti vax kid should never have mixed with ours.

Blaise: You don't understand. We don't discriminate against unvaccinated children, or working moms, those who don't co sleep, those who bottle-feed. In other words, we support moms, not intolerance. Imagine how a mom would feel to be rejected because of her parenting philosophy.

Maxine: No, Blaise, you don't understand. My kid didn't catch someone else's cosleeping, bottle-feeding, work-life balance. She caught a preventable childhood disease. And look how it spread. None of us had ever even met Eloise, yet our kids have it.

Blaise: We all have different parenting philosophies, and we have to be respectful of them.

Mandy: Did that bitch respect my kid's health???? Now they're talking about him being on a ventilator. FUCK YOU

Blaise: I'm shutting down this chat right now to give everyone a chance to cool off. I'll turn it back on tomorrow. Good night. Hope Teddy feels better soon.

Blaise: Okay, this chat is back on. Please keep it civil.

Maxine: Teddy just coded in the pediatric unit.

Maxine: He didn't make it.

Maxine: Mandy is screaming.

Maxine: They gave her a shot. She's quiet now. They're driving her home.

Correspondence 19

Cordelia Links for the Battlefield Times

(February 2020)

Infant Death in South Central Pennsylvania

LIPPINCOTT - This morning, an outbreak of measles that began in Littlestown claimed its first victim signaling a resurgence of a disease that hadn't caused the deaths in Adams County since 1960, before the measles vaccine had been introduced.

The victim, an eleven-month-old boy, was just one month shy of being administered his first dose of the measles-mumps-rubella (MMR) vaccine. The first dose of the MMR vaccine is typically administered for children aged twelve to fifteen months, with the second dose typically given between four and six years of age. Babies six months or older who travel internationally can receive a dose of the MMR vaccine, then continue with the standard immunization schedule as advised by Centers for Disease Control.

The baby died at Lippincott Medical Center of acute respiratory distress syndrome and doctors could not revive him despite several attempts. A week prior to being admitted to the hospital, the victim had visited the following locations:

Sunday, January 26, 2020 - Lippincott Lutheran nursery from 9am to 10am church service

Tuesday, January 28, 2020 - Lippincott Lutheran nursery from 9am to 10am nursing mothers group

Two other patients at Lippincott Medical Center have been confirmed to be carrying the measles and visited the following locations:

Tuesday, January 21, 2020 - A private playdate at the residence of 204 Longstreet Avenue, Gettysburg, PA 17325

Tuesday, January 28, 2020 - Lippincott Lutheran nursery from 9am to 10am nursing mothers group.

Wednesday, January 29, 2020 - Battlefield University Daycare 7am to 5pm

Thursday, January 30, 2020 - Adams County Healthy Oils 2pm to 3pm

Saturday, February 1, 2020 - General Lee's Buffet 5pm - 6pm

Anyone who was at those locations during those times or up to two hours after is advised to call the Adams County Health Department if any of the following symptoms present:

- High fever
- Runny nose
- Watery eyes
- Cough
- A rash that appears to emanate from the hairline or face, then spreads downward to the neck, trunk, arms, legs, and feet.

If not treated, measles can cause encephalitis, acute respiratory distress syndrome, and death.

Currently, Battlefield University Daycare and Battlefield University are under quarantine as dictated by Adams County Health Department. At this time, four suspected cases are associated with the daycare and no suspected cases are associated with the University.

In recent years, the measles disease has spread primarily among those who are not vaccinated against it. The MMR vaccine has an effective rate of 94% with just one dose and 97% with the second dose. The MMR vaccine has a proven record of safety to protect against disease since its inception in 1963. By contrast, the anti-vaccine movement is rooted in conspiracy theory and unscientific practice.

The original patient who had contracted measles in Western Samoa has been sent home under quarantine. The victims' parents are Eloise Voldesing and Ronald Stillman who reside at 496 Pickett's Boulevard, Lippincott, PA 17329. They may be charged by the Adams County Health Department for willfully withholding information contrary to the public health of Adams County residents, pending further investigation.

Adams County Health Department advises MMR vaccination for anyone who is not protected against the disease. Please call your primary care physician for more information.

Gobbledygook WRUMIRS

(February 2020)

Blaise: Dear WRUMIRS,

As you know, we have lost little Teddy Vero. He will be missed. I'm trying to reach Mandy and she doesn't seem to be answering her phone. Do any of you know how to reach her or if she has family in the area? If worse comes to worse, should we do a welfare check?

Warmest regards,

Blaise Ayers,

President of WRUMIRS

Georgia: I dropped off a casserole on the front porch and rang the doorbell. It was gone when I drove by again later.

Blaise: Then maybe we don't have to do a welfare check. Is there a funeral to attend? Maybe we can connect with family there?

Marisol: I'll look at Lippincott Lutheran's bulletin board tomorrow.

Blaise: Yes, please keep us updated.

Marisol: Just circling back to update - according to the bulletin board, Lippincott Lutheran is holding a funeral for Teddy on Thursday at 3pm, burial in the churchyard.

Blaise: Okay, I'll try to make that. Is anyone else planning to attend?

Georgia: I can come, and I'll leave Mosi with my husband.

Marisol: I can come, but I'll have to bring Maximus.

Blaise: I don't know if bringing children is a good idea.

Marisol: Okay, I just won't go. I kind of don't want to anyway.

Blaise: Understood. I think it's fine if it's just Georgia and me.

Letter 23

Amanda Vero to Amy Hood (deceased)

(February 2020)

mom

Correspondence 20

Chase Evergard, M.D. to the Editor of The Battlefield
Times

(February 2020)

Dear Editor,

In the heart of every pediatrician lie the scars of the children
we couldn't save - victims of cancer, genetic complications,
SIDS, car accidents, and the like. To do everything in our
power to save those children is exactly what we train for.
Pediatric residencies, discounted bike helmets, ordered tests,
waiting room pamphlets are just some of the tools we use in
these efforts to prevent devastation. Try as we might,
tragedies come along, jarring in their surprise, as in the case
of accidents, deeply aggrieving in their lifelong timetable, as
in the case of genetics. But, in addition to the scars, there is
Hope. Hope that the suffering of those who went before was
not in vain, but in advance of treatments for the next victims.
Hope that previous victims can lend understanding to
prevent further tragedy.

Pediatric geneticists toil to find ways to prevent lifelong
issues. Orthopedists, rheumatologists, cardiologists,
psychiatrists, and medical professionals of every other
discipline in the realm of pediatrics work to correct
complications from a host of ills. We might not march
lockstep, but we move in the same direction, to keep, to
advance, to advocate the health of the child. We want the
best for them, for we are all too familiar with the bad
outcomes, not only from our own experiences, but those of
our peers. We read all of the data of the threats against
children. If we can't lend our expertise in person, we write
up our research for mutual benefit, we donate money. We
want children to thrive for when children thrive, so does
society.

However, I am not just a pediatrician; I am a parent. I am a parent who takes his child to another pediatrician. Because I have the humility to know that I don't have the expertise of every pediatric specialist, that I must lean on their vast knowledge and experience for the complications that arise outside of my general practice. They are the same people to whom I refer your children when the need arises.

And now, I must add another scar to my heart. A baby boy shaped scar who, through the lack of humility on the part of others, died of a preventable disease. Not a lack of humility on the part of his parents, but a lack of humility from other parents. Parents who thought they knew better than those of us steeped in the protection of children. Parents who thought that it wouldn't be that bad, or that no one would know. Parents who never cared to plow through the actual facts and figures, the research, the anecdotes from peers, exhausted by trying to fight the spread of disease.

Please, please, I beg of you, as your community pediatrician, but also as a fellow parent – please have your children vaccinated. If you have questions about our practice, the ingredients of vaccines that we administer, the effects of receiving vaccines, the pharmaceutical companies we partner with, please come to my office and I will gladly go over these things with you. And it is not enough that you know them. To ensure the safety of all our Little Ones, check in with those around you – family, friends, care providers, places of worship, indoor play communities.

Because if you don't, we all pay a terrible price.

Sincerely,

Chase Evergard, MD,

Lippincott Pediatrics

Email 73

Maxine Epipedo to Blaise Ayers

(February 2020)

Dear Blaise,

I am writing to inform you that I will no longer be a part of WRUMIRS. I cannot belong to a group that sabotages moms by letting diseases run rampant. I thank God for the hospital workers - the doctors, respiratory therapists, nurses, the pharmacists, and even the sanitation workers who worked tirelessly to save my baby. Yet you sit there on your high horse like it's all fine. It's not fine! Hephzibah may be home now, but we have to watch out for developmental delays and a fatal brain complication when she's older. Not only that, but the doctors also said that measles has disrupted her immunity so badly, she might catch types of illnesses that she had previously had immunity to for the next three years. And she isn't even the only one of our group under these threats. Every other baby who caught measles has the same scary future. Even babies who have never even joined could get it. Why? Because we have to support other moms who don't believe in science? Newsflash - you can't actually "raise up moms in real solidarity" if your inaction severely sickens or kills their children.

I'm only able to write this email because my daughter didn't die like Teddy did. If I lost her, I would be utterly devastated. My heart goes out to Mandy. You need to rethink your life choices.

Maxine

Email 74

Bela Rekker to Blaise Ayers

(February 2020)

Dear Blaise,

I just want to thank you for unwavering support in the face of adversity. When measles came calling for my Portia, I didn't know how rocky the journey would be, but I am pleased to say, we have turned a corner. She is breathing quite normally and is expected to make a full recovery in the next few weeks.

In that harsh hospital environment of masked personnel, beeping machines, plastic tubes, barking intercoms, cinder block walls, sharp needles, and disposable everything, I drew upon the warmth that is our moms group. Part of why she is still with us is because of all of the community she and I have received in this fellowship of moms. Every potluck, nursing group, tourist trip, moms' night out, and oil sales from trusting moms buoyed me when Portia's health was touch and go. We have traded so many stories about our children that I felt the love of everyone reaching through that unfamiliar place and holding up my Portia with their hearts. Our group has been uplifting when no other form of society was there for us. Don't get me wrong, my husband loves and supports us, but only mothers know what mothers go through.

I have never felt more acceptance and care for my child than in those moments when her health was touch and go. Now we are back in our sanctuary, and I can nurse my child, just like Mother Nature intended.

I don't know what the future holds, but I highly doubt the negativity of the faceless hospital staff. It's as if they're trying to suck us back in, preaching more vaccines, etc., when really, those questionable ingredients would put Portia right back into the hospital. Just because a bunch of corporate "healthcare" workers decided that Mother Nature won't protect her from illness for the next three years doesn't mean it's true. And last I checked none of them could read the future with any certainty, or they wouldn't be slogging away in a hospital setting to begin with. All I know is that whatever Great Power exists, I am grateful for Her care of my Portia. I don't know what I would do without her.

Again Blaise, thank you for keeping an open heart.

Your Fellow Mom Friend,

Bela

Email 75

Blaise Ayers to Amanda Vero

(February 2020)

Dear Mandy,

I am so sorry for the loss of your only child. I know how much he meant to you. Please know that Teddy meant much to us also. His sweet smile is captured in many photographs of our group, and he will not be forgotten. In case you don't know, the other children in the group who contracted measles seem to be on the mend. I would have told you about these things in person, but you didn't attend the funeral of your own child and you didn't answer your door when I knocked.

I am also writing this email to you to let you know that WRUMIRS has removed you from our roster. Though it's certainly no fault of your own that you are childless, that very condition prevents people, like yourself now, from being a part of our group, no matter how nice you are, or whether you were with us before. I'm sure you understand.

If you ever have another child, please consider reaching out to our group again because we would love to have you. We wish you the best of luck in all of your future endeavors.

Warmest regards,

Blaise Ayers,

President of WRUMIRS

Correspondence 20

Cordelia Links for the Battlefield Times

(February 2020)

Pennsylvania Woman Electrocutes Self in Mid-Flight

PHILADELPHIA - A 45-year-old woman was electrocuted yesterday at 8 am when she came into contact with a power line while flying a homemade contraption. The incident happened in West Philadelphia on Osage Avenue, just blocks from where the MOVE bombing occurred in 1985.

The woman, confirmed by her fingerprints on record from her last job as a bank manager, was identified as Amanda Hood Vero of Lippincott in Adams County, Pennsylvania.

According to investigators, Ms. Vero is presumed to have flown from her house in Lippincott all the way to Philadelphia. It is not known whether she made any stops along the way as her small size and low altitude appear to have evaded detection by rural and municipal radar scans.

Witnesses, primarily commuters in their cars and on the Philadelphia transit system, noticed a dark shape contrasted to the swirling snow in the morning sky, and assumed it to be a large bird. Several messages were left for the Pennsylvania State Game Commission at that time. The Pennsylvania State Game Commission has since confirmed no bird of that size exists in the state of Pennsylvania, nor anywhere in the United States and no bird as large as the ostrich has been known to maintain flight of that duration and height.

Witnesses recorded videos of the victim swooping across the sky until she collided with the power line. The collision produced a large bright spark on the videos and made a "crackling noise" according to neighbors who immediately lost power at that moment. Ms. Vero then fell approximately fifteen feet to the ground below. Coroners, however, determined that her heart had already stopped due to the electrocution prior to the fall. Ms. Vero's remains were also found with large containers strapped to her body and coated inside with a red residue of some sort, whose reason for being there is unknown.

"At this time, the investigation has not concluded. We are asking the public to bring forth any information that could explain the existence of the containers and/or their contents," said Bill Mine, chief of police for District 18. No suicide note has been found, though it cannot be entirely ruled out. Investigators will sift through any information they receive from the public to ascertain the purpose of Ms. Vero's flight.

Recently, Ms. Vero suffered the death of her only child, Theodore Vero, and that of her husband, Peter Vero.

Family is in the process of being contacted, but due to the unusual circumstances of her death including her successful flight costume and the mystery involving the containers, her name has been released. If Ms. Vero's flight occurred exactly as recorded by witnesses, it will be one of the exceedingly rare human powered flight contraptions capable of flying such a distance. According to investigators, the contraption seems to have been created out of ordinary and accessible materials in the garage of the home Ms. Vero and Peter Vero had owned together, prior to his death.

Osage Avenue is no stranger to extraordinary events and this incident drew several neighbors out of their homes to express their feelings.

"I never know what's coming," said Doreen Maven, longtime resident. "I was here when they did the MOVE bombing and I['ve] never been the same since. I saw those police cars and ambulances pull up and my pressure went up," she added. Earl Washington, her longtime partner, echoed the same. "After you go through something like [the MOVE bombing], you never want to go through it again. Those sirens yesterday morning was just nerve wracking," he finished.

Police have since cleared the area and the power company has repaired the broken line, but scorch marks remain where the dangling line had brushed against the wooden support pole. Yesterday's snowstorm blanketed the rest of the scene.

This investigation is ongoing. Updates will occur as new details emerge.

Correspondence 21

George Speculos for The Battlefield Times

(April 2020)

Assault from Above

LIPPINCOTT - In the grainy footage on a small black and white security screen, a swooping figure gradually emerges from the ice fog above the Lee Monument. The mist beats back and forth with the movement of the wings that hold the black hooded figure in cloudy suspension. For a moment, the grace of this heavenly body is admirable, but one furtive gesture dashes all admiration to the ground. Judging by the scowl on John Graves' face, this creature isn't heavenly at all, but demonic.

"That right there - that is when she damaged the monument irreparably" he grunts, as if the viewing of this crime causes him physical pain.

By now, every American paying the least bit of attention to the news knows the story. On a foggy night in February, just prior to a freezing rain and ensuing blizzard, when tourists would be scarce the next few days, Amanda Vero, known as "Mandy," in her former circles, dressed in black, donned prehensile wings of her own creation, flew over the National Military Park of Lippincott, pumped a mixture of salt and tomato juice whose combination is lethal to bronze statuary of the Victorian and Edwardian eras, and ruined thirteen Confederate state monuments forever.

Shifting his eyes downward, past the National Military Park patches on his uniform, John continues in a low tone, his voice cracking from time to time.

"We didn't know that anything had happened until weeks later. By then... it was too...late. Had the sensors picked up on her movements, especially if she had moved along the ground, we would've had a team out there with [helicopters] equipped with heat cameras and everything searching for her. As it was, she came from a direction that we were only equipped to detect when the [flying] machinery was more substantive." he said. "We've upgraded our radar equipment now to detect flying costumes, small drones, and the like,

317

though," he added, but the small hope contained in the comment was lost in the grief that consumed him as a large tear slid down his red cheek.

The devastation to the Military Park, or The Battlefield, as locals refer to it cannot be understated. In a town of twenty-five thousand citizens, everyone is touched by events that happened over one hundred fifty years ago. The Visitors Center of Lippincott receives over one million visitors a year who, after spending time on The Battlefield, then spend their money on lodging at the many hotels, restaurants, and shops within the town, or the amusement park, campgrounds, and other venues outside the town's perimeter. While the monuments didn't exist during the battle, they serve as touchstones for those who wish to remember. On any given day, small Confederate flags can be found at their bases. Busloads of "Southern Ladies," often in Civil War regalia, frequently make the pilgrimage here to honor their Confederate ancestors. Reenactment fervor abounds from mild skirmishes throughout the year, reaching its zenith on June 20th-21st each year, the anniversary of the Battle of Lippincott. Motorcyclists often journey to Lippincott, over scenic country roads, past the stone fruit orchards, and circle the Lee monument as a highlight of their trip. But none of that will happen today.

In the aftermath of the attack, when the damage began to appear, structural engineers were summoned to the monuments. Because the tomato slurry had gone unnoticed for several weeks, it had caused erosion in both the metal figures and the granite bases. Structural engineers determined these "etchings" in the granite and the bronze rendering the monuments too unstable to continue to stand. "The instability of the monuments is too great of a risk to the public. They must be removed," stated Freddie Stans of Lippincott Engineers, Ltd, in a letter to the Director of the National Parks, George Collins, appointed by President

Trump. Director Collins lamented the removal of the monuments in a recent press conference, stating, "Look folks, I love these monuments more than anyone and it pains me to remove them, but we have to get them to a safer environment until we can determine what can be done to save them." Invoking politics, Director Collins continued, "No lefty liberal is going to erase our Confederate heroes. If we have to station armed guards around these precious monuments, if we have to reduce funding to education or transportation to save our history, we are going to do it and no woke mob will stop us."

But not every American agrees with the sentiments of Director Collins. Marisol Esperanza, who had been in a mother's group with Mandy, weighed in with a different point of view. "When Mandy talked about these Confederate monuments, I didn't quite get what she was saying, but I understand now. These monuments don't celebrate America, but threats to Black Americans, our democratic ideals, and the unity of our nation. I get now why the North was called the 'Union troops,' they were literally trying to save the Union that already existed. I don't agree with what Mandy did, but I wish I could tell her now that I agree with her premise. It's too late to save her, but at least I can speak out about these blights in our National Parks."

If Ms. Esperanza is subdued in her rhetoric, Shirley Jackson is not. "[Amanda Vero] perioded all over them monuments and it was glorious. My ancestors were enslaved by the Confederates. I never, never want to see that [expletive] celebrating the Confederacy anywhere. Not the monuments, not the flags, not this both sidesism. It's sad she died, but I approve of what she did."

For every approval for Ms. Vero's action in the Black community, there are equal numbers of disapproval.

"The Black community does not need any white savior to swoop in and solve the Confederate monument problem for us," noted longtime resident Georgia Zuri who was also in the same mothers' group as Ms. Vero and Ms. Esperanza. Ms. Zuri reflected, "Defacing those monuments on federal property constituted a federal crime. Our Civil Rights groups have a proud history of non-violent means, including those regarding racist property. We are pursuing legal removals through an Act of Congress which will have a greater and long-lasting impact." She continued, "Additionally, [Ms. Vero's] impulsive actions directly caused us unpleasant, well downright frightening, and unnecessary interactions with the FBI. I mean, I know she just lost her husband and her only child, but our community is a bit shook. Everyone passed these interrogations, though they were very intimidating. I'm just grateful she didn't communicate her plans with anyone ahead of time."

"However," Ms. Zuri, putting a positive spin on such an uncomfortable situation, then referred to future consideration for local memorialization, "with the removal of the Confederate monuments, there is a greater possibility to install a new monument to honor those free Black people who were hunted by disgraced Lee's forces up and down the Mason-Dixon Line." At this time, sketches have been submitted to various artists, but nothing has been contracted.

In Gettysburg, desperate gun-enthusiasts are planning to gather around the Confederate monuments and at the National Cemetery to defend against rumored attacks against those monuments. The FBI, the Department of Homeland Security, Gettysburg Borough, and Pennsylvania State Police have decried these rumors as simply a hoax, but that has not deterred hundreds of supporters online who claim they will be there. "If I see a Black Lives Matter symbol on anyone, I'm gonna shoot him in the...head," wrote one anonymous poster.

Both the Adams County police, and the National Park Service are teaming up with the Dept. of Homeland Security to increase security measures both in the National Military Park of Gettysburg and the town itself.

Correspondence 22

Christopher Decapente to the Editor of the Battlefield Times

(April 2020)

Dear Editor,

THAT WOMAN had no business damaging them monuments. How else can we remember what the Confederate boys did? Now, I can't even see them under them tarps. I can't see how much they gave, how the angels loved them. That really gave me comfort, you know? If she hadn't died in what she did, God rest her soul, I think she would have died somewhere else.

No one nowhere has the right to destroy monuments that are important like them Confederate ones. How are my children going to learn about their ancestors like Uncle Jaspar? From some boring panel of words. She killed those monuments because she had hatred in her heart for the Confederate boys who had nothing but love for America, just like their ancestors before them. I would like to show her what hatred looks like at the muzzle of my AR-15.

 Then she would know.

Don't take down the monuments. Fix them and soon so women like her can learn they have no business with men's wars.

Chris Decapente

Lippincott

Correspondence 23

George Speculos for The Battlefield Times

(September 2020)

End of An Era

GETTYSBURG - Today has been a day of epic proportions. No one account of the events can quite capture its magnitude, but something must be written. Does it begin with Ms. Colvin's 81st birthday today? Perhaps it began earlier, on that fateful bus, when her brave actions kicked The Civil Rights Movement into high gear? No, no, it begins farther back, past the Montgomery Bus Boycott, through the sermons of Dr. Martin Luther King, Jr. Look beyond the desegregation of Brown versus The Board of Education of Topeka, Kansas. Swing through The Jazz Era. Harken the eloquent words of W.E.B. Dubois and Frederick Douglass. Journey with me, through the Reconstruction period, dance past Juneteenth, dodge the bullets at Gettysburg where the tide of the Civil War changed for Good, hike with Harriet Tubman to the North, read Solomon Northrup's injustices, grieve the many failed rebellions, cheer the escapees, suffer through the Middle Passage until we arrive at last to 1619 and that first black fist raised in defiance of a philosophy begotten by Evil and until today, cloaked in glory and granite.

Today, fists were again raised, not in defiance, but in unity, though with as just a cause as that first raised fist, and linked, brothers and sisters, descendants of those enslaved, while many descendants of enslavers pouted in the background. In a check of one of the most sordid histories of the United

States of America, the symbols of its glorification were rightly removed.

In what can only be described as "Equality's Tsunami" waves of Black leaders, members of Civil Rights groups, and every progressive person who believes in the fulsome defeat of the Confederacy reversed "Pickett's Charge," not only by direction, but by moral purpose. As tens of thousands of Americans linked arms and walked from Cemetery Hill, across that same Gettysburg battlefield to what is now Confederate Avenue, they sang several rounds of "We Shall Overcome" until they stopped at the Virginia monument, often called "The Lee Monument" after disgraced Robert E. Lee.

The crowds fell silent as the lone crane, arranged for such a purpose, pulled the bronze statue of Lee on his horse, freshly unscrewed from its base, off of its granite pedestal. When the metal sounded its grounding on the truck bed with an awkward clang, a great cheer arose from the Battlefield, for in that moment, this altar to white supremacy was dismantled. The crowd then dispersed east and west along Confederate Avenue, soon to be renamed Civil Rights Row, to witness the simultaneous removals of all of the Confederate State monuments, the Confederate Soldiers and Sailors Monument, and the few monuments dedicated to specific Confederate regiments. Cranes that had parked to the sides of those monuments swung into action, and every few minutes another roar would erupt from the crowd, announcing their removal. The following state monuments were removed this day:

The Virginia monument, erected 1917

The Alabama monument, erected 1933

The Tennessee monument, erected 1982

The Texas monument, erected 1964

The North Carolina monument, erected 1929

The South Carolina monument, erected 1963

The Arkansas monument, erected 1966

The Louisiana monument, erected 1971

The Maryland monument, erected 1994

The Georgia monument, erected 1961

The Florida monument, erected 1963

The Mississippi monument, erected 1973

Other monuments slated for removal later this week are the Confederate Soldiers and Sailors monument and six others honoring Confederate brigades and regiments.

Today, September 5, 2020, corrects the false narrative that the Daughters O' the Dang South and the Hoopskirt Hunnies had been telling since the Confederate States lost the Civil War. With cognitive dissonance, these women had failed to grasp the true horrors of what their ancestors fought for, foisting tall tales on the American public through the decades to suit their purpose - that the Confederate States only fought for States Rights not slavery, that slavery wasn't brutal, that the Confederacy consisted only of "genteel" Southerners, that plantations were paradises lost, that the Confederate flag was simply a flag of "heritage, not hate."

But we are no longer victims to their selective memories, nor their gaslighting. Credit to every person who ever fought for equality, but also their megaphone of the Internet, for now, We the People have access to primary sources that were once largely viewed by the private eyes of quiet historians. Never again will the Constitution of the Confederacy, nor the Letters of Secession (Ordinance) be hidden from our scrutiny. We the People know that the states who attempted to carve out a country for themselves from The United States of America did so in order to preserve that Evil institution known as "slavery." We can read their horrible words like those of Mississippi anytime we need that reminder. Released "slave schedules" from plantations recorded the deaths of enslaved babies, children, their mothers, and their fathers. Scanned burial grounds on plantations support those documents. No longer will we support kicking up one's heels in a wedding jig on a plantation because we know such behavior literally results in dancing on the graves of babies

For those threatened, intimidated, brutalized, beaten, mobbed, raped, robbed, shot, hosed down, and lynched during slavery, the Jim Crow and the Civil Rights Eras, this moment has come too late. In fact, it had come so late that Nazis, inspired by American slavery and the Jim Crowe Era had studied such practices in order to marginalize and kill Jewish people during the Holocaust, but it has come. No longer will the Confederacy be held high up in granite and bronze as beacons of gentility. Its place in American History is shameful and it is known. Across America, more monuments have yet to fall, but they will.

Make no mistake, the descendants of enslavers will voice their rage, their anguish, their belief in their righteousness, but middle Americans will no longer lend them the megaphone to do so. Social media have worked to silence their platforms of hate, lies, and calls for violence. There is more work to do, but they can no longer "both sides" the philosophies. All the quaint balancing of the Blue versus the Gray, the North versus the South, the Unionists versus the Secessionists, is crushed by the tidal wave of Truth. Anecdotes of enslaved ancestors come to the fore and are shared, freely. The book Barracoon: The Last Black Cargo by Nora Zeale Hurston is Canon for high school students of

American history as are the "Slave Narratives" from the Library of Congress.

Today, images that blocked our vision of the past have been taken away by crane and by tow truck. We have removed that blight of Confederate mythology from this hallowed ground and stopped equating the sordid causes of the Confederacy to the American ideals of equality, justice, and democracy so that true racial equality will sweep across the fields.

Let Freedom roll, indeed.

George Speculos

Gettysburg

Correspondence 24

George Speculos for the Battlefield Times

(December 2020)

New Monument Erected

GETTYSBURG - At just after 9am this chilly morning a large, somber group gathered in Gettysburg at McClellan Woods to dedicate a statue to the mothers and children kidnapped by the Confederacy. The bronze statue which measures ten feet tall, including a two-foot pedestal, depicts a fleeing African American mother tightly cradling her toddler. In this captured moment of desperation, the mother's head covering has slipped down, and her hair has burst forth, springing from her forehead in tall points not unlike a crown set upon her head. The toddler's gender is indiscernible, but their bare legs and feet attest to their extreme vulnerability.

"I wanted the spectators to use their own idea of horror," sculptor Justina Swope explained. "It's much more powerful when we fill in details about what is missing." Certainly, spectators' imaginations could easily fill in the barking dogs, thundering hooves and sweaty flanks of muscular horses, loud shouts, and every other force that pursued innocent people who did not agree to be enslaved.

The swishing skirts, the foot upraised mid-stride lend credence to the stress of the moment, yet in it, a mother's fierce love shines with a steadfastness the Confederacy never knew. Having only existed for four years, the Confederate States of America petered out, but in the National Military Parks, their mythology had stood solidly until last Fall when their bronze and granite effigies were finally removed. Removal of Confederate monuments was only half of the correction though. Americans can never again be mistaken about the aims of the Confederacy and since they have been so swayed by three dimensional depictions, it is only fitting that the Truth of the enslaved and Free Black American experience be set before us.

"But frankly," Ms. Swope said looking around the McClellan Woods, "There's a whole lot of detail missing from the Gettysburg Battlefield. It's atrocious." Ms. Swope couldn't be more right.

Of course, Ms. Swope is referring to the thousands of enslaved people who were forced to slog along with Lee's army or face brutal consequences if they didn't. But most white Americans don't know anything about them. Ask anyone within spitting distance of a Confederate grave and they'll tell you their ancestor fought for the Confederacy because they didn't know how awful slavery was. Not infrequently do these uninformed Americans punctuate their defense with the phrase, "My [ancestor] didn't have any slaves."

Oh, but they did, Good Sir or Madame. You see, when Confederate soldiers served in the Army of Northern Virginia, they availed themselves to the thousands of enslaved people who chopped their firewood, pitched their tents, cooked their food, and tended to them medically. They were called "servants," in a genteel fashion, but they were not paid, and if they chanced to escape, they were hunted down. In pursuit of escaped enslaved people, Confederate soldiers rounded up anyone of color, enslaved or free.

"She's free, but she's running," informed Ms. Swope, "because she was hunted too. And God only knows what would happen to her baby."

While most spectators will see the statue of one of despair, it equally recalls the universal protective nature of motherhood. No matter what forces are after a child, a caring mother will work to protect her baby.

The "contraband" lists from every Confederate unit detail hundreds of women and children whom they caught. We pin our hopes on this statue for the people who weren't captured.

George Speculos,

Gettysburg

Email 76

Eliza Dupont to Adams County Moms...In Progress Members

(August 2021)

Dear Adams County Moms...In Progress,

Please join me in welcoming our newest member - Imani Johnson! Imani, her husband Bob, and their twins Mahalia and Aaliya, aged ten months, have just moved from Baltimore, MD, where Bob taught high school history. Bob will teach Civil War History at Battlefield University next month, so reach out to him there if you're affiliated! Imani is currently staying at home with their twins and is open to outside playdates with social distancing.

Per usual requirements, Imani's AAP-certified pediatrician faxed us up-to-date immunization records for both children. She and Bob belong to a church whose nursery also requires current immunization records, though it is currently closed while services are live-streamed. Furthermore, both Imani and Bob are currently vaccinated against COVID-19. Like the rest of us, they also plan to have the children vaccinated against COVID-19 when the FDA authorizes a vaccine for their age group. If you are looking for another mom to invite to your outdoor event, please think of Imani.

As a reminder, next week's Travel Tots is heading to Sacred Ground Orchard to pick apples. Masks are required for everyone over the age of two years and social distancing is strongly suggested, even for the vaccinated. Remember to twist, *then* pull to pick the fruit. Collecting windfalls is discouraged. Watch out for bees!

See you soon,

Eliza Dupont,

President of ACMIP

END

www.ingramcontent.com/pod-product-compliance
Lightning Source LLC
Chambersburg PA
CBHW030416180626
46812CB00005B/2035